DEBORAH TOMKINS

Deborah is an award-winning author of fiction, short stories and flash fiction. Her novella *Aerth* was a joint winner of the inaugural Weatherglass Books Novella award in 2024, judged by Ali Smith.

Her work has also been long listed for the Mslexia Prize (2015), the Eludia Award (2020), the Bath Novella-in-Flash Award (2018, 2019). Shortlists include the Siskiyou Prize for New Environmental Literature (2018), the Yeovil Prize (2019), the Sandy River Novella Award (2020).

In 2017, she founded Bristol Climate Writers, a local network of writers of all genres, from poets to travel writers, novelists to journalists. She is also a member of ClimateCultures, an extraordinary worldwide network of artists and scientists.

She lives in Bristol with her family.

First published in the UK in 2025 by Aurora Metro Publications Ltd.

80 Hill Rise, Richmond TW10 6UB, UK

www.aurorametro.com   info@aurorametro.com

Follow us X: @aurorametro FB/AuroraMetroBooks

Insta: @aurora_metro

The Wilder Path copyright © 2025 Deborah Tomkins

Cover images: *Port Mulgrave* and *Cormorant* © 2025 Michelle Hughes /Michelle Hughes Design www.michellehughes.co.uk

Cover design: Aurora Metro Books

Editors: Cheryl Robson and Jill Russo

With thanks to: Sally Mears, Diya Gracias Velho

Printed on sustainably resourced paper by Short Run Press.

ISBNs: 978-1-910798-68-3 (print)

978-1-910798-69-0 (ebook)

MIX
Paper | Supporting
responsible forestry
FSC
www.fsc.org   FSC® C014540

THE

WILDER PATH

Deborah Tomkins

AURORA METRO BOOKS

For Ian, Alexandra, Christopher, and Nathaniel,
with all my love

ONE

Rain Bomb

I shoulder my son's ancient 70-litre rucksack, Tate St Ives Gallery behind me, and walk west past the small car park above the surfing beach. Skirting the bowling green, I arrive at a wide grassy area where people are taking photos of a view I could draw in my sleep: distant misty headlands stretching into the grey-blue sea; closer, a small promontory overlooking the town's beaches and the harbour lined with tourist shops and boat trips. It's a glorious midwinter afternoon, gentle with sunshine and a soft breeze.

Over the ridge the clifftop path will become wilder, trickier, rougher, its slopes steep and unforgiving for elderly thighs like mine. It's old, this path, once used by Cornish smugglers and customs men, but its first half mile has been tamed, flattened and widened, surfaced with tarmac for families and pushchairs and those who like an easy stroll.

One mile further, it becomes difficult, even treacherous, and only the most determined walker manages the seven miles to Zennor, up and down the ravines, crossing streams, clambering over boulders and stiles. Hugo and I did it before the children were born. It took us six hours. We ate fish and chips at the pub, our feet sore, our spirits triumphant, and took a taxi back to town.

It's not too late for a walk, just after lunch on one of the shortest days of the year. I want to get up on those cliffs and back to town before the sun sets soon after four. There's an ancient stone circle I'm keen to see again. After that, I'll find a guesthouse, call Flora and let her know where I am, arrange to meet tomorrow, on New Year's Eve. She'll roll her eyes at me: 'Mum... what possessed you to come down here without telling me?'

I'm looking forward to New Year, despite my misgivings a few days ago, and to seeing Anne's new home and meeting her new husband. I'm a little nervous, still – who wouldn't be? – but my arduous and unbelievably challenging journey just makes me thankful to be alive. I'm determined to enjoy myself and bring joy to everyone else. No moaning.

This path is dear and familiar. Gulls soar above, and there are the tiniest signs of an exceptionally early spring: spiky pink thrift flowers, a few primroses, green shoots of bracken like miniature shepherd's crooks unfurling beneath dead bronze foliage. It reminds me of family holidays when Flora and her brothers were young. We'd straggle along, taking our time: Hugo first, carrying the picnic, spare clothing, and water; then Jonnie, striding long-legged like his father; Flora, usually singing; our twin boys, silent and frowning; and finally me, with the first aid kit, sun cream and hats. We stopped for rests on rocks or little tussocks of grass at the side of the path, greeting the hardier walkers and their dogs. Each year we walked slightly further, as the children's stamina and legs grew.

In my memories the sun is gentle in a blue sky, although I also remember sunburn and rain showers, the weather down here always unpredictable. Today I'm unintentionally well-prepared. Winter coat, a few provisions, half a bottle of water.

Here's Clodgy Point. Great views in several directions. Vast granite boulders lean craggily against each other, vividly splodged with lichens in bright orange, yellow, green, grey, and cream. Little sedum plants crouch in the crevices, dark red and pink. But I press on, don't linger. As long as I'm back in town by five. *Keep going, Rosalie, you can do it.*

Another memory: Hugo sitting on a rock near a disused tin mine telling stories about the knockers, Cornish sprites deep in the mines that warned of danger. Miners who didn't heed the knocking lost their lives when the mine collapsed. The children loved Hugo's storytelling, his acting out of all the parts: the wicked mine-owner, the brave miners, the secretive and sinister knockers. I loved to watch him, watch their young faces. They enjoyed the stories even into their teens, although by then he seasoned the make-believe with real history about mine tunnels stretching for miles under the sea, terrible accidents in which dozens died, and he'd point out the old mine shafts dotted everywhere along the coast. Those huge mines operated until fairly recently. It makes me think, as I trudge along, that these cliffs are less stable than they look.

Ahead of me the sun is low in the sky. I stop for breath; the path's steeper now, snaking inland, punctuated by boulders and abrupt corners. To my right and far below is the sea, thumping and roaring. A fine spray mists my face. I step closer to the edge, careful of loose stones: there's a little track descending the cliff in a kind of zigzag that looks almost deliberate. A smugglers' path? What a story for the grand-children tomorrow.

I inch down, my new boots gripping well, sea spray misting my hair and Jonnie's old parka. It lost its waterproofing long ago, but I can dry it tonight in the guesthouse. High jagged cliffs rise above me and slate-grey waves crash against massive rocks below. Huge seismic events must have shaken those boulders loose, sent them rolling into the ocean. I stop for a rest and scan the cliffs, the horizon, the deepening clouds. My knees are a little wobbly, not used to this terrain. I like to walk, but it's pretty flat back home.

There's a split in the cliff face to my left that looks big enough for a person to squeeze inside. I scramble down to a flattish rock, only a few feet above the waves, where I kneel to peer in. Judging by its coating of fine green slime, this rock is submerged at high tide. The light from my phone reveals a tiny cave; the floor broken and uneven, scattered with miniature pools, the walls sloping towards each other, the ceiling low and bumpy.

The light's fading. I turn back to the track, lowering myself to my hands and knees to crawl when the loose earth and scree slips beneath my feet. Not one of my better ideas, exploring down here. Nobody knows where I am.

Back on the main path I'm suddenly cold and tired and hungry. Lunch seems a long time ago. I'd love a cup of tea. There's still just enough light to see my way.

I glance up for the reassurance of streetlights in the distance, and am startled to see a vast purple-grey cloud. It appears to bulge in several places. I can't at first work out what's going on. The bulges are growing bigger, then they explode in huge vertical columns of water like waterfalls, thunderously loud, and racing towards me.

A rain bomb. I'm not waiting to see what happens next. I've seen these things on YouTube.

I stumble back the way I've just come. Lightning flashes, thunder cracks. My half-empty rucksack catches the wind and shoves me forwards. It feels like I could be lifted off my feet, sent sailing over the cliffs like a paraglider before plunging into the gigantic waves below. I trip, slide down a large piece of slate and fall onto my front.

Great drops of rain bounce off the ground like rubber

balls. My hands loom white in the weird purple light. I crawl into a sort of hollow place surrounded by boulders. Hailstones smash onto my head, my shoulders, the path, the bracken, and I can't see anything under this falling water and ice. My hair whips round my face and into my eyes. It's no longer beautiful, this place. It's horrendous. I crouch, listening to the explosion of noise, and watch in relief as the columns of water veer away from me and out to sea.

I turn once more towards St Ives and shelter.

But now I hear a new roar. I stop, turn, stare at the sky in all directions, see nothing obviously dangerous, walk on. The sound's getting louder. I seem to be following it.

I turn a corner to find a flash flood racing across the path, deep and wide and furious, funnelled by a steep gulley into the ocean below – mud and water and rocks and bushes and trees, planks and bits of shed roof, blue tarpaulins, orange pails and white plastic barrels, a lawnmower, great chunks of moorland granite swept down from the fields and the dry-stone walls. It's a fast, turbulent, terrifying mass of energy. The ground shudders beneath my feet.

I stare at the torrent, my legs trembling, my breath ragged and shallow. My one route back to town is impassable, and behind me are miles of cliff path, hours of walking in the dark until I get to the next village. I need shelter urgently. If I'm out here all night, the very least that will happen is some kind of exposure.

I turn again, retrace my steps in these last minutes of daylight, desperate to find a way onto the stone-walled fields, willing to shove through the bracken, the brambles, the gorse, the sloe bushes and razor-sharp thorns. Even if I manage this, the fields are largely abandoned, unlighted, uneven underfoot, invaded by nettles and yet more gorse and bramble.

I find myself back at the tiny zigzag track. In this deep

twilight I have no choice. I slip and slither and skid down the slope on my bottom, cross the slippery green rock, and squeeze through the narrow gap in the cliff onto the uneven floor of the cave, pebbles and shells crunching under my feet. Water slops into my new walking boots. I'm shivering uncontrollably, close to tears, chilled to the marrow of my bones.

Outside, the wind rises, rain begins to fall.

TWO

Cavelet

I'm suddenly awake, choking, gasping, spluttering and wheezing, my heart racing, the panic rising within me like nausea. I don't immediately remember where I am or why I'm here.

I'm crouched at the very back of this minuscule cave partway up a cliff at almost the very tip of Cornwall, waiting out a violent storm on this viciously cold New Year's Eve. The wind died down overnight, the sky cleared and I even saw stars, but now the wind howls, it groans, it screams, it roars. Between gusts there's the smell of clean salt air mingled with rotting seaweed. I occasionally get a whiff of my underarms when I shift position. The tide is rising and seawater crashes in every couple of minutes, the spray drenching my feet and my legs. So I couldn't get out if I tried. I can't even get close enough to the entrance to see out.

I am very cold, and very wet. But I know these Cornish storms. They blow themselves out in a few hours, and as soon as that happens, I'll be up that cliff. If I can't get to St Ives along the cliff path I'll cut across the fields and make for the road.

It will probably have gone by now, that flash flood. A few hours of mayhem and terror, cars gliding down rivers that used to be roads, patio doors caved in by the weight of water, people standing on rooftops filming the devastation with their mobile phones. A few hours of chaos, many months of clearing up.

I've just realised I'm not alone in here. I've been aware all night of small noises and shufflings while I've been half-awake, half-asleep, and I thought it was simply the wind. But now there's just enough daylight to see a large bird on a narrow ledge above the high-water mark, watching me like a baleful god, its emerald-green eyes half-closed, wings folded tight against its body for protection, or warmth. It must have been here already when I crawled in yesterday afternoon dragging Jonnie's battered old rucksack behind me, my hands red and swollen with cold, my hair plastered to my head, my clothing soaked through.

'It wasn't the sea that made me so wet, it was the rain bomb. Not technically the correct term. That would be *wet micro-burst*, if you're interested.' The bird turns its head at the sound of my voice, and eyes me suspiciously.

There's a bleak beauty in this place, in this early morning light: the stripes of coloured rock – elephant-grey, burnt umber, blood-red. The little rock pools with blue-black mussels and yellow-and-white sea snails, barnacles spread across the rocks like spilled oatmeal. The crimson jelly blobs of sleeping sea anemones waiting for high tide. The eddies and swirls as seawater swooshes in and out. The fat vein of fool's gold above my head. A smear of fresh water trickling down the rock at the back of the cave. An entrance that's a mere slit in the cliff face, invisible from above, hardly visible from the sea. It's a miracle I found it.

I can't believe that I slept at all, what with the cold and the damp and the lumpy shingle that digs into my back and buttocks. I dreamt of Jonnie as a small child, four or five years old. He was running through a meadow, laughing, holding his hand out to me. 'Run, Mummy, run…!' I jogged alongside him, laughing too, neither of us out of breath, skimming the wildflowers and grasses, and then somehow he was outstripping me, running ahead, racing up the hill, disappearing over the top. When I reached the crest, he was no longer in sight.

These dreams come and go. I have one every few weeks. Not exactly the same, more a variation on a theme. Jonnie is sometimes older, sometimes younger, but each time I lose him. I've lost him in the cinema, in supermarkets, in woods, at his graduation, the graduation he never attended. I've seen him mingling with guests at Flora's wedding, when he'd been dead ten years. In that dream, I lost him several times. He walked behind a pillar in the Cathedral and didn't emerge the other side; he took a plate of food from the buffet and turned towards me, and was a different guest, not my son; he drove the happy couple away from the reception in a chauffeur's uniform, his face expressionless, intent on the road ahead of him.

I stand and stretch my cramped legs, gaze at the bird on its ledge. Its wing feathers are decorated with bronze lozenges, its bright yellow throat ringed with white. The beak is long and hooked, ideal for catching fish when diving. I move a little closer. It shuffles away, distrustfully, and then I see its leg stretched out behind it, the webbed foot at an awkward angle, injured, perhaps broken. Poor bird. I think it's a cormorant. It can't have a great chance of survival. Maybe I can get it to the RSPB.

'Do you ever dream? Of what, I wonder? Sailing the oceans? Fishing? The beauty of the cliffs?' The cormorant cocks its head towards me, closes its eyes. I can't say I blame it.

Jonnie would have loved a day here. It's a bit like camping – the wet and the chill and not enough hot food – and Jonnie always loved camping, making dens, exploring. He never lost his adventurous spirit. In many ways I wish he had lost it, had been a homebody like his sister, Flora. But then he wouldn't have been Jonnie.

I loved Jonnie more than the others. You're not supposed to, as a parent. From the moment he was born and placed into my arms and looked up at me with those dark-blue eyes that never changed colour he had a hold on me that my other children never had, a hold that tightened until it felt like his hand was around my heart. We could read each other's moods, and it seemed that I would always know what he was thinking, that we would always chime.

Memories of Jonnie have hit me out of nowhere for over twenty years. They side-swipe me, they knock the wind out of me, they trip me up, they make me lose my way. I'm walking along, or cooking or feeding the hens or making a telephone call, and then, quite suddenly, Jonnie is there before me, as real to me as the walls of this cave. I feel that I could reach out and touch him, rumple his hair, kiss his cheek.

Flora and Hugo used to think I'd gone into some kind of trance. Maybe it's a kind of post-traumatic shock, a flashback. Maybe I'm mentally ill. Maybe I'm simply zoning out.

Or, maybe, just maybe, it's the solidity and permanence of grief.

చ్ఛ

'What would you do in a zombie apocalypse?'

Jonnie sounded entirely serious. He was sitting opposite me, twelve years old, his eyes on the bowl of chocolate icing I was using to decorate Flora's birthday cake. He was getting over a cold, was well enough to go back to school, but I'd granted him an extra day at home. We never had proper time alone together and I missed him. By the time he got home it was chaos, running around with Flora's after-school activities and preventing for the most part the twins' periodic meltdowns.

'What's a zombie apocalypse?'

'You know, Mum…' He lurched from the stool and began stalking erratically up and down the kitchen, legs stiff, arms out straight before him, hands dangling like a hideous scarecrow, gurning, eyes lolling, moaning and dribbling.

I laughed. 'What are you doing?'

'I'm being a zombie!'

'But why?'

'Well, if there was a zombie apocalypse you'd need to know. You've got to run really fast because they can't run.'

'That's a relief.'

'And you've got to lock yourself into a building with plenty of supplies and weapons and food. Basically,' he confided, climbing back onto the stool, 'you've got to be prepared for a siege.'

'Really?' I raised my eyebrows.

'Mmm.' He nodded. 'A long one. Most people don't realise that. Most people think it'll be all right after about a week.'

'And it won't.'

'No. It might never be all right. Zombies can't die.'

'Ah.'

'But you can blow them up.'

'OK.'

'And burn them. With flamethrowers and things.'

'Yuck.'

'Oh, it's all right, Mum. They can't think or feel, so they

17

don't know anything about it.'

'So what are they after then?'

'Er…' He faltered for a moment, then brightened. 'Oh, they want to turn us into zombies too.'

'I see. Like a sort of virus.'

'Maybe. Can I lick out the bowl yet?'

'Here you are.' I pushed it across the counter and watched as he bent his dark tousled head over it, intently scraping out the icing with a teaspoon.

'I'll make sure you're all right, Mum. I'll take you with me. We can run together.' Absorbed by the bowl, he didn't look up.

'Thank you, darling.' I smiled, my heart melting.

❧

It's been terrible weather these past few days, I hardly need to remind myself: storm after storm after storm from the northeast – all that snow – and from the west – all that wind and rain. But this storm feels worst of all, because I'm trapped in here with only a bird to talk to. It truly feels like it could be the end of the world – squalls of rain and wind lash the cliffs, thunder bursts overhead, flashes of lightning briefly illuminate the filthy dark clouds that roil above. Fanciful, of course. The end of the world won't come so dramatically, so quickly. The end of me might come, though, if I can't get out pretty soon. I'm fortunate to be safe in here, despite the dank chill and the cramp in my legs.

I take a few deep breaths, pull myself together. There is absolutely no need to panic. There's probably a little path on the other side of this cave. There wasn't time to look last night as I scrambled inside.

I'll text Flora. No need to mention what's happened, at

least not in detail. That can wait. I don't want to worry her. And when we're cosy around the fire at Anne's, I can mention my little adventure on the cliffs. I might embroider it a bit, tell the children about the smugglers' cave, the spooky bird, the creatures in the rock pools: diminutive crabs and tiny fish, small translucent shrimps scurrying from one hiding place to another, fronds of delicate seaweed like a miniature forest.

Terrible weather! Am sheltering on cliff.
See you later at Anne's!
Have a safe journey! xxx

My phone goes black and dead. My own fault. I've been using it as a torch. I hope Flora doesn't worry too much when she can't get hold of me.

I search the rucksack for Jonnie's old wind-up torch. We gave it to him when he was about eight. I begin winding it, charging its battery.

I can wait out the rain in this cave for a few more hours. No longer than that. At my age I need a few home comforts. I'm sixty-seven, you know.

'Ah! Do I detect a little surprise in your eyes? Perhaps you think I look good for my years? – or maybe you think I'm too old for this caper. But then you've seen better days too, my friend.'

I'm far too old, you're quite right. I shouldn't be here at all. I should be at my friend Anne's, sleeping in her comfortable spare bedroom, enjoying her delicious food, gazing out at the Cornish countryside, so beautiful even in winter. But instead of luxuriating in the comfort of a warm and convivial home, surrounded by loving family and friends, I'm huddled on this strip of wet shingle, all broken shells and pebbles, my spine against the rocky wall, my knees drawn up tight under my chin, eking out my apples and walnuts while I wait for the storm to pass.

19

I'm incredibly thirsty, too. I might be able to fill my bottle from that trickle just here at the back, or there are the torrents pouring down outside. Neither seems appealing. I expect there's mud and grit mixed in, and I bet it'll taste disgusting.

The cormorant shifts uneasily, moves awkwardly on its shelf, stretches its wings as if it's about to fly. It's huge, its wingspan as wide as my outstretched arms. It opens and shuts its long, hooked beak. I back away, stumbling a little on the uneven floor of the cave.

Then I feel what the bird's reacting to. The ground's vibrating... there's a gritty grating and rumbling over my head... a thunderous scraping... The whole cave's shaking... it feels like an earthquake. The vibrations run up my legs and my back, right into my head, into my eyes. Instinctively I duck and hold my forearms tight to the top of my head, protecting my skull from the grit and pieces of rock that drop from above, crash around me, smash onto the rocks and into the pools... I need to get out before I'm crushed or trapped... on hands and knees I crawl across the trembling floor towards the entrance, gripping the barnacled rocks with sore fingers...

My lungs are blocks of stone, my throat's closing up... Breathe out, Roly... all the way out, that's it... empty your lungs... Now breathe in, very slowly, easy does it... Well done... Well done...

Slow, steady, breathe... Don't think, don't panic. Breathe... breathe... I wish I had an inhaler. But my specialist said there was no need. It's just panic, she said. Just panic. As if that means nothing.

And... breathe...

And... breathe...

Aaagh!

☙

There's been a landslide, a rockfall. It's massive. I can hear earth and rock and gravel still tumbling down the cliff. I lie on my front and peer outside. Dust and sea spray swirl around me in a kind of mist, and I can't see much at first. Then I do. I see enough to make me gasp. I stare, for minutes, while small rocks and a few barrowloads of soil continue to trickle downwards.

A huge section of cliff has disintegrated and crashed into the sea. All my handholds and footholds and that little animal track – they're gone.

The boulders below me are treacherous, smooth and slippery with that slimy green weed, the sea heaving around them.

Sheer vertical cliff. Sheer horizontal rain.

I haul myself back inside, shaking with shock, and only now do I notice blood pouring out of a massive gash in my thigh, soaking my jeans. I don't remember when that happened, maybe when I slipped down between those two narrow rocks as I crawled along. It's agony, a sharp throbbing pain that seems bigger than the wound itself, a long open slice along my inner thigh.

I feel a bit faint, a bit sick. I'll just sit here for a bit, have a think. Gather my resources. Bathe my leg with sea water. Tie it up tight with my scarf. Rummage for painkillers.

What a mess. What a bloody mess.

I grab my rucksack, crawl back to where I was sitting. Oh, and there you are, still there on your ledge. Still staring at me, still suspicious of me.

'Look at you, barely moving, barely alive. I think you've got a broken leg.'

Look at me, trapped, bleeding, talking to an injured cormorant.

THREE

He Won Medals, You Know

It's calm now, tonight. The wind has dropped, the sea is quiet. The sunset was stunning. Streaks of red and gold interwoven with violet cloud.

But it's dark and late, how late I don't know – I've no way of telling the time. I don't bother with a watch. I please myself in my daily life; I don't have to be anywhere or do anything. Besides, there's the kitchen clock, and the one in the hall, and my alarm clock on my bedside table.

I'll get out on that rock tomorrow to look for another way up the cliff. Low tide is mid-afternoon. Fortunate this little cave wasn't swept away with everything else – the boulder, the bushes, the bracken, the footpath. Me.

This coast is wilder than I remembered.

Occasional vibrations rumble through the rock. The cliff is still fragile. I mustn't panic. I must hold on, hold tight, hold fast to – what? What exactly can I hold on to now? My sanity? Precarious, at the best of times. The love of those I hold dear? Maybe. The hope of rescue?

I have no certainty that any of these things is true and

solid. Everything feels insubstantial, like sea mist. But the cold closes like a vice around me, like I'm turning into ice, apart from my leg, which is hot and sore and stiff, although it appears to have stopped bleeding.

However old I am, however mature – although Hugo might have something to say about that – there's something creepy about being here alone at night. I find myself wondering what's hiding in the darkness beyond this tiny pool of slowly dimming light from my torch. I have to wind the torch every few minutes, and meanwhile the shadows creep closer when I'm not looking. The rocks freeze when I swing my torchlight onto them, like a game of grandmother's footsteps. Like the worst kind of nightmare. Because I feel a sudden terror that I'll never get out of this cave, that my bones won't ever be found, that my family will never know what became of me, and that I'll never know what became of them.

I gasp, a long shuddering gasp, raucous in the sudden silence of this space, a deep wheezing rasp that startles me as much as it gives me relief. I hadn't realised I was holding my breath. I've always done it, held my breath when concentrating, or if I was in pain or frightened or shocked, and someone would tell me to 'Breathe!' – a teacher, a parent, a friend, or most irritably, Hugo.

I must breathe very slowly... out... and in... and out... and in...

I must concentrate. I'll time my breaths to the waves coming in... and out... and in... and out...

There... there... there...

∽

This sea, this sea... the slow heavy rolling of the waves that crash grey and white on the rocks below... This sea reminds me of Jonnie's last moments. Six thousand miles away, my most beloved son. Twenty-three years ago, give or take a few weeks. Twenty-three years. I remember it so clearly.

It was played over and over on the news, a few seconds of blurry footage – two people on a ship, holding a banner which billowed and flapped like a sail in the strong wind. You could barely make out the words 'Stop Whaling!' They seemed to be swaying back and forth in a kind of slow-motion dance, taking a step back, then another step forward or to their left or right. Then I realised it was the ship swaying from side to side at the same time as it was going up and down. There was no horizon, no sky, or maybe the sky and the water were the same colour. Enormous white and lead-grey waves broke over the guardrail at the front of the ship and the two people swayed and stumbled, trying to stand upright in the wind.

Then one of them tripped and fell and slid slowly along the side of the deck. Water crashed over them, and, when it cleared, he or she was no longer there.

The video footage swung back to the other person, on their knees, crawling towards us.

The film cut out at this point, the news anchor gravely explaining that the first person had fallen into the sea, was still secured to the ship by their safety line, and the rescue operation was ongoing.

That's how I found out. The news. It couldn't be Jonnie, I was sure, as I stood rigid in front of the television, iron in hand, watching the one o'clock news. No, it couldn't be Jonnie, someone would have contacted us; there would have been police at the door hours before. It couldn't be Jonnie.

When the reporter said that Greenpeace was trying to trace the family of the young scientist who'd fallen overboard, I dropped the iron. The scorch mark never came out, the carpet fibres crisped and blackened in the shape of an iron pointing south to the Antarctic. We replaced the carpet eventually – Hugo insisted – even though for me the burnt patch marked the time and date indelibly and I felt oddly disloyal, letting that carpet go.

When I saw the police at my front door, I knew it was true. I'd crawled over the carpet to the sofa and lain there desperately trying to suck air into my lungs. I realised after a few minutes that the room was filling with acrid smoke, and that jolted me into action. By the time the police got there the windows were open and the carpet was drenched by dirty water from the washing-up bowl, bits of cabbage and coffee grounds scattered around the ironing board.

I said to the policewoman: 'I never wanted him to go, you know. And what on earth was he thinking? Out there in that weather, that wind – did you see the wind? – and the waves, so dangerous. He's a good swimmer, you know,' I said. 'He won medals,' I said, 'lots of medals,' and I went to a drawer to look for them and they weren't in the drawer because I'd put them away safely in his bedroom a long time ago, just tidying up, you know, but at that moment, when I couldn't find the medals, I felt I really needed to find them, that my world would fall apart if I didn't find them right then, as if my world hadn't already begun to disintegrate just an hour before.

I started looking around the house – Hugo's study, the kitchen, the drawer in the hall table – and the poor young policewoman who'd been sitting with me while her colleague rang Hugo and made tea had to follow me around while I pulled out drawers and opened boxes and peered into cupboards. Every now and then she said, 'Would you like to come and sit down, Mrs Danborough?', but I ignored her because I had to find the blessed medals.

I was too calm. I was in shock, the kind of shock that leaves you functioning on the outside while your heart and mind are somewhere else entirely. And when the shock wears off, then, I found, the grief begins. The denial, the anger, the blame and regrets, the longing for that one last kind word, that one last smile, that one last embrace. I didn't cry, not then.

The last day I ever saw Jonnie, the day he left us, I didn't say goodbye to him. To my shame, I didn't watch him open the front door and walk out. I haven't even that memory to comfort me. I have to imagine how he looked, what he did. Did he put his rucksack on before he left the house, or outside when he stepped through the porch? It was raining – did he wear a hat, or did he let the raindrops settle like diamonds in his dark curls? Did he look back into the house as he left, hoping for a word of love?

He'd be back, he said, to take his final exams. That's one of the things we rowed about. Hugo didn't think he would. Hugo thought he'd never get his degree, never get the first he'd been working so hard for. Hugo thought Jonnie would bum around the world and ruin his life.

I backed Hugo up. We'd talked and discussed and argued all through Christmas, but we didn't know about the girl, the person we saw crawling towards us in the storm. Perhaps she was the real reason he wanted to go just then. I'll never know. I'll never know...

Jonnie was impetuous, like his father, but without that inner cool of Hugo's that seemed sometimes just, well, cold. He cared about it all, Jonnie told us – global warming, litter, pesticides, whaling – everything fed into everything else, and he meant to fight it with all he had. He had passion, fire, was impatient to set things right, impatient with us and our lukewarm lives, our endless complacency.

And I let him go.

And I didn't think about him more than once or twice a day.

And I refused to be the one to say sorry.

And often I couldn't breathe.

FOUR

Fuck the Career

Listen to me. Rambling on. Well, who cares? No one will ever know. Words echo in the air and leave no trace, except in the heart.

When I get out of here, I'll call Flora from someone's house, or I'll borrow someone's mobile. Tomorrow. I'll easily get out in daylight, in this calm weather. There will be some way up on the other side of this little cave, away from the landslide. Or someone will rescue me, and Flora will come and fetch me, and we will be back to Plan A.

Plan B – what I'm doing right now – was never on the cards.

Flora thinks she looks after me. She'll be worrying about me – she always worries about me, because that's what daughters do when their mothers get to a certain age. She'll be worrying because I've not phoned her for a couple of days, and I'm not at home in St Albans, and I'm meant to have travelled here with her and Peter, squashed into the back of the car with their three children. But – long story – I travelled down to the coast by myself.

I'm not really someone who likes to chat on phones. Not like Hugo, my sort-of ex-husband, although we've never actually divorced. Hugo and Flora both love the phone. They're people-people, chatty and gregarious, love parties and gatherings and all that kind of thing. The twins and I are pretty solitary types. Fergus and Dugald are physicists-turned-farmers, so laboratories and fields suit them very well. They'd probably be happy if they never saw another person in their lives.

And Jonnie? He was a people-person too. Everybody loved him.

We're supposed to have arrived at Anne's yesterday, Friday, and now be enduring her New Year celebrations – sorry, enjoying. What a silly joke. Just trying to keep my spirits up.

I hardly ever go to Anne's because it's such a long way and I'm not a party-lover. But this year Flora begged me to come, and I decided I would, not least because Anne's forgiven me, and it's high time we buried the hatchet and became friends again. Real friends, I mean, not just birthday-and-Christmas-card friends, but back to being the kind of friends we were when we were young. I shouldn't have accepted her invitation quite so grudgingly. She needn't have invited me, after the way I treated her.

တ

Now my eyes have adjusted to the darkness, there's something very beautiful about the way the water shimmers in the rock pools. The thin, slanting triangle beyond, slightly paler, is the entrance to the cave, so narrow that a skilled canoeist could just about get a canoe in. Jonnie would have tried – he loved a challenge. He and Flora adored sea-kayaking when they were teenagers. The twins didn't. They didn't like anything much, except maths. All the holidays we had down here... By the time they were teenagers they often simply refused to get out of the car. I used to worry about them baking to death while the rest of us were on the beach.

❧

The morning Jonnie left started like any other. It was just after the New Year, early January, and we'd had a lovely time – a traditional Christmas, turkey with all the trimmings, sprigs of holly perched over the pictures, a red-ribboned juniper wreath on the front door, a garland over the mantelpiece, pine-scented candles dotted around the place, neighbours in on Boxing Day for mulled wine. A marvellous Christmas. We always did Christmas so well, and we all enjoyed ourselves. Well, apart from the twins, who holed up in their room with mince pies and sausage rolls whenever the neighbours came round.

I don't exactly know what started the row. It was probably the Greenpeace trip. I heard raised voices in the kitchen and came in from the conservatory where I'd been picking dead leaves off the plants, to find Jonnie and Hugo yelling at each other. I couldn't hear what they were saying at first – they were shouting at the same time, and Flora, bewildered, sat at the kitchen table with her coffee, looking from one to the other.

'You're destroying the planet!' is what I most clearly remember Jonnie saying.

This was news to me, and I said so, laughing. I had an idea of defusing the row before it got serious.

Hugo weighed in with heavy sarcasm, wondering which bit of it we'd destroyed that morning while cooking our breakfast. He pointed out of the kitchen window, where the sun was shining in a pale wintry kind of way, and said it looked all right to him.

'You know what I mean,' said Jonnie. 'If everyone on earth lived the way we do we'd need three planets to support us all.'

'Thank God for peasants, then,' said Hugo.

For a moment I thought it would all be all right. It was a crass joke, but still. Jonnie could have chosen to take it as a joke, and could have made the effort to climb down from his moral high ground. He was only twenty-one, and rather prone to black-and-white statements about the world, unlike his father, who was more cynical, and prone to black-and-white statements about the youth of today, or when he was young. But I felt just then that in a few moments we would all have a mince pie or a chocolate biscuit and everything would be all right.

They were standing on opposite sides of the table, glaring at each other. They were the same height, but dissimilar in so many other ways. Hugo, solid, handsome and greying, was broad and becoming paunchy; Jonnie was slender and skinny, dark-haired and pale-skinned, beautiful enough to be a model.

'Fuck you,' said Jonnie.

Hugo's mouth dropped open.

Flora, at the table, pushed her coffee away. 'Jonnie!'

Hugo took a deep breath. 'I will not be spoken to like that, Jonathan, by my own son in my own house. Apologise.'

'Fuck you,' Jonnie said again.

'I'm warning you, Jonathan.'

'I'm warning *you*,' Jonnie said.

'What the hell is that supposed to mean?'

'You need to get your act together,' said Jonnie. 'You need to understand the planet's heading for disaster. The climate's changing because of us. Animals go extinct every day, did you know that? The sea's full of plastic. We're living on borrowed time, we have to act right now, we –'

'Bollocks,' said Hugo. 'Now, I expect you to apologise.'

'I've got nothing to apologise for,' said Jonnie.

'Apologise to Daddy for swearing at him!' said Flora.

'Stay out of this, Flora,' said Hugo.

'Hugo –' I began.

'Quiet, Roly. Let me deal with this.'

'Now, just a minute, Hugo –'

'Shut up, everyone!' Hugo pushed his arms out sideways as if conducting a symphony. 'Jonathan. Apologise!'

'It's no bloody good, is it?' said Jonnie. 'I mean, you ask what I'm interested in, and I try to tell you –'

'We were thinking about your career, Jonnie,' I said.

'Fuck the career! You don't know a bloody thing about me. You think you know best, don't you, all the time! You think you know everything there is to know about the world! You're self-satisfied hypocrites! You do your little bit of recycling and think that's enough! You give a few pounds to charity, but actually you're patronising gits! Buying your little souvenirs and watching local dancing and coming back and enthusing about how authentic that bit of Thailand is or whatever!'

'I don't think we –' I began.

'Fuck off, Mum. You're no saint, you're as bad as –'

'Jonathan!' roared Hugo. 'Apologise to your mother! Right now!'

'I'm going back to Oxford.' Jonnie glanced briefly in my direction. 'Today.'

That meant he would miss my birthday the following day. Deliberate, it had to be. He didn't have exams to go back for, term didn't start for another week or two.

'Stay right there!' bellowed Hugo.

They met in the kitchen doorway. Hugo grabbed Jonnie's shoulders and pushed him back against the door jamb. He'd gone very red and was breathing through his nose like a bull.

They were staring at each other with hatred, faces set, mouths tight.

'Daddy!' screamed Flora. I saw it too. He wanted to beat the living daylights out of his eldest son.

Upstairs a door clicked shut.

'Hugo…' I wheezed. My chest was closing up. They both turned towards me.

'There are millions of people like you, Mum, who can't breathe because of pollution. Kids die. Think about that.' Jonnie wrested himself free from Hugo and ran up the stairs.

Hugo charged into the hall after him. 'Apologise!'

There was a muffled yell from Jonnie's room. 'No!'

'Come down here at once!'

'No!' Jonnie's voice was louder and clearer. He was standing in the door to his room. 'I'm packing!'

'Don't even think of asking for a lift!'

'I'm going by train!'

'And don't bother to come home until you apologise!'

'I won't!' His door slammed.

Flora began crying. I just stood and watched her, paralysed with the shock of it all. I could hear Hugo muttering in the hall as he went into his study. He too slammed the door.

Jonnie left within the hour and never came home again. And I didn't know – how could I know? – that this was the last time I would ever see him.

At the top of the stairs I found Flora, white-faced, huddled on the floor outside the twins' bedroom door. They were sixteen, then, and Flora was eighteen, about to do her A' levels. She was my absolute rock, when it came to the twins. If I didn't know what to say or do, she usually did. We were a good team.

'They won't let me in,' she said, without looking at me.

My heart sank. I stood close to the door. 'Boys, let me in. It's Mum.' I spoke quietly, staring at the crack where the door met the frame, unwilling for Hugo to hear there was another crisis in the house.

There was the slightest sound from inside the room, like someone creeping across to the door to listen.

'Boys,' I whispered hoarsely. 'Boys.'

Not a sound. I strained to hear. At my feet Flora was completely still.

'Boys.'

All I could hear was my heart thumping. I was scarcely breathing, holding myself taut against the door, ready to fly in, out, or downstairs at a millisecond's notice.

'Rosalie! ROSALIE!' Hugo's bellow made me jump back hard against the doorframe. 'Roly!'

'Yes?'

'I'm off to fetch your mother.'

Oh God, I'd forgotten. We had at most twenty, twenty-five minutes to make everything as normal as possible. He slammed the front door as he left. I felt, rather than heard, someone move on the other side of the bedroom door and I leaned against it once more.

'Boys, let me in. Fergus. Dugald. It's Mum.'

There was silence for another five, ten seconds, then unexpectedly, a whisper. I couldn't make it out.

'What?'

'Has he gone?'

'Who?' Stupid question. Stupid me for asking it. They might clam up again. I didn't know which boy it was but most likely it was Fergus, who, if either of them spoke at all, was the spokesman.

Another silence.

'Boys. Jonnie left about half an hour ago. Dad has gone to pick up my mother from the railway station.' It occurred to me that Hugo and Jonnie might see each other at the station. I hoped that if they did, they would make up.

I waited. There were footsteps from inside the room, walking away from the door. Then they came back. The bolts were shot back – one, two, three – and the door opened a crack. It was Fergus. He peered at me through the crack.

'Hello,' I said.

He gave a single nod, the kind of nod you give when passing an acquaintance in the street.

'Are you all right in there?'

He opened the door three inches. There was just enough gap for me to see Dugald sitting cross-legged on the carpet, rocking backwards and forwards, whimpering, his eyes scrunched shut. A little runnel of dribble trickled from the left corner of his mouth.

'Duggie!' I pushed the door open. Fergus didn't resist. I crossed the room and knelt down before Dugald. He was having a panic attack, closing down rather than lashing out as he did when he was a child. Any stress, any unexpected shouting or anger, this is what he did.

'How come you're all right?' I heard Flora say.

'I took a pill as soon as I heard shouting,' Fergus said.

'Good for you.'

'I'm not all right though. Neither's Duggie.'

'No. None of us are, Fergie. It's OK not to be all right.' She glanced at me. 'What can we do, Mum? Dad and Granny'll be back soon.'

I didn't know. I looked at them all blankly.

'We have to lie,' said Fergus unexpectedly. The twins never lied. They saw no point in it, they told me once.

Flora and I both turned to face him.

'We have to say he's got flu.'

'Dad won't believe us,' said Flora.

'No. But Granny won't want to see us if we say he's got flu. She won't make it worse.'

By some complicated algorithm he'd decided that a lie was acceptable today. The needs of the many outweighed the needs of the one, perhaps. Peace in our home versus social niceties. Whatever it was, I was grateful.

'Can you cope with that?' I asked.

'I have to,' he said. 'I'll have flu too. Please leave so I may undress.'

Flora and I got to our feet and turned to leave.

'Please bring us some food, Mum.'

'I'll do it,' said Flora. 'I might be going down with flu too.'

'Don't you dare!' This slipped out before I could stop it. She turned to look at me in surprise, then giggled. 'What about you, Mum? Don't you want flu too?'

And that, surprisingly, was a happy moment. We sniggered like naughty schoolchildren hiding from a fearsome head-teacher. Fergus regarded us stonily until we left the room and ran down to the kitchen, where we hastily assembled trays of food and drink, trying to provide the twins' favourites – Coco Pops, bananas, celery, bread and ham and prawn cocktail crisps, tomatoes and apple juice. We had just delivered the supplies when Hugo arrived back with my mother.

ↄ

I don't remember much about the rest of that day. It would have been the usual. My mother droning on about her travels, the hotels, the bars, the eligible silver-haired and silver-tongued bachelors (I never believed this – they surely had to be divorced, or gay, or on the run from their wives) with whom she'd nearly had a fling. And the drink she consumed. As slim as ever, eating very little, but drinking gallons of Hugo's better wines as well as the compulsory aperitifs and digestifs. She wouldn't have been the least bit interested in the boys' flu, merely determined not to come into contact with them. And dear Flora would have made an effort, as she always did, rewarded by a few perfunctory comments, mainly about what she was wearing.

We endured her visits, Hugo and I, and now I have no idea why. When life is so fragile, when those who matter get a raw deal, why should others take up all our attention, so much energy and time?

I do remember, though, that we lay side by side in bed that night, not touching, as straight as a lord and lady on their tombstone.

Hugo said: 'He won't do it, you know.'

'Mmm.'

'He won't risk his degree. He's got too much sense for that.'

'Mmm.'

'Five weeks in the Antarctic. Not a chance.'

'Mmm.'

'Should never have let him do all that sailing. They wouldn't have had him then.'

I believed him. What's more, I believed in him. I thought that Hugo had such a grasp on reality that in this, as in everything, he was right. It was as simple as that. It's the old story, isn't it, that people who confidently assert something to be true and act as though they believe it themselves, well, they sweep everyone along with them. They can even change their minds, and no one notices.

So, when Jonnie went straight to Heathrow from Oxford, and got on that plane to New Zealand without even phoning us to say goodbye, and Hugo clapped his hands to his head and said, 'I knew it! I knew it! I predicted this. The boy's an idiot!' there was only the tiniest part of me that thought: 'No, Hugo, you didn't predict anything of the sort.'

❧

I have never forgiven myself for that row, for not speaking loving words before Jonnie left, for not ever writing or phoning him during the whole of that term. I suppose I believed that he would come home before the Antarctic trip, or that he wouldn't even go on it. I believed the row was a storm that would blow over. I thought Jonnie would crack first, phone and apologise, and everything would go back to normal. But it seems it was one of those storms that herald something new, something different, although none of us could have predicted how things would turn out.

FIVE

How Things Stood

Sunday morning, early. New Year's Day. A stiff breeze is blowing through that gap – whistling, moaning, wailing. It sounds like I feel, like the cave itself is in pain.

Good weather, despite the wind, but high tide. Not a chance of getting out. I'd drown, for sure. The water's right up against my bit of shingle and completely covers the rocks. I'm sitting sideways to the water, my knees drawn up to my chest, keeping as dry as I can. Just as well this little cave slopes up at the back.

'So, how are you doing, my friend? How was your night? You're hungry, no doubt, thirsty too, and does that leg hurt?'

I'm famished. We say that kind of thing all the time – famished, starving, ravenous – but so rarely do we mean it. I'm so hungry my stomach hurts. My hands are shaky too, and I feel wobbly when I stand up, a bit light-headed.

So, food for us both. I'll investigate the biggest pool when the tide goes out and see what I can find for the bird. Cockles, maybe, or mussels. Not sure I want to eat anything like that, myself. I'm not really into raw seafood. I worry about sewage.

For me, well, I've two apples, half a bag of walnuts, and a stale bar of chocolate which I found in one of the pockets of the rucksack. It has a bloom on it, a pale coating of white, but I never heard of anyone getting poisoned by chocolate. And there's one bagel left in its plastic wrapper, and a small piece of cheddar from the Co-op, and the jar of peanut butter, which I can scoop out with my fingers. It's all keeping quite well. It is January after all.

They'll be wondering where I am. Probably phoning home, ringing around my neighbours. Did I tell Flora where I was? I'm not certain I did. I passed some people on the path – they might remember me. And maybe there's GPS or something on my phone to tell people where I am. The police or the coastguard.

I'll make a plan. Keep calm. There must be some way of signalling to people outside. I need to draw attention to myself, to the fact I'm here, trapped. Perhaps there's something I can use in the rucksack.

Here we go: sponge bag with toothbrush, toothpaste and flannel, a small hairbrush, three sets of underwear, my damp spare trousers, two damp spare shirts and a smart sweater, four pairs of socks – also damp – my long black silk dress and a red embroidered shawl, and a pair of smart shiny evening shoes with diamanté buckles, because Anne always likes people to dress up. I also have my pearl necklace and my sparkly diamond earrings in their little leather case.

Nothing of any help whatsoever, apart from the wind-up torch. I could try waving it around at the entrance tonight. No matches or candles. Not even a mirror to signal with in daylight.

To think I used to be a Girl Guide.

ↄ

I needed some kind of closure after Jonnie's death. I needed someone to blame. Not Jonnie, who had clearly made some wrong decisions, and had suffered for them, and couldn't now explain himself, couldn't now reassure me that he still loved me. I couldn't reasonably blame him.

But although people told me it was an accident, and they meant well, nobody understood my need to let myself and Hugo off the hook – and my need to find a scapegoat, someone who had pushed, cajoled, persuaded, somehow influenced my son to put his life in danger. I didn't blame the people on the ship, although I could have. I wanted someone closer to home, someone tangible, someone who would end up weeping with remorse. And then I could have forgiven him.

 batch

Someone on the ship packed up Jonnie's olive-green 70-litre rucksack for us, and sent it home, grimy, battered, and oil-spattered, the same rucksack I have with me now. They had carefully folded Jonnie's clothes, wrapping a bottle of vodka in a T-shirt so that it wouldn't break, slipping small items into the pockets and compartments. Part of me was thankful for the care this unknown person had shown; most of me resented it, resented a stranger's hands on my son's poss-essions, resented the whole tragedy, the fact that this needless accident had ever happened, that we – I – had been reduced to a crippling semi-existence.

I would find Jonnie's phone, I thought, look at the contacts, work out who it was that had set my son on this terrible path. And I was pretty sure I knew. His friend Ollie.

On a dank Monday in June, I stood in the door of Jonnie's room. I wrapped my arms around myself, chilled through by this room filled with Jonnie's ghostly presence, and stepped over the threshold. I'd been in his bedroom many times since his death, but that morning the room felt utterly different. I wasn't dusting away non-existent dust, straightening the books on his shelves, changing his bed linen, as I'd done so often. It wasn't that I expected to see him again. In my head, I knew he'd never be coming back, I'd never hold him again, laugh over a joke, share a bag of crisps. But the ache in my heart told me otherwise, and I needed to keep his room ready for him.

The rucksack was just as it had come home to us months before, and I stood before it, my stomach churning, daring myself to unclip it and to open it and to inhale the Jonnie smell of sweat and musty unwashed clothing and salt and stale waterproofs. I approached it eventually as if it were a venomous snake, slowly and from the side; I laid my hand on it and stroked it, placating it, willing it not to strike me dead. Trembling, I unclipped the top section and pulled it open. The first thing I saw was the half-finished bottle of vodka. A gift of Dutch – Russian – courage from my son to me. I said 'Cheers, Jonnie!', unscrewed it and gulped a mouthful, which brought tears to my eyes as I spluttered and coughed from the acrid burning in my throat.

But then I began to laugh, at first quietly, in relief at finally being brave enough to confront my fears, then wildly, manically. In a kind of dervish dance I pulled and pulled the stuff out of the bag, tossing it around the room – socks, underwear, T-shirts, long johns, sweaters, a woollen hat, padded trousers and jacket, biscuits, chocolate, paracetamol, gloves, jeans, trainers, boots, his four-season sleeping bag, a torch, a penknife, a first aid kit, his sponge bag and towel, more thick socks, a compass, dried fruit. But there was no phone.

I stared at the chaos around me in dismay. I turned back to the rucksack, groped desperately inside every single pocket and compartment. Urgently I turned out everything that remained, chucking it on the bed and the floor, thrusting my hand deep into all the pockets – tissues, coins, a wallet, his front door key, a small Bible, a battered paperback thriller, but no phone.

Without Jonnie's phone, how could I get in touch with Ollie, his so-called best friend, the idiot who'd filled his head with juvenile half-baked theories? Who had no knowledge of how the world really works, whose influence had persuaded Jonnie to risk his life in dangerous places, and who most certainly hadn't risked his own life?

Some might think that I jumped the gun about Ollie, made assumptions that I couldn't possibly verify. But I had evidence: emails on Jonnie's chunky old laptop, the one Hugo insisted on giving him for university and which he hadn't taken with him on that last, fateful trip. A heavy Toshiba, laughably slow and unreliable by today's standards, with its black and red screen and its disk drive. It was still plugged in, still, when I lifted the lid, on standby. Password protected, of course, but that was easy to guess: 'L18hty3ar'. To infinity and beyond.

Ollie's emails spoke earnestly about ecocide, parts per million of carbon; palm oil and plastics; ice sheets and glaciers; algal blooms, alternative economics, climate cycles; ocean acidification and coral bleaching. All this and more. He went on and on and on, relentlessly, humourlessly, boringly. Reams and reams about things I didn't understand, didn't care about, and dismissed.

Extremist nonsense. Dangerous rubbish. That's what I felt. Hugo felt the same, I knew; I'd heard him say it. That's partly what all the arguing had been about at Christmas.

I didn't bother to read Jonnie's replies. I felt I had found the person I could blame for his death.

I swigged more vodka and talked aloud, pacing up and down the room, bed to desk, desk to bed. I rehearsed telling

Ollie precisely what I thought of him, putting him in his place, spelling out my arguments about life and responsibility and blame, about his youth and my maturity, about how a mother feels when she loses her son.

When I swung away from the desk and found Hugo staring rather bug-eyed at me from the doorway, I was just sober enough to say that I'd been thinking it was about time I sorted out Jonnie's things.

'Right,' he said. 'Right.' His eyes veered to the bottle in my hand. 'I'll give you a hand, shall I?'

'No, it's all right, darling. It's all under control.' I grinned at him reassuringly, showing all my teeth.

'Right,' he said again. He took a step into the room, his briefcase in his hand, looking about him. He leaned over and picked Jonnie's front door key off the bed. I couldn't see his face. He slipped the key into his pocket and straightened up.

'You're back early!' I gave him a bright, wide smile.

'No… not really.' He glanced at his watch. 'A bit later than normal, if anything.'

'Heavens, I had no idea! It's these long summer days! I got quite carried away! Doing the sorting out!' My face was beginning to ache.

'Right.'

Relentlessly cheerful, I exclaimed: 'Pizza for supper, then!'

I hadn't even thought about our evening meal. Flora loved to cook, made shopping lists, pored over cookery books, experimented with things like pomegranate seeds scattered over roast lamb, exotic spices and herbs, edible flowers. She used to come straight into the kitchen after school and add her own touch to our meals. Now she was away at university my cooking was basic, to say the least, more often than not thrown together at the last minute. The twins had only ever been interested in food as fuel, and since Jonnie's death they always took their food upstairs and ate in their room. I didn't stop them. There seemed no point. They'd simply have bolted their meal as quickly as possible, said not a word and left the kitchen. Not much fun for any of us. And I didn't really pay attention at the time, but they'd begun staying as late as possible in school, then going to the public library until it closed. That should have told me something.

'Right. OK, then.' Hugo nodded. 'I'll, um, just go and change.' He nodded again. 'Actually, Roly, why don't you come down and I'll phone for a takeaway? Hmm?' He was still nodding, like one of those fluffy toy dogs in the back of cars. 'What d'you think? Chinese or Indian?'

'Ooh, I don't mind,' I said breezily. 'I'm not particularly hungry, actually.'

'No?' He glanced around the room, somehow taking in the vodka bottle once more in a swift view that lasted barely a second. I dangled it carelessly from my fingers. 'You must have had a good lunch.'

I hadn't eaten all day.

'On second thoughts, I'd love some Chinese tonight. Can't think when we last had a takeaway.' As I said the words I remembered, and I knew Hugo did too. Our last family meal at Christmas, the night before Jonnie left. Our eyes met.

'Come on, old girl,' he said, after a second. 'We have to do normal things.' He stepped towards me and caught me as my knees gave way and I crumpled to the floor. 'It's what he'd want,' he murmured into my hair. 'It's all right, it's the first time, another first, but it'll be OK.'

But it wasn't all right. Every mouthful almost choked me, and I wanted to spew up the whole meal and run screaming from the house and throw myself under a train. Hugo watched me and knew how I felt, I could see it in his eyes, but for him

45

the meal was a mark of love.

Very early the next morning I stumbled my way downstairs, sleepless, at dawn. I was badly hungover from the vodka and the bottle of red wine we drank alongside the Chinese takeaway, but I went out anyway, too nauseous and dizzy to eat breakfast, my head thumping, and I waited outside the hardware shop until it opened. There I bought a bolt and padlock for Jonnie's bedroom door, which I fixed that same day. From then on, I kept it locked. Hugo must have noticed but he said nothing. At the funeral, his sister had told us to be gentle with one another. No doubt that was what he was doing. Being gentle.

I avoided Jonnie's room for a few days. When I did venture back in, I saw it through Hugo's eyes, and was embarrassed at the state I'd left it in. *Be gentle*, I told myself. I tidied up the mess, folding the clothes, piling them in heaps on the bed ready for washing, when I felt up to it, placing his notebooks neatly on the desk. I sat for a long time on the floor, burying my face in Jonnie's jumpers and T-shirts, smelling him, the strongest scent of him I would retain before it slowly faded with exposure to the air.

I was reluctant to leave his room, to leave him, ghostly, alone. I felt that I was on some mystical journey. A clue would, if I waited long enough, reveal itself to me and set me off in the right direction. I had an important task to fulfil, a task that would make sense of everything that was so horribly wrong and somehow put it all right.

That day I didn't have any idea of what lay ahead. I could see nothing beyond that hour, that minute, that second. I wandered about Jonnie's room, staring out of the window at the scudding clouds, watching people walking past the house, opening and shutting the desk drawers, twitching his duvet straight.

I suddenly realised that I'd overlooked the obvious. I could email Ollie, and that would surely be better than calling him out of the blue from Jonnie's phone, which I never found. It's probably at the bottom of the South Atlantic with half a mile of sea above it. Or sculling about the Greenpeace ship, an ancient phone that everyone thinks belongs to someone else. Or the girlfriend took it and it's now in a box in her attic and one day when she's dead or in a nursing home her children will find it and throw it out.

Instantly the room felt full of Jonnie. It seemed to me that he was just out of sight, that if I turned my head quickly enough, I'd catch a glimpse of him, if I listened hard enough, I'd hear his laugh, if I closed my eyes, I'd feel him brush past me. I took this as a sign, a blessing on my endeavours.

Dear Ollie,

I'm sure you remember me. I'm Jonnie's mother. I have been wondering how you are. We are all well.

Yours sincerely,

Rosalie Danborough

It took me an hour to compose this short message, deleting, rewording, writing almost my life story at one point. I'd just sent it when Hugo came home. He was expecting supper, I'm sure, although he didn't mention it, just poured himself a gin and tonic and kissed me on the forehead as he passed me on the way upstairs to change.

I put four frozen pizzas in the oven and rootled around in the fridge for salad. There wasn't much – a couple of tomatoes, a courgette and some white cabbage. The twins took their meal upstairs as usual but paused before leaving the kitchen.

'You've been crying, Mum,' said Fergus. Dugald stood behind him, staring at something to the left of my shoulder. I turned to see, but it was a cupboard, closed and blank, like his expression.

'Yes, I have,' I admitted. 'I'm very sad.'

He nodded. Dugald turned his attention to the floor tiles.

'We're sad too,' he said. 'But we decided not to cry, because crying can't bring Jonnie back.'

True enough.

'Don't you want to cry, sometimes?' I asked. 'I mean really want to cry, let out your feelings?'

He stood for a long moment, dropped his gaze to the floor, thinking. Dugald closed his eyes, tray in his hands.

'Yes,' he said. 'We understand, Mum.'

They both turned and left the kitchen. Their tread on the stairs seemed heavy and slow. I wanted to ask them so much – how is it for you, boys? You've lost your big brother, what does this mean for you? Can you see the cracks in my sanity, Hugo's resolute life-must-go-on attitude, our struggle to find our feet? Don't you miss Jonnie, deeply, viscerally? Doesn't your breath catch at the very thought of him? But I knew they would tell me nothing.

Hugo ate the inadequate meal with every appearance of enjoyment, washing it down with a couple of glasses of Valpolicella.

He didn't ask what I'd done with my day. I didn't ask him about his. That was how things stood.

SIX

The One I Blamed

Ollie replied to my email politely, perhaps warily, I don't know. He said he often thought about us, he thought about Jonnie constantly, that he missed him, he'd been a good friend, one of the best. Yes, yes, I thought testily, I know all that. What do you really think, Ollie, what do you really admit to about your responsibility for my son's death? How well do you sleep, Ollie?

'Would you like to meet?' I asked.

As I intended, Ollie said, yes, if that was all right.

I prepared for him, oh yes. I was so sure of myself – possibly the last time I ever was, before everything turned on its head and came crashing down.

But this was before all that. This was a time when my strong conviction told me that I was right and Ollie was wrong. Back in the late nineties, we all thought – well, most of us, apart from the prophets and the eccentrics and madmen, and lone scientists and hippies and pagans and earth mothers and geography teachers – we all thought that the only way was up, better and better, more and more progress, into a shiny, wonderful future. Everyone I knew thought the same way. There were seemingly balanced articles in the papers, and documentaries giving both sides of the argument: global warming either was, or wasn't, happening. I found it so easy to ignore reports from big international conferences halfway across the world about the dangers of an overheating planet. It didn't once occur to me that it was being taught in schools because it was important. If I'd thought about it at all, I might have concluded that it was of mild and passing interest, like learning about the Vikings.

So I prepared for Ollie's visit, knowing exactly what I was going to say:

What kind of friend are you, Ollie? Not brave enough to sail dangerous waters yourself? Not a good sailor, Ollie? You nasty little toe-rag. I wish it had been you. I wish it was your mother mourning her son. I wish I could wring your bloody neck. I wish I could drown you in the Antarctic myself…

Yet even as I thought all this, it felt too extreme. There's such a thing as politeness, after all, and whatever else I may be, I have always been immensely polite. I don't like rows and scenes and public distress. But I planned to tell him off, and he would apologise, and we would be reconciled in some gracious way – he would always owe me a grovelling gratitude for my forgiveness.

At one time I was immensely fond of this boy, Ollie. Oliver Henderson. Jonnie's best friend from junior school. The Hendersons moved away when Ollie was eleven. Jonnie was distraught and kept asking when he and Ollie could get together. It wasn't so easy – they'd moved to Scotland, and we were in St Albans, and I had three other children to look after, but we did manage to meet up once on a beach in France one summer when we were all on holiday there. That was about as much as I could manage, back then.

And now that I'm being honest, I'll admit something else. I was jealous of Sarah Henderson, God knows why. Ollie was her only child, a late and most welcome arrival in her mid-forties after years of miscarriages and investigations that yielded no answers. Jealous? What stupidity. She was the sweetest woman, kind and generous with her time and friendship. What I envied was the calm of a home with only one child, the favourite.

I wasn't prepared for the young man who turned up on the doorstep a couple of weeks later. I remembered him as a child, Jonnie's inseparable companion, so close and so alike that people mistook them for twins as they romped and charged around the local park. I always wanted to say, no, those aren't twins, those beautiful healthy boys, no, look at those weird kids over there, those two arranging leaves by size or screaming with terror at the *bottom* of the slide, those are the twins, yes, and they're mine.

Ollie was both taller than I'd imagined, and broader. The biggest surprise was his long wavy dark brown hair and beard, wild and bushy, the hair swept back in a loose sort of ponytail reaching far below his shoulder blades. His beard curled luxuriantly down to the middle of his chest. He was wearing jeans and trainers and a heavy checked shirt over a brown V-necked jumper and what seemed to be two T-shirts. His fingernails were dirty, with black grime deep in the crevices around the nails.

'My goodness,' I said, before I could stop myself. 'You look like Davy Crockett!'

'I don't know who he is,' said Ollie. 'But that's better than what my Mum says.'

There was a fraction of a second's pause, and then we both laughed.

In that moment my intentions were undermined, my

rehearsed speeches scrubbed. This living breathing boy, his veins pumping warm blood, his glands releasing hormones, his nerves conveying sensation, his eyes, ears, lips all acting as they should – he was standing in front of me, waiting for me to speak, and I thought, if this were Jonnie standing in front of Ollie's mother, Jonnie who had lost his best friend, I would want her to be kind to him. I fought the impulse to ruffle his hair and kiss the top of his head as he sat at the kitchen table while I walked past making tea and finding plates for cake.

I showed him round the house and garden, some of which he remembered well and some of which he didn't remember at all. Then I invited him to stay for lunch and he looked pleased and ate so well of the cold supper I'd got in for myself and Hugo and the boys that I mentally scanned the drawers of the freezer to see what I could pull out and microwave that evening. I loved it. I loved the reminiscences, the easy banter we fell into, and, in the end, I lost myself for an hour or so in the sense of normality, enjoying the company of a young man who could possibly have been my son.

Of course, we got onto what he was doing now, at the age of twenty-two, and it was more than troubling when I realised that he left school at sixteen with almost no qualifications. Sixteen, well, that explained it, I thought. At that age people are easy prey to ill-educated rubbish garnered from hippie-type websites, written by pagans and druids and the sort of people who dangle crystals in their windows and bits of string and twig behind their beds to catch their dreams. People who believe in astrology and folklore and fairies. I felt it wasn't surprising that someone like Ollie would fall for it. I silently bemoaned the lack of rational thought. How ironic it seems now, to think I believed that I was the rational one.

'What did your parents think? What did they say?' I asked, agog.

'Not much,' he said with a grin. 'My grandparents gave me some money, so I went off travelling for a bit. I woofed.'

'Sorry?'

'I woofed. Worked on organic farms.'

'Really?'

He nodded, scooping up coleslaw with his fork. 'Yeah, it was great. I made some good friends. I spent four months in New Zealand, and a couple more in Australia. Then about a year in Spain. It was great, I loved it.'

'And what did you do?'

'All sorts. Fencing, sheep-shearing, apple-picking, tree-pruning, nursing orphan lambs, digging potatoes, weeding – you name it. I did it all.' He shook his head slightly, as if over the folly of his youth.

'But what about qualifications, Ollie? A Levels? A degree?' I was horrified. It was worse than I'd realised. An intelligent boy like him, working as a labourer. I couldn't see the point. Jonnie had gone straight to university after school. He played with the idea of a gap year but Hugo and I had thought he might lose momentum, forget what he'd learned at school. It wouldn't be gainful, we said, to not get his degree straightaway.

'A Levels?' said Ollie. 'I'm not at that place right now, Roly. I don't see the need.'

'Don't see the…?'

'What would I do with a degree when I'm happy doing what I'm doing now?'

'Well, Ollie, one day you might want to settle down and have a family and provide for them. You'll need to do more than just be able to shear sheep!'

He smiled and shook his head. 'I'm learning to be self-sufficient. I like growing my own food. I've got a family. We have a lot of fun.' Seeing my dubious look, he added: 'It's cool.'

'And your parents?'

'Yeah, they're cool with it.'

'Really, Ollie? Can you really say they're whole-heartedly in favour of this... experiment?'

'Yeah. I'm not costing them any money, after all. And I'm not scrounging off the state, not claiming benefits. And Mum came to stay a few weeks ago.'

'Or is it, Ollie, that they realise they have no choice, and that whatever they say you'll ignore it?'

He grinned. 'Yeah, well. Maybe.'

∽

He said it first, a kind of half-request that we'd both skirted around and yet knew had to be asked and answered, like some sort of exam question.

'I don't suppose I could see his room, please, Roly?'

'Of course,' I said, and jumped up from the table, leading the way upstairs with a curious feeling of lightness and expectation. I went in first and turned immediately to see Ollie's reaction. I don't know what I expected – guilt, perhaps, or grief, or maybe a stolid acceptance of loss, like Hugo.

Ollie just looked amazed.

'It's almost exactly the same! I didn't expect it to be the same.'

He took a step into the room.

'Oh my God. It really brings it home.' He stood gazing around, and then brought his fist up and wiped both his eyes, first one, then the other. It was a clumsy gesture, reminding me of a bear I once saw on a wildlife programme. Flora had thought the bear was crying, when it only had dust in its eyes.

Do bears cry? I don't think they do. I tried to harden my heart.

'I don't know how you manage it,' he said.

'I don't.'

I must have sounded brittle then, and hurting, for he stepped towards me, and I found myself enveloped in a strong hug, my face pressed against his chest and beard. I stood stiff and still, allowing him to hold me. We stood there for ages, Ollie sighing heavily once or twice, his chest heaving. Then he broke into racking sobs, weeping into my hair. My son, another woman's son, what did it matter? Ollie needed to weep with and receive the comfort of a mother; I needed his grief. And for a few moments, listening to his heart and feeling the heat of his chest and arms, I could pretend this boy was mine. Apart from his smell. He smelt of woodsmoke and sweat and mud. That wasn't a Jonnie smell.

I pulled away eventually and let him compose himself. He turned and took a couple of steps towards the desk by the window. I watched as he brought his sleeve up to his nose.

'There are tissues in the bathroom,' I said.

I ought to have been moved by this display of emotion, wept with him, taken his hand and helped him tell me how he felt about losing his best friend. But at that point I wanted him to leave my house and to take his crocodile tears with him. How dare he shed tears for my son, how dare he mourn him, in front of me, his mother? He was utterly to blame for Jonnie's death. Utterly. The more Ollie seemed upset, the more enraged I became. I wanted him to suffer.

When he'd recovered, I asked him quite deliberately if there was anything he'd like to take with him, any memento.

Ollie took his time glancing round the room. He shook his head once or twice and sighed again. 'Only if you're sure. It's really kind of you.'

'Quite sure, Ollie.'

He chose a small Spiderman figure, that was all he wanted. I lifted it down from the shelf. But when Ollie held out his hand for it, I held it back; cruelly I asked him a question.

I said – and I can barely believe it of myself, this pettiness, this power-play, after all we'd been through that day – I said: 'You can have this, Ollie, if you tell me what all those ridiculous climate change emails were all about. I hold you responsible, you know, for Jonnie's death. Ultimately.'

You'd have thought I'd slapped him. He looked more than shocked; he looked devastated. He sat down abruptly on Jonnie's bed with his mouth hanging slightly open, his eyes wide.

'What do you mean?' he whispered. 'I didn't tell him to go on that ship…' He shook his head. 'I can't be held responsible for his death, really I can't.' He looked up at me, bewildered.

Of course he was confused, I see that. I'd greeted him warmly, we'd had a lovely happy few hours, eaten together, laughed and cried together, and now I seemed a different person altogether, hard and tough and accusing.

'So you didn't encourage him, then?'

'No… no… not really…' He tailed off, looking uncertain. He blinked, and frowned, and shook his head. 'No…'

'You can't tell me it was his idea.'

'But it was,' he said. 'It was. Honestly.'

'Honestly?'

'Yes,' he said more robustly. 'Honestly. He had the idea for years. He said he'd do it when he felt ready, when –'

'Years?' I raised my eyebrows, gave him my most sceptical look.

'Yes!' He was nodding vigorously. 'We must have been about fourteen, you know, that summer when we all met up on the beach in France. We talked about it then.' He stood up, took a step towards me. 'Honestly, Roly, that's when we first talked about it, that's what made me interested.'

'He got you interested in all this environmental stuff?' I snorted. 'I don't believe it for one minute.' Ollie was so scruffy, grubby, unkempt, just the sort of person you saw on the news, up trees, in makeshift tents, protesting against new roads, trying to protect scrappy bits of woodland or bog – and Jonnie had always been immaculately turned out. He loved his clothes, loved choosing new things. Except – and just a tiny splinter of doubt crept in – I couldn't think what had happened to the beautiful sweaters, the cotton shirts, the jackets, the smart shoes. They weren't in his bedroom, didn't come home from university, certainly weren't in the rucksack that came back from the South Atlantic. I shrugged it away.

'But it's true.' Ollie seemed to be weighing something up, frowning, looking down at his feet, his hands thrust deep into his coat pockets. He'd always done that, I now recalled; he was always pulling things out of his pockets – string, a compass, a torch, a fossil. After a few seconds he nodded. 'Yeah,' he said. 'What Jonnie told me, you know, about global warming and the sixth mass extinction and rising carbon emissions, you know, all that stuff, it sort of changed my life. I wasn't academic at school, and it gave me a way out.' He waved vaguely at the bookcase and desk. 'I couldn't have done all this, Roly, university and things. It gave me a plan, which I've stuck to and I'm not failing at. I'm a success, actually, in my own small way. I'm turning out better than anyone predicted, aren't I?'

He must have said that to his parents.

'And I've put all that other stuff behind me.'

I didn't know what he was talking about.

'You can see that, can't you?'

He was appealing to me, tears once again in his eyes. 'I'm

not the person everyone thinks I am, Roly, really, I'm not. I'm responsible. I'm a father. I've got a child. You should see her, she's beautiful. I'm thinking about her future all the time, Roly, all the time.'

A father?

It was my turn to sit down heavily. I groped for the desk chair behind me, but it swung away from me, and I found myself sprawled on the floor, staring at Jonnie's metal Buzz Lightyear waste-paper bin.

Ollie crouched down and gently raised me. We knelt side by side on the carpet, as if at prayer.

'I don't believe you,' I managed at last, not looking at him.

'It's true,' he said softly.

'But he had everything he could possibly want! Why go off on some wild goose chase, some tree-hugging nonsense – how did he even know about it?'

'School,' said Ollie.

'School? Oh no.' I shook my head. 'Oh no, no, not at all. Hugo and I, we chose his school very carefully. There wouldn't have been any of this rubbish there.'

'Geography lessons,' said Ollie.

'Nonsense.' I got to my feet, hanging onto the desk to steady myself.

'Debating society.'

'And he was a good debater. You wouldn't know that, Ollie.'

'School trips,' said Ollie.

'This sounds like desperation, Ollie,' I said, turning to face him. 'You're just scrabbling around looking for excuses.'

'Fundraising for charity,' said Ollie. 'Christian Aid, Oxfam, the Red Cross, Save the Children –'

'And we support them too, they do humanitarian work,

Ollie, humanitarian, do you know what that means?'

I looked up at him, feeling, it has to be said, rather smug. I'd been so proud of Jonnie's fundraising – the sponsored swims, the concerts he put on with his little band, selling cakes to our neighbours when he was ten – and his enthusiasm and desire for justice had influenced me, and Hugo too. We still supported all of Jonnie's charities: the RSPCA, Guide Dogs for the Blind, Great Ormond Street Hospital.

But there was something in Ollie's eyes, a kind of deep sadness, and it didn't seem to have much to do with Jonnie. Looking into his eyes it seemed to me that sorrow was at the heart of him, despite his pride in being a father. So young, how could he be mature enough to bring up a child? I began to feel less triumphant about winning the argument. There was something wrong, something not making sense to me. But I couldn't be deflected by sentiment, so I continued to put him in his place.

'Humanitarian work, Ollie, is the sort of work you do rebuilding places after natural disasters, and sending in doctors and nurses and people like that. Natural disasters, Ollie, tsunamis and landslides and hurricanes. Do you understand?'

He nodded.

'And they have ongoing work too, bringing in food when the rains fail, or there are floods and things. Am I right?'

He nodded again and let out a breath that sounded like a small sigh.

'And disease. They have immunisation programmes. Desperately important, wouldn't you agree?'

'Yes.'

'Of course it's important to look after the environment. After all it's what the National Trust does. All those trees, and sheep, and things. But to become fanatical about it, well, that's wrong-headed and leads to all sorts of trouble. As we know.' My heart had begun thumping, and I was beginning to breathe quite fast. The footage of Jonnie being swept off the ship flashed into my mind and I suddenly had to hold on to the desk.

I took another shuddering breath, decided to quote Hugo, who never had any moments of doubt about what was right and what wasn't. 'You have to understand, Ollie, that global warming is overstated. If it's happening at all it will be completely beneficial.' I breathed out, then in, out, then in. 'For the economy. Which will be a benefit to all.'

I was finding some comfort from Hugo's words. So solid. So certain. So sure of the bright future before us.

'Where do you get your information?' He spoke quietly, his tone serious, thoughtful.

'What?' I wheezed. 'Hugo knows all about this stuff. He's very well-informed, you know, Ollie.'

'Is he a scientist?'

I glared at him and took a long gasping breath. 'You know very well that he's not. You're being extremely impertinent.'

'No, I'm not,' said Ollie, to my astonishment. 'Where does he get his information?'

'He's very intelligent, very well-informed, and I don't see that it's any business of yours.'

'It's the business of everyone on this planet,' said Ollie obliquely.

'This is bonkers! We're going round in circles! I can't make any sense of what you're saying. It's just hippie nonsense, and for heaven's sake, look at you! Look at what you're wearing! That – what is it? – donkey jacket? That, that lumberjack shirt? You haven't a hope of being taken seriously looking like that!'

I stopped.

Ollie was standing very still, his face expressionless.

'Appearances do matter,' I said lamely.

'If you say so,' he said, and gave a small smile through the thicket of his beard. He held out his hand for the Spiderman. After a moment, I gave it to him. He closed his fingers over it and over my hand too.

'Jonnie was doing geology. He loved it – it was his life,' he said gently. 'Thank you for lunch,' he added, when I didn't reply. 'If you ever – if you ever want to have another chat, discussion, whatever, it's OK, I'd be up for that.'

I was taken aback by his gentleness, his respect. Ollie was looking round the room, still holding my hand. Then he nodded, pulled me towards him and gave me a one-armed hug.

'So long,' he said. He and Jonnie had always said that to each other. So long. He kissed the top of my head. 'Come and see us, if you like,' he said into my hair. I could feel the warmth of his breath. 'We've got plenty of room.'

'I don't know where you live.'

'I'll write it down for you.' He pulled away, let go of my hand, slipped the plastic figure into his pocket. 'Thanks for Spidey.' He patted his pocket. 'I'll keep him safe.'

He let himself out. I watched him from Jonnie's window, swinging his way down the road, and I turned over and over in my hands the little scrap of paper where he'd written his address. I could have offered him a lift to the station, but I didn't think he would have accepted it. I felt, obscurely, that I had let myself and Jonnie down. And, of course, there was no getting around the fact that Ollie had behaved a good deal better than me.

SEVEN

It's Not Fixed

The tide's as low as it's going to get, but I could so easily slip off these slimy rocks into the sea and drown, my body found somewhere along the coast in a few weeks' time. I feel like I'm about to sky-dive for the very first time; my stomach's tight, my breath comes in short gasps.

I've left the rucksack propped against the back wall of the cave. It's too dangerous to wear in this wind, which buffets me, pushing me back against the slanting layers of granite. Hugo and Jonnie used to point out these rock formations as evidence of earthquakes millions of years ago. I begin to feel – not optimistic, exactly, but that this might be possible, all things being equal: good weather, easy climbing, me not getting too tired or scared, someone spotting me. I rather wish this old parka of Jonnie's was a fluorescent orange, not a dull beige.

The landslide behind me is a shocking scar on the cliff face, a long fragile slope, bright and clean against the weathered granite. In the sea below lies a large block of the headland, small bushes perched atop as if it's a long-established island. As I watch, stones and earth slide gently down the slope and topple into the sea.

I turn back to my task. Around the corner I find great boulders, tumbled who-knows-when from above, lying across each other at angles. Waves roll around them, white surf breaking. The cliff must be two hundred feet high. There's no beach below me, no obvious path, but there are ledges on the cliff face that seem almost like steps. I've never climbed a rockface in my life, but it might not be as bad as it looks. I begin to climb diagonally, a few centimetres at a time: one foot, then the other; one hand, then the other, ignoring the pain and stiffness in my thigh.

Slowly does it. Don't look down. My legs tremble, my breath comes in short gasps, my fingers are cold and sore, but I'm concentrating, my eyes focused on the next place to grip, my face so close to the rock that I could kiss it.

Five minutes, ten, twenty. But now it's getting dark and I'm finding it hard to see where to place my hands. Low tide comes twice a day, half an hour later each time. The next low tide will be at night, when it's too dark to see. The one after that, after sunset. So my next chance to climb out will be in a few days' time, early in the morning.

My chest has tightened up at the thought of several more days before I can try again to escape the cave. I lay my forehead against the cliff, close my eyes, breathe, breathe.

After a few moments I glance up at the towering cliff, then look down between my feet, at the sea and the boulders. The water is very close. I've hardly achieved anything in an hour.

I grip my little outcrops of rock, my hands suddenly so weak that it would be easy to simply let go and fall into the waves rolling against the base of the cliffs. Images of Jonnie being swept off the ship flash into my mind. It would not take much to give up, end this ordeal. I briefly wonder how it would feel, being swept away by waves stronger than me, pushed down below the surface and dashed against the rocks.

I pull myself together. People will be looking for me. I've got to stay alive, stay safe, for them. I turn into the increasing breeze, climb down to the boulders and back up to my cave, fighting tears of frustration and disappointment. It has started to rain, a drizzle, but the clouds are black and fast.

'You know, I'm not enjoying this cave experience. I didn't expect to be here more than a couple of hours. You clearly have a lot of patience. I don't think patience was ever my strong point.' The bird raises its head and opens an eye briefly at the sound of my voice.

I had a bit of a panicky moment when I got back. For a short while I felt as if I might die here. As if. The weather will change pretty soon, and I'm only a mile or so from St Ives. It's no distance at all, half an hour's walk if you don't linger on the cliff path to stare at the view. Someone will hear me, someone will come. A fishing boat. I'll sit out on the flat rock at low tide tomorrow and wave. There will be walkers if it's good weather. I'll yell, call for help. And there are lights at sea, a huge container ship anchored in the bay. I'll wave my torch, do an SOS.

I'm feeling calmer now. I've pulled myself up onto this narrow ledge at the back, almost at the same level as the bird so I don't get splashed at high tide. I wouldn't bother otherwise. It slopes quite sharply, too.

'Your ledge is better than mine, you know. No slope.'

❧

Hugo never knew that Ollie had visited. It would have led to all sorts of questions – what he was doing, where he lived, horror at the lack of A Levels, and so on and so forth – and I was too tired to go through it all again. His indignation would have been directed at me, in the absence of Ollie himself, and I didn't have energy for the vigour with which Hugo would have addressed the problem of Ollie.

I did a kind of hearty vegetable soup for supper with what I could find in the fridge and freezer – a couple of wrinkled parsnips, an onion, some celery, frozen petit pois – all thrown in with tinned tomatoes and butter beans and a sprig of mint. Hugo poked around in it for a few minutes and asked if it contained any meat. Eventually he pushed it away half-eaten and went to make himself four slices of cheese on toast which he ate in front of the TV in the sitting room. The twins, as usual, said nothing, ladled soup into bowls and took it upstairs.

Slumped at the table I stared out into the garden as the evening darkened to chilly twilight. There was no sunset, just the promise of drizzle from the flat, grey clouds. At the edge of my mind, scurrying around like a shy woodland creature, was a half-formed thought that Ollie's visit was significant in some way, that it had importance beyond the obvious, although what even the obvious was I struggled to articulate. It might be helpful to see Ollie again. I found it hard to believe that Jonnie had come up with all this stuff by himself, although when I looked back at the blazing row the three of us had had the previous January it now seemed all too likely.

And now, seated alone in the kitchen, the heart of our home, I remembered other things, things that hadn't made a lot of sense and which I'd put down to teenage bolshiness: Jonnie aged fifteen insisting that we travel by train to Italy rather than fly, for example. Hugo and Flora had been enthusiastic for this adventure. I'd dreaded the whole expedition, imagining all kinds of disasters: hornet stings, trains being cancelled and our getting stranded, the twins having public meltdowns. But all went well. Hugo gave the boys notebooks, new pencils, a phrasebook and a guidebook.

Jonnie's mid-teen vegetarianism was suspended from time to time. We all kept healthy and it was a wonderful holiday. Who knew you could visit Pompeii on the train? The twins needed extra notebooks for that visit.

Other things came to mind, too. Jonnie informing me about acid rain, which sounded so outlandish I didn't believe him at first. There was no sign of it here in the UK. No, he said, we export it – it's pollution from our fossil-fuel powered industry blown into northern Europe, and it comes down in the rain and kills the trees and all the leaves fall off. That could be winter, I said, which I truly believed until he showed me a textbook from Oxford University Press and I had to concede that they probably knew what they were talking about.

We should eat less meat, he announced one day. I said of course, no problem, I'd buy more fish. He glanced at me and I could tell he wanted to roll his eyes. Lentils, he said. Beans. Nuts. Are eggs all right, I asked, annoyed at the idea of having to learn a whole new way of family cooking. Depends, he said.

There was plenty to look back on, now that I was excavating my memories. I mostly didn't want to look at them, but they knocked, insistently, at the door to my consciousness.

I went to the library a few days after Ollie's visit, wanting to understand climate change and global warming, wanting to disentangle the two and to find out what some people were so hot under the collar about. It was useless. I found little on the shelves – a 1997 flood assessment of Bedfordshire, a couple of books on population, a small pamphlet discussing rare orchids in East Anglia. When I asked the librarian, she pushed her glasses up her nose and swept her hand over her wispy hair, and said, hopefully, 'Science fiction?'

I regarded her. I'd gone all the way to the central library, and this is all she could offer. Facts, that's what I wanted. Facts.

She gave me a tentative smile. 'We don't have much call for

that sort of thing. I can order you up to three books at a time. There's a charge, I'm afraid. Is there anything in particular?'

'But this is a library.'

'Yes.' She looked past me, at the small queue that was beginning to form.

'Aren't you supposed to carry books on everything?'

'Well, yes, but the cuts, you know, there's not so much money around as there used to be.' She pushed her glasses up her nose again. 'I can order in anything you want. It's quite quick, only about a week or so.'

Things would be different now, more than twenty years later. So many books have been published in the past five, ten years. And the information online – astonishing. Who needs books? But back then, it was impossible. I tried bookshops too, and got the same answer: the general public wasn't interested, and quite frankly bookshops didn't have the shelf space to stock books that wouldn't sell. Try a library, they said.

∾

I sat on Jonnie's bed and looked helplessly at the boxes of books on the floor. They'd been sent back from college in a van, together with his files and folders, his climbing gear, clothing, boots, sports stuff and hockey stick.

The college had written to us – a beautiful sympathetic letter that made me cry – and asked if we wanted to pack it up ourselves. Although Flora said yes, she really wanted to, she would take a week off university and come down and pack it all up for us, Hugo and I looked at each other and knew, without words, that we couldn't do it. Too raw. That bloody row. Hugo got his secretary to compose a short letter, and someone, I don't know who, went to the house Jonnie shared with friends and boxed up our son's brief life and it was driven down in a Bedford van by one of the college porters. He was a nice man, who said how sorry he was. I gave him a cup of tea, white with two sugars.

Geology. Earth Sciences. I always thought geology was just mountains and valleys, coastal erosion and volcanoes, exploration for gas and oil and coal, with the occasional excitement of an Antarctic meteor shower thrown in. It's all that and more, I discovered, and Jonnie had chosen to specialise in the impact of human activity on Earth's environments.

Nobody in the family wanted to open those boxes, perhaps afraid of what might be let out – I think they were waiting for me to make the first move, my privilege as a mother, one of the few I possessed, it seems to me now. Hugo always decided the interesting things about our lives: where to live, holidays, schools. I did the mundane: the meals, the laundry, the clothing, the doctors, dentists, playing fields, parents' evenings, the school run. So now I had the privilege and pleasure of being the one to dispose of my dead son's effects.

The twins didn't touch anything, of course. I invited them into Jonnie's room about a month after his funeral, and they stood in the middle of the room, arms stiff by their sides, looking, eyes swivelling from side to side without moving their heads. At that moment even I didn't know which one was which.

'You can have something,' I said.

'Something?' asked Fergus after a pause.

'Anything you like. A book? An object? A toy? One of Jonnie's posters?'

There was a long silence. I bit my lip and tried not to feel impatient.

'Why?'

'Well, to remember him.'

After a few seconds Fergus said, 'We remember him anyway.'

'Well, yes, of course you do. But would you like anything of Jonnie's? Like a sort of gift?'

'Who from?'

'Jonnie, I suppose.'

'But Jonnie's dead.'

'Yes, I know.' My heart was beginning to pound, and I could feel the pulse in my head. 'I know Jonnie's dead, boys, I know that.' I took a deeper breath, tried to control it – in, out… in, out. To give them their due, these days they had the patience of saints – perhaps it was the medication – and it was me whose temper frayed. 'We all know Jonnie's dead. We went to the funeral, remember?'

'We saw his body.'

'Yes.'

All of us, trooping in together. Hugo, ashen-faced, Flora, clinging to his hand and weeping, the boys, faces set – who knew what they were feeling? – me, last of all, fearing that I might faint. We had all, together, decided to see our boy. My last image of him, and it didn't look like him at all, five days dead, his features somehow flattened and sharpened at the same time. Only his head was exposed, the rest of his body covered by a sheet.

'It didn't look much like Jonnie.'

'No,' I said. 'You can have something of his, if you like, each of you. Or several things.'

'How many?'

'As many as you like,' I said desperately, wishing I hadn't started this conversation. 'Anything you like.'

The twins stood quietly in the centre of the room, and then both shook their heads.

'No, thank you,' said one.

'We remember him anyway,' said the other. He turned to look at me. 'We won't forget him, because he was our brother. You won't forget him either. But,' he added, and I found this curiously cheering, 'thank you for asking.' Flora took Jonnie's fluffy dog and tucked it into her bed. Hugo said he would look some other time, and I carefully closed the door, as if Jonnie was sleeping and shouldn't be disturbed.

I took nothing. I would leave his room intact, guardian of his shrine.

⁂

The boxes of books from college remained where we left them, pushed out of the way behind Jonnie's desk.

But now, a year later, I was becoming sensitised to the language. I began to notice the references to climate that were everywhere beginning to pop up, however contentious – and it did seem contentious, at the time, with lots of arguments and controversial opinions and people telling us there was no evidence that the climate could change fast, that we had centuries before we needed to worry, that the whole thing was overstated. Radio 4, newspapers, Oxfam, Christian Aid Week, Save the Children, Médecins Sans Frontières, some of the charities we supported... It was like a sort of eczema. The rash popped up because I was sensitised, and the more I scratched, the more it itched.

I mentioned it once or twice to Hugo, and he cautioned me to be careful, that I shouldn't believe everything I read.

'You have to ask, Roly, what are they gaining from this? A

research grant? A book deal? A movie contract?'

This last one seemed unlikely but I didn't interrupt.

'Any number of things,' he added. 'Being employed on a nice fat salary by a solar panel manufacturer. Or even just getting themselves noticed, getting their names out there. And don't forget confirmation bias! That's when people look for a result and find information that seems to confirm what they're looking for. That's junk science.' He wagged his knife at me, satisfied. 'I do believe, if it was that serious, this global warming thing, everyone'd be jumping up and down about it.'

'Jonnie knew a lot about it. He did geology, Hugo.'

'Yes, and there's a lot more to geology than changing climates. Personally, and I'm not alone in this, I think the bigger problem is peak oil.'

I stared at him, dumbfounded.

Hugo speared a bit of fish with his fork. 'The world's running out of oil, and we need to find more. Can you imagine the economic mayhem if we don't secure a good supply? Oil companies are crying out for prospectors. Jonnie could have...' He paused. 'Well.'

I took a breath, suddenly didn't feel like eating. We sat in silence while I slowly finished my meal. I accepted the glass of red wine Hugo poured for me, and drank it swiftly, almost in one go. At the end of our meal, he rose and came around to me and gave me a hug. 'Sorry,' he whispered. I leaned into him for a few moments, gave him a tiny dry kiss on his cheek. Not enough, but better than nothing.

A couple of days later I opened a couple of Jonnie's boxes but found to my enormous relief that everything was far too technical for me to skim through and absorb. I'm not saying I couldn't have worked my way through them eventually. But what would have been the point? It was Jonnie's life, Jonnie's choice of subject, not mine; it would have looked even to myself as if I was competing with him – and Hugo – and Flora, also on track for her first – and trying to prove that I wasn't after all the dumb mum-at-home I seemed. I'm not stupid, after all. I just made a stupid mistake, not bothering to work for my degree, believing that love would conquer all.

What I needed was an overview. Teach Yourself Climate Change. Environmentalism for Dummies. Eco-Lite. I gave Jonnie's books to Oxfam.

℘

I tried talking to Hugo again a few days later, but it was a mistake. He laughed, and ruffled my hair, like he'd done with Jonnie and Flora when they were little. 'You don't need to worry about all that, old girl,' he said. 'The science,' he said reasonably, 'isn't even fixed, it's still being debated.' He pulled me to him and kissed me on the forehead. 'Don't worry your pretty little head about that.'

It was a joke, I knew it was a joke, the pretty little head thing, a reference to a sexist lecturer of mine at college, and we'd often laughed about it, each of us referring to the other's pretty little head. But I was wounded when he then said, 'What's for supper?'

'A takeaway,' I said offhandedly. 'I'm not hungry, actually.'

A small victory, a miniature retaliation, but I'm not sure he even noticed. And I was hungry. In fact, I was ravenous, having spent the entire day in Jonnie's room and forgotten to eat.

So the science wasn't fixed. I asked the boys the next morning. Is science ever fixed?

They turned from their twin desks and peered at me owlishly through their specs. It was the summer holidays, sixteen months after Jonnie's death, and they were working on something mathematical together. The height of fun. They hated going away on holiday, not much liking the change in routine and rather loathing sand and sea. Flora was away with Peter – her first serious boyfriend – and Hugo had suggested that he and I could have a break some time when the boys were back at school. They wouldn't have minded, he said, and I knew this was true. As long as there were meals in the fridge or freezer, they would have been absolutely fine. Even if I missed them, or worried about them, I wouldn't have been sure that they missed me. They seemed utterly self-contained – but maybe that's unfair. They were simply mysterious to me.

'No,' said Fergus. 'Science can't be fixed. It's empirical, it works on evidence being gathered and theories being made and testing those theories and then the theories have to change sometimes.'

'So, is it a bad thing, when science isn't fixed?'

'It depends what you mean, Mum,' he said. 'I mean, we have to assume that we're right about gravity, and the speed of light, and important things like that.'

It felt for a moment like they were teachers, and I was a primary school kid. I rallied.

'That's not what I was thinking,' I said. 'I meant new things, like what chemicals do when they're mixed with other chemicals…' I trailed off. They had both turned to face me and seemed to be regarding me with interest.

'No, it's not bad when that's not fixed,' he said.

Dugald shook his head. 'No,' he said, 'it's good. It means that scientists are still finding out about things. Although of course we want to get to a point where it's as solid as it can be.' He said we. A clue about their future direction, I noted. 'Our hypotheses or theories may have to change if new evidence is found.' He gave me a quick smile and looked down, clasping his hands between his knees. A long speech for Dugald.

'I thought so,' I said. 'Do people debate things in science?'

They looked at me. 'What do you mean?' asked Fergus.

'I mean, do they argue about what's true or not?'

'Not usually,' said Fergus. 'They discuss the results. That's different.'

'So, you don't have debates about the results and what they mean, whether they're true or false?'

'No, that wouldn't make sense,' said Fergus. 'You don't have true or false results; you just have results.'

'What about global warming?'

'The planet is clearly heating up,' said Fergus.

'Why is that? How can people be sure?'

'Human activity.'

'Really? – Dad says –'

Fergus jumped in, interrupting. He didn't want to hear what Dad said. He'd heard it already, I assumed. All ears, those boys. As silent as the grave. 'Ninety-seven per cent of scientists agree that recent rapid global warming has been caused by human activity. Roughly.' He blinked rapidly. Approximations were outside his comfort zone.

'Yes, I heard that, it was in the news. You're sounding just like the headlines!'

Fergus blinked again, turned half away, looked down at his textbook.

Why had I said that? Why had I teased him? For half a minute I tried to think of what to say, how to engage him. I didn't mean to upset him, and even now I feel hot at the memory of how he must have felt, belittled, patronised. From the set of his shoulders and the back of his head, bent earnestly to his book, Dugald clearly didn't want to take part any longer in this conversation. But he'd been listening.

74

'Sorry, Fergus,' I said. 'That was silly of me. A silly joke. But can you explain something to me?'

He half turned back, looked up.

'The three per cent who don't think it's to do with human activity, what about them?'

'They've got other theories. But they're probably not looking at all the evidence.'

'What sort of theories?'

For a moment, he seemed to falter.

'Some of them are really strange, Mum,' said Dugald. They glanced at each other.

Then Fergus, suddenly animated, said: 'There's this guy that thinks it's all a conspiracy for world domination by the United Nations.' He began jigging his foot up and down.

'What, he thinks the UN is creating climate change in order to take over the world?'

'No, he thinks the UN is making it all up.'

'Other people think it's made up as well,' said Dugald. 'They think it's a fashion and it's dangerous.'

'Well, it is dangerous,' I said. 'Isn't it?'

'Yes. But no, they think it's bad for the economy to believe in climate change.'

The economy. Conspiracy theories.

'But proper theories take into account cyclical climate change and sunspots and Earth's magnetic core and meteors. And other things,' Fergus added.

More than I wanted to think about.

'And some religious people say Earth is only ten thousand years old, so we can't ever have had an ice age.'

'My goodness, do they really?'

'Yes.' Fergus looked solemn. 'But they're not taking account of ice core samples.'

'Well,' I said. 'Thank you, Fergus. Thank you, Dugald.' My futile attempt at differentiating between them. As far as I could tell they never wanted to be separate, but they deserved that dignity. 'It's been an interesting discussion.'

'Yes,' said Fergus. 'It has.' They looked at each other and then back at me. 'We're glad you're getting into science, Mum.'

❧

Getting into science wasn't quite how I thought of it. I wondered about the three per cent, the people that called the ninety-seven per cent junk scientists. Majority consensus hadn't always been right – was that what the three per cent were saying? If the maverick three per cent were right, and global warming wasn't happening, or even if it was, it wasn't caused by humans, then we could all breathe a sigh of relief and carry on as normal. And, of course, as I was hearing everywhere right now, the climate had changed before, many times, without any help from humans.

I went downstairs and put the kettle on, conscious of a huge weight lifting from my shoulders. Just because a majority believed something was so, that didn't make it true. Black people are not inferior to white people; we don't get flu from the influence of the moon; the sun doesn't go around the Earth. These ideas were all believed by majorities, once.

So maybe, I thought, Jonnie had been on the wrong tack. Maybe Hugo was right, and the boys were wrong. They were still teenagers after all, still working things out. They could easily have got hold of the wrong end of the stick. Maybe, like Galileo, reviled for decades because of his opinion that the Earth moved around the Sun, the three per cent were up against junk scientists, more concerned with their grants and jobs and not rocking their academic boats than dealing with the truth.

Maybe it was all going to be all right.

I made tea in my favourite mug, the one Jonnie had given me at his last Christmas, and stood at the window and watched the rain hit the glass almost horizontally. It was a grim day, the westerlies promised by the weather forecast already gusting across the country and blowing tiles off roofs. The boys, upstairs on the other side of the house, wearing their white-noise headphones, were oblivious.

But what if the ninety-seven per cent were correct? Sometimes the majority was in the right, after all. Brushing teeth is helpful, despite the woman I met once in the health food shop who told me all I needed to do was drink milk at every meal. We should all definitely eat our vegetables. And I recalled the flat-Earther I met one day handing out leaflets, passionately sincere that the Earth was a disc, not a sphere.

I cradled Jonnie's mug in my hands. It was pink and white – not my colours; I prefer russets and ochres and olive greens, earth tones – but I loved it anyway for the thought and love. 'Best Mum in the World' was on one side, and a cartoon mother juggling dishes and laundry and a cat on the other. He might not have meant it, of course, that I was the best mum in the world, but I preferred to think it wasn't a last-minute gift picked up on Christmas Eve because he couldn't think of anything else. He slightly anxiously asked me if I liked it, and sat back with a smile when I said I did.

I watched the darkening sky, the wind bending the trees at the bottom of the garden so that I could see our neighbour's garage, normally invisible. I traced in my mind the course of the last year. We'd had various birthdays, all without Jonnie, but those had been just about manageable, as they were in term-time when we were used to him being away. The night before each birthday I shut my phone off and put it in the drawer in the hall table, so I wouldn't be reminded that he wasn't going to ring. I was trying to be kind to myself. I wanted not to feel that pain. I wanted to wall it off, bury it so deep that even archaeologists couldn't find it.

But Christmas had been a different matter. We rose early, opened stockings by the fire that Hugo always made on Christmas morning, ate croissants and drank hot chocolate, a ritual that had started when Jonnie was a toddler. I'd tentatively suggested a few days before that we could do something different, but Flora had been so horrified I immediately retracted it, and said I was sorry, and I hadn't been thinking. Hugo took me aside before we left for church and said, 'Don't you see, Roly, tradition is more important than ever, this year? Hmm?'

Of course I saw. I just didn't want to do it.

The boys were bemused, as ever, by the contents of their stockings. I'd given up buying jokey things for them as they never understood the jokes. I tried to get scientific items and food. Einstein calendars and maths puzzles and satsumas. Flora's stocking was full of girly stuff, hair scrunchies and eye shadow and things; Hugo's had quite a lot of chocolate and socks. I'd sort of lost my direction, getting it all. My mind hadn't been on the job. And I'd forgotten my own, so even though Flora and Hugo had bought a few bits and pieces – tissues, make-up remover, nougat and a chocolate orange – it was rather meagre, and Flora noticed, and was sorry, and came over and gave me a hug and said, 'Poor Mummy, we'll do better next time.'

We went as usual to the cathedral for the morning service, sang 'Once in Royal David's City', listened to the Dean waffling on about I don't know what, and came home for lunch, by which time my mother had arrived and let herself in and was making Buck's Fizz with real champagne. All the time there was this hard lump in my throat and another in my stomach and a tight pain in my chest, and I didn't see how on earth I could eat one mouthful.

I cried only once, when my mother toasted Jonnie.

But how I cried.

'To absent friends,' she said, and we raised our glasses and then I pushed my plate away – food hardly touched – and laid my forearms on the table and my head on my arms and wept. I found myself being held by Hugo, kneeling next to me on the floor, rocking me backwards and forwards. He stroked my hair and kissed my cheeks and forehead and murmured comforting things that I couldn't hear through my sobs. He helped me up the stairs to our bedroom and tucked me gently into bed and held my hands. 'We'll get through this, Roly, all of us. We'll manage, somehow. We'll look after each other.'

Then he sobbed, just once, a single racking heave of his chest, and I watched tears trickle down his cheeks.

EIGHT

Normal at Elevenses

Standing by the sink and watching the weather, Jonnie's mug in my hands, remembering the previous Christmas, I felt my chest tighten up with anguish. A sob rose in my throat, and I swallowed it back, holding my breath, holding my body tight, telling myself not to cry because it wasn't fair on the twins, what if one of them came downstairs and found me crying?

I was scarcely breathing when a pigeon crashed into the kitchen window, blown off-course by a sudden gust, its head smashed so hard against the glass that it left a smear of brains and blood as it slid downwards. I jumped and dropped my tea at the noise of the impact, a loud bang followed by a second of gut-churning horror as the pigeon flapped its wings feebly once and then fell out of sight.

I stood paralysed, shaking with shock, my smashed mug at my feet, my slippers sodden with hot tea, jeans splashed up to the knees, before I fell keening on the floor amid the broken shards of pottery, scarcely able to draw breath.

Hugo roused me, my fingers cut and bloody from gripping the broken mug. I had wept myself into unconsciousness. He was called home by the boys who found me at lunchtime and covered me with a blanket. They kept an eye on me, they told him, they made sure my airways were clear and that I was breathing. They didn't know why I had collapsed, they said, I was normal at elevenses.

છ

I took to my bed, something I should have done perhaps after Jonnie's funeral, except back then I was too busy making sure that everyone else was all right, that meals kept coming at the right time and that everyone had clean clothes to wear, and that people were thanked for their kind wishes and condolences and that the house stayed tidy and organised.

I had been so very brave, said Hugo, I had been too brave; he'd been watching me and hoping that something like this wouldn't happen. I should stay in bed until I felt better, he said, give myself a few days' rest. He and the boys would cope. And he would buy me another mug.

'It will be all right, Roly,' he said. 'I promise.'

છ

I stayed in bed for weeks, mostly asleep, the curtains closed against daylight. Hugo moved into the spare bedroom. Why he didn't call the doctor or get me to hospital, I will never fathom. I asked him once, and he said that I hadn't seemed too bad, that he thought that all I needed was a long rest.

I woke one day to see Jonnie sitting on the end of my bed. I was thankful to see no trace of his injuries. He was reading. I lay and watched him in the late afternoon sunlight drifting in through the gap at the top of the curtains. I could smell his favourite shampoo – coconut – and it was obvious that he had just stepped out of the shower and dressed quickly, as he always did, too impatient to dry himself properly. His curls were wet. He glanced up, saw me watching, and smiled.

'I thought you might need a visitor,' he said.

I smiled back, suddenly relaxed, my whole being suffused with joy. I hadn't lost him after all.

'You've got to get your strength up,' he said. 'Do you want anything?'

I shook my head. I felt so grateful to see him, so warm and happy, so strong. I needed nothing.

He gestured to the tray on the bed beside me.

'I know Dad'll be sorry he can't run to a cooked meal.' He raised one eyebrow and grinned. 'Even if he did,' he continued, 'it'd be burnt.' But he said this kindly, our shared family joke. We all knew Hugo was a terrible cook.

I looked at the tray. Grapes, a banana, a small carton of apple juice, a tomato and a triple pack of supermarket sandwiches nestling together on a dinner plate. Two *Snickers* bars and a box of half a dozen jam tarts, strawberry flavour.

The bed shifted beneath Jonnie's weight as he stood. 'Got to go, Mum, sorry. Get better,' he said. 'See you tomorrow.' He bent over me and leaned towards me. I closed my eyes as he kissed my forehead. When I opened them, he was gone.

I felt that kiss, you know. It was solid and warm.

Hugo wrinkled his nose when he came in after work. 'What's that smell?'

'Coconut,' I said. 'Jonnie's shampoo.'

'I don't think so,' said Hugo. He bustled around me, moving the tray away from the edge of the bed where it had somehow slipped while I'd been asleep, selecting a shirt and tie from his wardrobe for the next day. 'It's coming from the bathroom.' He disappeared through the door. 'Ah!' He reappeared with an empty bottle. 'Got tipped up in the shower.' He waved it at me. 'I want you to take care, Roly, in there. Have showers when I'm around? Hmm?'

Jonnie came to visit me several times. I didn't speak to him. I was afraid that he would disappear. Sometimes he talked to me, sometimes he wandered around the room, sometimes he worked on his laptop, sometimes he stood in front of family photos and studied them as if committing them to memory. Sometimes he was as solid as Hugo. Sometimes I could see right through him.

Sitting at the end of the bed one morning Jonnie looked up from his laptop. 'You need to take this seriously, Mum. Dad won't. It has to be you. You're the one. You've always been the one. Don't forget.'

I nodded and closed my eyes. I felt the bed shift as he left. When I opened my eyes, Hugo was sitting in Jonnie's place.

'Good sleep?'

I nodded.

'I've ordered some home-made food from that catering place, you know, the one that makes things to order. That's why I'm home early. They said between one and two for delivery. So, we'll have proper meals in the evenings, what d'you think of that? Hmm?'

I nodded again.

'Good. Lasagne and shepherd's pie and coq au vin and things. I'll do salad too. We'll get along just fine, Roly.' He clapped his hands together and stood up. 'How are you feeling?' This seemed a bit of an afterthought.

I closed my eyes and shook my head. I meant I didn't know. I could hear Hugo breathing. Then I heard him go downstairs.

As I got used to Jonnie's visits I tried communicating with him. I never spoke aloud, but I tried to convey in thought and feeling, how proud I was of him for living – and dying – according to his principles. How much I loved him. How sorry I was.

Jonnie smiled and said, 'I know.' He sat by me and stroked my hand until I fell asleep. And when I sent thoughts to him of my intention to make a difference, to change the world, or at least my own small part of it, Jonnie nodded and said, 'I knew I could count on you, Mum.'

The last time Jonnie came that autumn he stood at the end of my bed and pointed out of the window. He was holding his laptop under his arm.

'Ollie and me,' he said, 'we've got it all worked out. It's all in here.' He patted the laptop. 'Don't forget,' he said. 'You know what to do. So long.'

'JONNIE!'

He was gone, and I was awake, wide awake, my heart pounding, panting as if I'd just run five miles uphill. I lurched out of bed, crashing onto my hands and knees on the floor, and scrabbled around under the bed behind my slippers and balled up handkerchiefs and overdue library books. The laptop was there, covered in a layer of dust with not one fingerprint on it. I opened it, kneeling in my pyjamas on the carpet. You may think me mad – I know Hugo did – but I believed I had a commission from my dead son, a last wish, if you like. I thought: *Jonnie's laptop, it's his last will and testament. It's all I need.*

౬౩

I got up that day, got up properly, I mean, not just for the toilet or for food. It was a clear beauty of a day, with a deep blue sky and the faintest tinges of copper and gold on the trees along our road. I took a long shower and afterwards regarded myself in the full-length mirror in the bathroom. My build is long and skinny, slender and lithe like Jonnie, but now my ribs stuck out and my knobbly knees looked like they'd been stuck on and belonged to some other bigger animal. But although I was tired, I felt well. Something had happened to me. I was a new creature. I had shed a skin and emerged not only alive but stronger, able to take flight, no longer crawling about on the ground like other earth-bound grubs. And the thing about flying is that you can see a long, long way.

෬

Hugo was delighted to see me up and about. He said that he always knew I'd be better for Christmas, all I'd needed was a good long rest and in fact he'd told Flora so even when she started talking about doctors and clinics and things. I know you, Roly, he said, you're as strong as an ox, all you needed was a good long rest.

I agreed with him. I told him I was ready to move on. I'd finally acknowledged and accepted that Jonnie was really gone, never coming back. What I didn't tell Hugo was my new mission.

I went back to Jonnie's computer and switched it on.

NINE

Misinterpreting the Signs

'Well, my avian friend, our New Year hasn't gone very well. You don't seem to like cockles very much, and my wounds are going to take a while to heal. I'll be more careful next time. If there is a next time.'

No plasters in my bag, of course, or antiseptic. I wasn't expecting to be camping out away from home.

I feel really sick too. I was so hungry I ate a couple of raw mussels. The worst thing was prising them out of their shells. I gouged away with my car key like Hugo getting a tiny battery out of his watch with his penknife, but less efficiently, not a quick flick and ping as the battery shoots out of the watch but stabbing and skewering and scraping so that the mussel was shredded into little stringy bits. It was disgusting, but I couldn't stop because I was so hungry, and it'd somehow be worse to leave them half-dead, dangling in little bits from their shells.

Do mussels feel pain? How would anyone ever find out? I didn't enjoy them. They were revolting, salty and slimy and chewy. I should have stuck with my walnuts and my one remaining apple, but I was scared of completely running out of food, so I tried the shellfish instead.

Then the cockles. I tried giving these to the cormorant, scattering them on its ledge. It stretched its neck, opened its enormous wings, then opened its bill and grunted at me, a deep, guttural, annoyed-sounding grunt. I thought it didn't understand what I was trying to do, so I went closer, careful to make my movements slow and deliberate. I pushed the cockles around on the ledge, picked one up, tried to get the bird interested. Then it lunged with its long, hooked beak, and stabbed the back of my hand.

The wound has stopped bleeding now. I've bathed it with salt water, sucked it a little to get out any poison before it enters my bloodstream – that's what I learned as a child, but I'm not sure it'll make any difference because of the deep cut in my thigh, which is now throbbing in time with my heartbeat.

I'll keep talking. It passes the time, helps me deal with my anxiety. The bird gives a good appearance of being interested. It occasionally lifts its head and gives me a long stare, whether of approval or disapproval, I can't say.

‹›

I had another long chat once, with my boys, well, as much of a chat as they've ever indulged in. They'd probably rather have been playing chess.

I got them outside one summer afternoon, thinking the sun would do them good, help give their pasty faces more of a glow. I made them sit at the patio table, facing the sun, placed mugs of tea and chocolate digestives before them. They squinted at me suspiciously.

'We haven't got time to mow the lawn,' said Fergus.

'We've got some programming to do,' said Dugald.

'You've always got programming to do. Why not enjoy the

sunshine for a bit? It's going to rain tomorrow.'

'We don't really mind,' said Fergus.

'Well, I mind. It's a bit lonely sometimes, with you upstairs chained to your desks, and me pottering around down here. I could do with the company. You can do your good deed for the day, keep me company for half an hour.'

They looked at each other. 'Twenty minutes,' said Fergus.

'Twenty-five,' I said, 'and no arguing. And it'll do you good, sunshine and fresh air, what's not to love?'

Dugald sneezed.

'It's quite nice,' said Fergus politely.

'For heaven's sake! It's beautiful! Not a cloud in the sky, and just look at Dad's roses. Glorious. I'd quite like to make a water-saving garden, like Spain. Do you remember that holiday when we saw all those cactus things by the road?'

'Prickly pears,' said Dugald.

'We could grow those, and aloe plants and herbs and things. Maybe oranges, and dates and star fruit, oh, and melons, they'd be easy. And why not pineapples and lychees too? It'll be a kind of fusion of east meets Mediterranean. And a pool would be great at the bottom of the garden.'

I was showing off, demonstrating that I did read the news, did notice what was going on. Five degrees warmer was the prediction, by the end of the century. Just like Spain, some people said. The boys munched their biscuits and watched me demonstrate that I didn't know what I was talking about. Fergus dipped his chocolate digestive in his tea, fished it out just before it disintegrated. It had taken him years to perfect that timing.

'We'll be just like Spain or Greece, won't we? We can have gravel instead of a lawn, lots of pots, paving, maybe an awning just here – actually, a pergola would be better, and we can grow grapes up it. I'll get you two to help me build it. You're so practical.'

'No, Mum. You don't understand. It won't be nice. It could be really wet, anyway.'

'Really?' My head was full of Mediterranean sunshine and barbeques and swimming and mango trees.

'Five degrees is an average,' he said. Behind him Dugald nodded.

'Yes, I know that,' I said. 'Some years it will be four degrees warmer, other years six. That's what average means. So we might have one year which is four degrees warmer, and another one that's six degrees warmer, but overall, it's five.'

'No,' he said again. He shook his head. 'No, mum, that's not how these averages work.'

I took a deep breath. Much as I loved them, these very odd boys were, I thought, teaching me to suck eggs.

'Tell me,' I said. I poured more tea, prepared to spend a long time listening to a convoluted explanation that would go over my head, but it was worth it, just to spend time with these boys. They were shy of company, so wrapped up in their ideas, so self-sufficient. I liked not feeling superfluous for half an hour, even if it was an illusion. I'd listened to them so many times as they worked out ideas, watched their faces become animated, alive, alert: computer science, economics, further maths, all the stuff they loved, couldn't get enough of, stuff that really made no sense to me at all. I've always been more artsy, love a good concert or exhibition, although to give them their due, they did like music, the more obscure the better.

We sipped our tea. I nibbled my biscuit. The boys stared at each other. I sometimes wondered if they were telepathic.

'OK,' said Fergus. 'These average temperatures, Mum, are from thousands of readings from all over the world.'

'OK.'

'That means Equator to ice cap.'

'OK.'

'Night and day.'

'OK.'

'Sea and land.'

'OK.' So far so good. Easy-peasy.

'So five degrees doesn't sound so bad, when you're thinking about twenty degrees on a summer day in the UK, and then the next day being twenty-five degrees?'

'Exactly,' I said. 'That's exactly my point.'

'But it's not like that,' he said.

'So what, Fergus, is it like? Tell me. Put me out of my misery. I don't understand why five degrees is going to be such a massive problem.'

He blinked. I'd sounded tetchy.

'Sorry, darling.'

He smiled, briefly, his eyes on me but not seeing me, seeing something beyond me, a chart or a graph, most likely.

'Can you estimate, Mum, how much colder the world average temperature was at the coldest point of the last ice age?'

'No.' I shook my head. 'I'll guess. Twenty degrees colder. Thirty.' I sipped my tea, wondered whether to have a third biscuit.

'It was about six degrees colder than it is now.'

I frowned at him. He gazed back, expressionless. Beside him Dugald stirred sugar into his tea. That was one of the few differences between them, that half teaspoon of sugar.

'I don't think that can be right,' I said.

'It's right. You can look it up.'

'So…' I paused. They were always accurate, the twins. They didn't exaggerate, obfuscate or lie. They relayed facts like walking encyclopaedias. Hugo had the enviable gift of being able to tune them out.

The boys let me work it out.

'So if six degrees colder means an ice age,' I said at last, 'what does six degrees warmer mean?'

'Hotter,' said Dugald.

'Well, yes, I –'

'Warmer is too gentle,' he said. 'We shouldn't say six degrees warmer; we should say six degrees hotter.'

'OK. Six degrees hotter. What does that mean?'

'It means the extinction of virtually all land-based life,' said Fergus, matter-of-factly. But his pale skin was flushed – the sun, maybe, or emotion. 'It'll be too hot to live. The seas won't be far behind. It's the sixth mass extinction, and it's already underway.'

I pushed my chair back and stood, quickly, and the plastic chair fell behind me with a clatter. I felt ambushed, although he hadn't meant it like that. He was trying to break it to me gently, get me to see it for myself, get me to own it.

'You needn't sound so bloody pleased about it!'

He blinked rapidly, looked down, stared at the table. Dugald began rocking slightly.

'I'm not pleased, Mum. It's tragic.'

I was sorry then. Don't shoot the messenger. It wasn't his fault. I leant forward and reached my hand across the table to him. His eyes flicked towards it and away.

'I'm sorry, Fergus. Dugald. My dear boys. I'm sorry. It was a shock, that's all. I'm not cross.' I bent down and retrieved the chair, pulled it back to the table, took my time in seating myself, gave them time.

Dugald's rocking began to slow. Fergus began to breathe. I didn't realise until that moment that he also sometimes held his breath in moments of stress.

'Tell me,' I said. 'Tell me more about it.'

Then the lecture began. For about an hour and a half they talked me through the historic records of previous extinctions at similar temperatures, the poisoning of the seas and the atmosphere, the sedimentary layers of dead vegetation and animals. Quite a lot went over my head, but I got the gist.

They said that after a few million years complex life would re-emerge from the sludge that was left of our geological age, the Anthropocene, the age of humans. I found that small comfort.

They said that planetary temperature rise was not uniform – the Equator and the Antarctic and Arctic were warming much more rapidly. Dugald rushed off to get his laptop and show me charts of atmospheric carbon. They explained about greenhouse gases, the blanket effect of clouds, positive and negative feedbacks, and by now I had lost my way.

I just knew that it was bad.

And how fast, I wanted to know, will all this happen?

'Well,' said Fergus, and he and Dugald looked at each other. I recognised that look. It was a look that Hugo sometimes had, when he was considering what to tell me. 'Some estimates say the temperature could rise six degrees by the end of this century. Or sooner.'

'Fahrenheit or Centigrade?' I said fatuously.

Fergus frowned. 'Centigrade, of course. Celsius. It's an international scale.'

I took a moment to absorb this.

'So there's no hope?' I said eventually.

'I don't know,' said Fergus, after a few seconds.

Dugald gave a tiny shrug and raised his eyebrows.

'I don't know either,' he said. He paused, then patted me on the shoulder. 'I'll mow the lawn after supper, if you like.'

❧

You can imagine the effect this had on me. My clever scientist sons were telling me it was bad, so bad they couldn't say whether there was any hope at all.

I was shocked at the starkness of their vision, lay awake for at least a few nights, but then I rationalised it once again. They were only boys, teenagers, what could they possibly know? It didn't occur to me that I was repeating the mistakes that Hugo and I had made with Jonnie: assuming they had no understanding because of their youth, assuming their lack of experience meant lack of intelligence, assuming that I knew better. I dismissed our conversation, the statistics they'd told me, the books they'd read, the science, the scientists, and felt a sense of huge relief. When I looked at the world around me, it all seemed pretty normal. The trees looked the same, there were birds in the garden, the supermarket shelves were still well-stocked. Nobody else seemed worried, nobody else seemed to be talking much about global warming or climate change. It didn't seem to be mentioned much in the news or in speeches in Parliament.

But perhaps I wasn't looking, perhaps I didn't want to look. Perhaps I was deliberately looking the other way.

TEN

Of Course, They Lived in a Field

The following summer, a full year after Ollie had visited me, two years after Jonnie died, I texted Ollie and said I'd like to visit. Hugo had gone abroad somewhere for a week or so, for work.

'Cool,' was his reply. 'How long for?'

That threw me. A couple of days? It's quite a long way from St Albans to rural Dorset, and I was no longer confident behind the wheel of a car.

I said a night, if they had the room.

Loads of room, said Ollie, come for as long as you like. Kiss.

Well, they lived in a field, of course, Ollie and his girlfriend. They'd built a kind of hobbit house, all tree branches and dried mud and a grass roof, with mismatched aluminium windows that looked as if they'd come from a 1960s toilet block, and a wooden door that had evidently been salvaged from a shed. There was an old metal bathtub sitting under an oak tree, incongruous with its lion feet and unusable gold taps, and a crooked fat metal pipe trickled smoke from the roof of the dwelling alongside a couple of solar panels. Sheets of plywood and planks of wood were stacked against one of the walls. Old tyres and large plastic containers lay strewn about the place.

It was summer, and they were sitting outside on a large log when I arrived, watching a toddler splash around in the bath.

I pulled Hugo's car over to a less muddy and churned up piece of grass near the hedge. Ollie strolled over to the car.

'Roly, hi! Welcome!' He gestured behind him. 'Come and meet the family. You're just in time for lunch.'

Oh no, I thought, *shoes,* and glanced down at my suede moccasins and jeans. Perfect for a day in the country, I'd thought.

'Have you got anything else for your feet?'

'Slippers,' I said ruefully. 'I didn't think.'

'No worries. We've got loads of wellies. So,' Ollie continued, as I picked my way through the mud behind him, choosing tiny patches of grass to zigzag my way to the dwelling, 'this is Polly, and this is Dorcas.'

'But we call her Moonbeam,' said Polly, and smiled at me. 'She was born during a full moon. Our little moonbeam!' She stood next to Ollie, a pretty young woman, with long blonde hair and brown eyes, the kind of girl I'd sometimes thought Jonnie might have married, except she wouldn't have been dressed in outsize wellingtons and filthy dungarees and a flowery blouse, wet from holding the toddler. The child didn't look like a beam of moonlight at all. She was solid and grubby, with rosy cheeks and dark bedraggled hair. Typical of Ollie, I thought, giving his child a silly nature name. One of those irritating little alternative things, something that marked him out as somehow more authentic than the rest of us. I was already half-wishing I hadn't come, what with the mud and the hut and the wacky lifestyle.

'Dorcas. You could have called her Dolly,' I said as a kind of joke. 'Rhymes with Ollie and Polly.'

'That's an idea,' said Ollie.

'Or Molly,' I added. Polly raised her eyebrows.

My nerves were making me babble. 'She's beautiful,' I added.

They both nodded at this self-evident truth. I could tell already this was going to be hard work. And I'd committed myself to an overnight stay. The child stared at me solemnly. She was naked except for an amber necklace, and now clamoured to be put down. Polly lowered her to the ground and watched as she toddled over to the bath and peered in at the grimy water, her little white feet streaked with mud.

'I should get her sun hat, Olls,' she said, and squinted up at the sky. She sounded incredibly middle-class, as if she'd stepped straight out of public school. I wondered how a drop-out like Ollie – charming though he was – could have managed to start a family with this young woman. I smiled at her. She smiled back.

'Have you lived here long?' I asked.

Polly made a little face while she calculated. 'Mmm… just over two years. We moved here a few weeks after Moonbeam was born.' Seeing my surprise, she added, with a little smile, 'All winter too.'

'Really?' I glanced quickly at the hovel. 'Isn't it cold?'

'A bit. But perfectly possible. You wear loads of clothes –'

'Except at night,' said Ollie and grinned at me.

I didn't look at him. I could see him smiling out of the corner of my eye. I wasn't sure where this conversation might go.

'It's only fairly recently that central heating was invented,' Polly continued. 'We shouldn't forget that Celts, Anglo-Saxons, medieval people – they all lived a similar kind of lifestyle.'

'It must have been terrible,' I said. 'Such a hard life. People died so young.'

'Not always,' said Polly. 'My research shows there are multiple factors in mortality, and chilly living conditions aren't that high up the list.'

Her research? I couldn't imagine what she meant.

Ollie said, after a moment, 'Polly's doing a PhD.'

'Really? But why are you living here? With your baby?'

'It's free! The field belongs to my grandfather,' she said cheerfully. 'No rent.'

'Good thing too,' said Ollie.

'And how did you meet?'

'Oh, a re-enactment thing up in York,' said Polly. 'I was there doing some interviews, and Ollie was being a Viking.' They smiled at each other, and he bent to kiss her on the lips.

'So, lunch,' said Ollie, straightening up. 'Stay there, I'll bring it out.'

'Could I wash my hands?'

'Oh, of course,' said Polly, and gestured to the bath. 'I'll get you a towel.'

'Actually,' I said hastily, 'I meant…'

'Oh! Sure!' Polly was smiling. 'Sorry! Yeah – over there.' She pointed to a tall hut at the far end of the field, half hidden by various bushes and spindly trees. It had steps leading up to a door about five feet above ground. 'Compost loo,' said Polly. 'Don't forget the sawdust. Sprinkle,' she said, when I looked confused. 'And remember to take a torch at night.'

In borrowed size eleven wellies I squelched over the field to the hut. I prepared myself for a stink but in fact there was very little smell at all. There were two wooden lavatory seats, both shut. One had a paper notice stuck to it with Blu Tack – 'do not use' in curly orange lettering – so I didn't use it. There was a bucket of sawdust to one side with a trowel, and a large plastic bin full of straw. I was thankful to see toilet paper, off-white and no doubt recycled. I disliked the idea of recycled toilet paper – it sounded wrong somehow – but I did use it and dropped it down the hole into a deep pit which smelt faintly farmyardy, and then sprinkled sawdust into the hole too, and closed the lid.

Back to the bathtub, to the grimy water, and to the clean but stained hand towel that had appeared at the end of the log.

It was just like camping, I reminded myself. I glanced around me. Almost like camping. I had a fleeting image of Olly's mother, the elegant Sarah, now in her late sixties, perched on the end of the log.

'Our own salad,' said Ollie, 'and new potatoes. Local cheese. Our own eggs. A few very early tomatoes. Raspberries from our neighbour. We feed her cat, so she lets us pick stuff when she's away. Meringue and cream from up the road. Birthday present.'

'It all looks delicious,' I said, genuinely. It did. It looked fresh and appetising, a medley of colours and textures. The yellow tomatoes were sweet and tart, more tomatoey than anything I'd bought in a long time. There was rocket and red lettuce, parsley, young spinach leaves and chives and red and yellow nasturtium flowers, which Ollie and Polly ate whole. After spotting a couple of tiny black beetles crawling around inside the flowers, I made sure to inspect them. I knew they were edible – I'd read about them in magazines – but it was the first time I'd tasted the nose-teasing pepper flavour mingled with the sweetness of the nectar. I hadn't realised how hungry I was. Then I thought: *How long since I've really enjoyed a meal?*

'Do you always eat this well?' I asked, after a few minutes.

'It can be patchy,' said Polly. 'Spring's tricky. You know, things have finished, and other things haven't started.'

'Oh. I think of spring as a time of plenty. New life, bees, birds, blossom.' I looked up from my plate. 'I suppose that's wrong?'

'Autumn. That's the time of plenty. That's when we try and get everything preserved. Pickles, jams, chutneys. Drying stuff.' Dorcas had started whingeing. 'We've got this dehydrator,' Polly added, hauling the child up onto her lap and pulling up her blouse. 'It dries things like tomatoes and mushrooms. Apples. Pears. You can't sun-dry things in the UK. Too damp. They go mouldy.' Dorcas began sucking noisily, her fingers twining themselves in Polly's hair.

It was a lovely day, both in terms of the weather – sunny, dry, not too hot for July – and my mood. I felt relaxed, carefree, almost as if I were on holiday. This little place felt like their own little historical re-enactment festival, where they were pretending to live an authentic medieval life, with adaptations such as tomatoes and solar panels, or as if I'd stepped back two hundred years to a bucolic idyll that had never in fact existed. I almost expected shepherds in smocks to wander down the lane past the field. Or perhaps it was more like a fairy tale, peasants living blameless lives in their sunlit hamlet in a clearing in the woods – dragons and witches and ogres and giants kept at bay by heroes striding through the surrounding forest.

We spent the afternoon wandering around the field, occasionally sitting on large logs in the shade. The bushes and trees were for nuts and fruit, said Ollie, and the chickens helped keep the pests down, and they grew herbs in the old tyres near the house, and they almost, at certain times of year, ate as much from the hedgerows and meadows as they grew themselves: dandelions, wild garlic, lime flowers, chickweed and meadowsweet, ground elder, goosegrass and young hawthorn leaves. I forget what else. I should think fat hen, and sorrel, and Good King Henry, and shepherd's purse, and horseradish, and jack-by-the-hedge, and berries and rosehips in the autumn. Of course, I didn't know these names back then, I couldn't recognise many of the plants. In my eyes they were mostly indistinguishable. Weeds.

They had beds of vegetables and salads and potatoes and fruit of all kinds – blackcurrants and redcurrants, strawberries and raspberries, young fruit trees no taller than my shoulder: apples and plums and pears. We peered at baby green peppers and minuscule black aubergines, at the tiniest broad beans, the white flowers falling away like tissue paper, at pinhead-sized green tomatoes. We glimpsed diminutive frogs and newts clambering over the weed in the pond. Blue and green dragonflies darted past, iridescent in the sunlight. They were lucky, said Ollie, the pond was fed by a natural spring. I thought of the tea I'd just drunk. But they also had a standpipe, he said, for drinking water.

I'd forgotten about staying the night. It was as dusk fell and we'd eaten a lentil stew, and I'd just realised there was only one bedroom and they all three shared a bed, that I wondered about my sleeping arrangements and whether I was expected to sleep in the car. But they offered me a choice: outside in an old canvas tent, or on the kitchen floor in front of the stove, made from an oil drum.

I made my excuses and went to find a bed and breakfast in Dorchester. My back, I said, it had never been good, and I needed a sprung mattress. They didn't seem surprised.

છ્ર

Ollie and Polly were bonkers, it was clear to me, and young and idealistic. It seemed equally clear that as Dorcas grew up, they would grow out of this romantic back-to-nature ideal and opt back into society, pay taxes, take advantage of free schooling and healthcare. But no, they said, they wouldn't. They weren't on benefits; they didn't feel it would be right when they had no intention of subscribing to an oppressive system. Doctors? No need. School? They would teach their child at home. She would learn far more that way, far more of real use than some of the propaganda kids had to absorb and memorise and regurgitate in state exams. Risky? Sure, they said. All of life is risky, after all.

And the PhD? I didn't find out a great deal more about that, except that it was to do with historical anthropology, whatever that is. I worked out, from things she mentioned, that Polly was in her late twenties, she'd had a previous relationship that had been a disaster, and that one day she'd publish her research. Her grandparents lived in a large bungalow a few fields away.

We skirted around Jonnie, not exactly the elephant in the room. More the ghost at the feast.

I'd just hinted that I'd better be on my way to Dorchester when Ollie blurted: 'Jonnie visited us, you know. Quite a lot.'

I was standing, about to go to the car, but my knees wobbled at the surprise of hearing Jonnie's name. I lowered myself to the log carefully, as if in a minor earthquake. I hadn't known he'd visited this place – and why would I have known? I felt a brief flaring of jealousy, like a stab in my heart. I looked away from Ollie and found Polly gazing at me.

'I'm really sorry,' she said. 'He was so sweet, so lovely with me when I was pregnant. I'm sorry he never met Moonbeam.'

I stared at her.

'It must be really difficult for you,' she continued. 'You

must be so proud of him, but you must miss him so much. I know we do.'

I couldn't speak. I was adjusting my mental picture of my son. A boy who knew how to handle pregnant women. Who had spent time in this fairy tale idyll.

'I know this doesn't make anything better,' she said, 'but we'd have loved him to be Dorcas's godfather. He'd have been wonderful. He was great with kids.'

It stunned me that I never knew he was great with kids. Or that I never knew he was loved and trusted enough to be godfather to a child.

'I'm sorry,' she said again. 'I'm making things worse.'

I shook my head.

'Are you all right?'

I shook my head, a tightness in my chest and throat. 'I don't suppose…' I shook my head again. 'I don't suppose I'll ever be all right,' I said. Tears pricked behind my eyes. I could feel my nose going red.

'I just think,' she said, and handed Dorcas to Ollie, and came towards me. I sat rigid, thought, *don't touch me, I'll cry.* 'I just think he was an amazing person. He was really brave and, just, I don't know, just full of kindness and really caring, and he was really thoughtful about things, in a good way. You know?'

I didn't know. I knew my son as my child, that was all. I stared at her, eating her words as if they could fill me and satisfy my hunger for Jonnie.

'You must be so proud of him, Roly.' She placed her hand briefly on my shoulder.

I nodded, dumbly, holding back the tears.

'He loved it here, didn't he, Olls?'

Ollie nodded. 'Yup.'

I took a breath, waited a few seconds, waited to be able to speak. They waited too. All of us waiting, even the child, staring at me with her blue eyes. 'But,' I said, 'but... but he died before you had the baby. I don't see how...'

'We planned it together,' said Ollie. 'We camped here a few times, planted trees, began building the house.'

'But when was this? When? I can't think when he had the time.'

'Weekends.' Ollie shrugged. 'He was planning to live here, for a while at least.'

My son the farmer. My son the hippie. My son the smallholder. My son the gardener.

Tick the right box, like a multiple-choice question.

My son the geologist. My son the oil prospector.

My son the eco-warrior.

∽

I went back to see them on my way home the next day. I'd parked in a side street overnight, lucky to find a space. The next morning the street was empty, apart from Hugo's car. There was a bright yellow plastic envelope stuck to the windscreen.

Ollie laughed when I told him. 'Expensive night in Dorchester, then.' He smiled to take the sting out of his words, his arm around my shoulders. 'But did you sleep all right?'

'Yes, thank you.' A lie. I'd spent half the night reading, pushing thoughts of Jonnie to the back of my mind, trying to find meaning in the women's magazines that had been left in a bedroom drawer by a previous occupant. How to make your home summer-friendly. Cauliflower, the latest superfood. Must-haves for the bathroom. Jonnie, squashed between letters and adverts, appearing at the edge of my consciousness as I dozed… his voice, his hands, his hair, his eyes, his smile.

'A good sleep, that's what matters,' Ollie said. He held out his hand. 'Look what's arrived.' Three small beetles: one was black with a large scarlet dot on each wing, the second was yellow with several black spots, and the third was almost chequered, red and black taking up equal space on its wings. Ollie turned his hand over and over, letting the beetles run up and down and crawl to the end of his fingers.

I leaned forward to see better. 'What are they?'

Ollie offered the beetles to me with a smile. 'They tickle,' he said. I held my hand out, ready to receive these beauteous creatures, feeling, I have to say, rather brave.

'They're harlequins. A type of ladybird. Very aggressive.'

'Oh!' I pulled my hand back instinctively, imagining stings and bites. Hugo was the gardener. All I'd ever done was raise feeble tomato plants in growbags and herbs on the kitchen windowsill that invariably caught whitefly and had to be thrown away. I'd done it for the children. It had been educational. What they took of any value from these abject failures is anyone's guess.

'Not like wasps,' said Ollie. 'They're not aggressive to us. Great predators. Great for eating the bugs, you know, greenfly and such. Trouble is, they eat the larvae of our native ladybirds too. They arrived today. Not there last night. Come and see.'

We walked through the strawberries to the climbing beans, which wound up long sticks in wigwams, red and white and purple and pink flowers intertwining. Small striped insects buzzed around, hovering close to the flowers like helicopters. I kept my distance, thinking of the wasps he'd mentioned, but Ollie beckoned me closer.

'Yesterday,' he said, 'all the shoots were covered with black aphids. Don't know if you noticed. It takes nerve not to reach for insecticide.' He pulled aside some leaves and there they were, these multicoloured beetles, crawling up the stems, on the underside of leaves, at the tips of the shoots, clustering around woolly masses of wriggling blackfly.

'Build it and they will come,' said Ollie. 'It's like that film,' he said, and gave me a sidelong glance, 'you know, where the guy builds a baseball field, and the dead baseball players come and then in the end hundreds of people turn up?'

'Jonnie liked that film too.'

'Yes. We watched it together. A lot.'

I had a vague memory of small boys in sleeping bags eating popcorn in a dark room and staring at a flickering TV screen. I'd had no idea what they were watching – it could have been anything at all – and how thankful I was they hadn't discovered porn or 18-rated violence at the age of ten. How neglectful I had been. But I wasn't neglecting the twins, who, most evenings, lost control over something as harmless as water in their ears during their bath, or the wrong colour towel, or their bedroom door not being left open precisely seven centimetres. Later they refused to have the door open at all and insisted on having bolts fitted to it so they could lock themselves in. Hugo calmed my fears of fire by keeping an axe under his side of the bed, to break the door down, if it ever came to it; and we fitted six smoke alarms.

'But how could you possibly know they'd come and eat all your blackfly?'

'Because it happens every year. You create the right environment for the pests, they come first, then the predators. Don't spray, whatever you do.'

'Hugo's roses.'

'Don't spray.'

'He wouldn't like that.'

Ollie smiled.

'Honestly? Does it always happen?'

'Pretty much. We let nature do the work. We're lazy.' He smiled again. 'But I can't help feeling sorry for our poor little natives. Nothing we can do about it.'

'Oh, surely there must be something. A special pesticide.'

'Giant nets,' said Polly. 'Stretched all around the coast to stop them blowing in across the Channel.'

For a moment I thought she was serious.

'They're here to stay,' she said. 'Nothing we can do.'

'Surely,' I said again.

'They come from warmer countries,' she said. 'The only way we could halt this is if global warming was reversed and we had global cooling. And that,' she said flatly, 'isn't possible.' She sighed. 'Anyway, they hibernate. We get them in the house all winter. Hundreds of them. They sort of huddle together for warmth around the window frames.'

I tried and failed to imagine this.

'We may have reached the tipping point,' said Ollie after a moment.

'What's that?'

'A perfect storm,' said Polly. She hoisted her child onto her hip and kissed her on the forehead. 'The point of no return. I don't know how it will be for Dorcas, but we're better off here than anywhere else. She needs to know what to do, how to survive.'

'I'm not sure what you mean,' I said. 'What's a perfect storm?'

'When everything comes together to create an unstoppable momentum,' said Ollie. 'When global temperatures have risen far enough that ice sheets melt and can no longer reflect heat back out to space. So the sea level's higher and there's more energy and moisture in the system, and the deserts get bigger… and all the time we're using more and more energy and creating more and more carbon dioxide and increasing the temperature.'

'You are?' I asked, confused.

'We're carbon neutral,' said Polly. 'It's not us. It's you, the rest of you, people like you, I mean. People with big cars and houses and foreign holidays. What we do here, the way we live, we've got tiny carbon emissions. Not nearly as big as yours.'

This stung. I lived modestly, I thought. Of course, I had no understanding of carbon back then, no real idea what she was talking about. She just sounded self-righteous and incredibly annoying.

'When it gets to a certain point it'll have a life of its own,' said Ollie. 'No one can stop it. The planet will heat up and it will burn. That's the tipping point.'

I looked at them. They had to be exaggerating.

'Some people think we've already reached it, the tipping point,' said Ollie.

It was time to challenge this, if it was that serious – 'So why are you having children?'

'Just one child.'

'No little brother or sister for Dorcas?' I was a bit shocked. 'Children need siblings,' I said. 'It's a bit selfish, otherwise. No one to play with, no one to share things with – that's important, learning how to share. No one to share the burden of elderly parents.'

Ollie shook his head again. 'Maybe it's a bit selfish having more than one kid, because of the strain on the planet.'

I didn't reply. I didn't want a row, didn't want to start a long journey home all shaken up and unsafe. I'd had four children, after all. But Ollie continued.

'I mean,' he said, 'every person in the UK has so much more stuff than the average African. We all consume more energy in a year than people in Africa do in a lifetime. We live so much longer than them. It's not really fair, is it?'

'I wasn't talking about fairness, Ollie. I'm talking about Dorcas and her needs. I mean, you've been showing me the way you live and how marvellous you think it all is. If it's all so perfect, you presumably don't have any scruples about extra children. You can do it without putting strain on the planet.'

'Every person puts strain on the planet,' said Polly.

'So what now?' I asked.

'We carry on,' he said. 'We want to run courses for people, teach them about using less energy, fewer resources, growing their own.'

'But all this –' I waved at the field and the dwelling – 'this all takes a lot of space. People in cities…'

'I know.' Ollie took a deep breath and let it out in a sigh. He scrunched his face up and squinted towards the wooded hills. 'It does presuppose that the planet's population will one day be a lot smaller than it is now.'

'How small?'

He made a face as if calculating the answer, but he knew it already. He'd said this before. He'd said it to Jonnie. I'd seen his emails.

'Two billion. Tops.'

'And how's that going to happen, Ollie? I mean, you're beginning to talk like you're enjoying this, you know.'

For the first time Ollie hesitated. He kicked the earth about a bit with his sandals, his dirty toes darkening with the drying mud. 'The usual,' he said, not looking at me. 'You know, disease, famine, war.'

'I'm sure we can be more optimistic than this,' I said firmly. 'Think of all those scientists beavering away on pro-jects, desalination and things. Energy from solar panels in the Sahara. I read about that the other day. There's lots to be optimistic about.'

'I'm afraid I disagree.' He glanced back at me, his blue eyes clear and serious.

'And you've brought a child into this hellish world of yours, where three-quarters of the people on this planet are going to die horrible deaths?'

Ollie appeared to crumple, just for a moment. He screwed his eyes shut and ran both hands through his hair, and shook his head very slightly.

He had to be mistaken. I didn't believe for one minute that things were as bad as he said. But to have children, and to blithely carry on in their little paradise, thinking one thing and doing another – it seemed to me that afternoon that he was confused and really didn't know what he was talking about.

'Well,' I said, 'I think we'll have to agree to disagree.' I didn't want to think any more about it. I didn't want my cage rattled any more than it had already been. I wanted to think of Ollie and Polly and Dolly as a little storybook family, living on their homestead, nothing to do with the real world. I wanted to put them in a box and leave them there.

The trouble with the subconscious, I have found, is that it doesn't like being contained. It breaks out at inconvenient moments.

∽

Hugo came into the kitchen a few weeks later holding an envelope in one hand and a letter in the other.

'There's been some peculiar mistake,' he said. 'It must be a scam.'

I looked up from the newspaper.

'Really?'

'Yes. Apparently, I have an unpaid parking ticket from Dorchester, of all places.'

'Oh!' My hand flew to my mouth. 'I forgot all about it!'

'Hmm?' Hugo peered at me over the top of his reading glasses. 'Dorchester? What were you doing in Dorchester? In my car?'

'Oh. I went to see Ollie.'

'Who on earth's Ollie?'

'Ollie. You know, Jonnie's friend from school.'

He shook his head. 'No idea.'

'Yes, you do. They were best friends in primary school. Ollie. Oliver.'

Hugo frowned at me, screwing up his eyes with the effort of remembering.

'They had sleepovers all the time.'

'The boy with the curly hair?'

'Yes! Ollie!'

'OK. Why did you go and see him? In my car?'

'Your car's more reliable than mine.'

Hugo nodded. This was true and he could see the logic. 'And?'

'I decided to look him up. See how he's doing... he...' I stopped, tried again. 'They...' A sob caught in the back of my throat. Hugo waited patiently, watching me, his glasses at the end of his nose. I took a deep breath, held my voice steady and said, 'They're farming.'

'Are they?' Hugo sounded distinctly more interested.

'Mmm. And they've got a little girl.'

'Livestock or arable?'

'Um, mixed,' I said.

'Good for him,' Hugo said robustly. 'Very sound. I always thought he had a good head on his shoulders, that lad. Sensible.'

I wondered if we were talking about the same boy. Ollie had rather loved computer games and the building of elaborate dens in the garden. I wasn't sure that Hugo had ever talked much to him.

'We should invite them up,' said Hugo, expansive now. 'Any time. It would be a pleasure to support a young farmer. Not many people appreciate farming, you know. Tough life.' He was imagining tweeds and green hunter wellies and a gun dog; I could see it in his eyes.

'Did you have a good time?'

I nodded.

'Good, good. I'm glad. I expect it took you out of yourself. Good idea to take my car. Make sure you invite them, Roly. Soon.'

'I'll do that,' I lied.

ELEVEN

The Fine Line

Sunday night. Still New Year's Day. Midnight? My chest is tight, my breath wheezing. I don't know if I have the beginnings of a chest infection or if it's just anxiety. Just. People can die from asthma, you know, although apparently I don't have asthma. It's just panic.

It seems clear to me now as I sit here in this cave: there are no heroes in this story, no one's coming to our rescue, no superhero or cavalry charge or magic wand will destroy the villain and put everything back the way it was. The baddies are us, and we're on the sinking ship.

We've always thought of ourselves as heroes, winners, gods. But we're more like toddlers with too much power. I can't rescue one cormorant, let alone myself. I'm exhausted, played out, nauseous with anxiety and fear and bad food, and in the last five minutes suddenly icy from being drenched in salt water and with no way to dry anything in here. Jonnie's rucksack is soaked too – all my clothes and my little bit of food are wet through. Salted apple. Yum.

❧

I sit with my arms wrapped tight around my knees, conserving what little warmth I have. I close my eyes, too tired to stand, too wired and cold to sleep.

But I must move, I must keep my circulation going. I push myself to my feet and start jogging on the spot, stretching my arms over my head and swinging them by my sides. After a few minutes of this I begin to feel less frozen, merely cold. My chest eases up.

I get the torch out of my jacket pocket and wind it. By its light I navigate the rocks and tiny pools strewn across the floor of the cave. The tide is going out now, and will reach its lowest point around five a.m. The lights of fishing boats seem miles away, although it's impossible to tell.

I crouch just inside the entrance and begin to flash my torch – three short flashes, three longer beams, three short flashes. Morse code, SOS. The only bit of code I remember. I do this for ages, until my thumb gets tired, then I swap to the other hand. I have to wind the torch every now and then.

My eyes get heavy. I'm exhausted. I put the torch back in my pocket. The fishing boats haven't moved. I feel helpless.

A movement outside catches my eye. I lean forward to see.

Jonnie is sitting on the big rock. He faces the sea, is gazing at the boats. The wind catches his hair, ruffles his curls. His skin gleams faintly in the moonlight. I haven't seen him for a couple of years, and now here he is, just when I feel most alone.

I watch for a minute or two, then whisper his name. *Jonnie.*

He turns immediately, smiles, raises his hand in a half-wave.

Mum.

What are you doing here?

Keeping you company.

I can't believe he's here. I stand, begin to inch forward over the seaweed covered rocks. He raises his hand again, palm facing me. *It's not safe. Stay back.*

I hesitate, gripping the side of the cave entrance. Look down at my sodden boots, at the slimy seaweed. Look up again.

Jonnie has gone.

I gasp. The shock is so severe that I wobble, suddenly aware again that I am dangerously exhausted. Then I hear a noise behind me. Hanging onto the rock wall, I turn and peer into the cave. It looks like Jonnie is sitting there, right at the back. Or maybe that's a rock.

I wobble uncertainly to the back of cave, treading carefully around the little pools.

There's another noise, a kind of shuffling. The bird. Of course.

I sit on the sloping patch of shingle, rest my head against the rock wall, listen to the waves, the bird rustling on its shelf, and a low humming, a folk tune I recognise from Jonnie's piano lessons.

A whisper.

Love you.

&

One night I couldn't sleep at all. I lay beside Hugo with my eyes wide open, watching a pale beam of moonlight move slowly across the room. The moon was full that night, and I felt restless, on edge. Eventually I rolled out of bed, unhooked my dressing gown from the door, and silently made my way down the stairs, avoiding the fourth creaky step.

In the kitchen, in the moonlight, there was Jonnie, sitting quietly at the table. He looked up I as came in, said, *Tea?*

I wasn't scared. It felt completely natural. So this was why I'd been so wakeful. My son had been calling to me.

'I'll put the kettle on,' I said, and he nodded, as if this was only what he had expected. I made two mugs, just dunked the teabag in and out, sloshed in milk, brought them to the table, placed one in front of him, and he smiled.

I can't remember exactly who said what, but the conversation went something like this:

What are you up to these days?

Oh, this and that…

Let's go for a walk…

And just like that we left our tea on the table and stepped through the back door into the conservatory and then into the garden. It was a warm night. Jonnie stopped by one rose bush. The colours were all bleached by the moonlight, but this had always been his favourite, a loose-petalled pale yellow, scented like citrus. He bent his head, inhaled, and touched the petals so gently with the back of his hand that they seemed to be stirring with the breeze.

Dad's not lost his touch. But what could you do with the garden?

Me?

He nodded. *You.*

I gazed at him, somehow grey and silvery in the moonlight, dark hair shimmering, like a sort of halo. He placed one hand, then the other, over his heart. *Feel it,* he said. *Love it. Feel it.*

I looked past him at the garden, remembering Ollie's smallholding. I couldn't do anything like that here, we didn't have enough space, but maybe an apple tree or two, maybe some cabbages or beans, tomatoes in pots.

More, there's so much more you can do. Remember food miles. Grow local, eat local.

Oh! You saw that too? In the health food shop?

He grinned. It's enough that you've seen it. Come on. He began walking around the side of the house to the side gate. *I want to show you something, Mum.*

To be called Mum was suddenly heart-breaking, and I closed my eyes with the anguish of it. This boy, so special, so missed – I suddenly realised this was odd, so peculiar that two years after he died, he'd come back. Perhaps I would be permitted to touch him, to hold him in my arms, tousle his hair, kiss his beautiful face. I opened my eyes, but Jonnie was nowhere in sight.

Later I sat at the kitchen table with two cold mugs of tea, wondering what exactly had happened. This was the beginning of something new, I could tell, something life-enhancing, exciting, worth everything that had gone before, even losing – no, not that. Not worth losing Jonnie. But I had choices to make, decisions. A new way of life beckoned. When Jonnie came back, I could show him what I'd been doing in his name, for the sake of the planet. I could win his approval as I had never done in life.

I didn't see Jonnie again for a while. But I asked Hugo about an apple tree – no, I demanded an apple tree. I told him that was what I'd decided we needed.

'Sure,' he said, without much interest. We were sitting at the breakfast table on a Saturday morning, toast crumbs strewn about, eggy plates and marmalade pushed aside.

He shook out his newspaper. 'November,' he said. 'That's the time. If we have one tree, it'll need to be self-fertile. You can look in the gardening books in my study and see what variety you'd like. There's more choice if we have two – they pollinate each other.'

I stared at him, aghast. This was my project, mine and Jonnie's. How dare Hugo be so all-knowing about apple trees.

'I'll think about it,' I said, coolly.

'OK,' he said. 'We've got a few weeks. The saplings won't be in the garden centre until late September.'

'Fine.' I turned away, but not before I saw him glance quickly at me over the top of his paper, his eyes sharp, observant, appraising.

❧

Every weekday morning I waited impatiently till Hugo had gone to work then ran up to Jonnie's room and turned on his laptop, continuing my mystical quest. I devoured information as I sat at Jonnie's desk, forgetting to eat, letting my mug of coffee cool beside me. I had Jonnie's blessing, I knew, as I trawled through websites and followed links. It felt to me then as if Jonnie was only in the next room, or downstairs, or in the garden. There were times when I smelt coconut, or something woody, of the woods, damp and earthy and fernlike, or smoky, like a campfire.

I found websites that showed me – in graphs and pictures and charts that even I could understand – all the periods of warming and cooling over billions of years. I saw photographs of the proof, the ice core samples and tree rings, the layers of sedimentary rock analysed and compared with other rocks. I found modern stories of sea-level rise in the Indian Ocean, wells poisoned by salt water, rains failing or coming at the wrong time, droughts and famines, floods and famines. I read predictions of how New York and London and Shanghai and Mumbai were going to fare when the ice caps melted. I studied maps of coastlines and how they would change when the sea rose by one metre, two metres, seven, fifty. I dismissed those maps. I wondered how anyone could possibly know how much ice is in the ice caps. But they haunted me when I closed my eyes at night.

I saw pictures from space of burning rainforests, the rainforests that – the twins explained – are the lungs of the world, that create oxygen, that clean the air, that hold half the world's species, that may hold cures for disease, that are home to untouched peoples, the rainforests whose secrets are yet to be fully revealed.

I began to understand how it was all connected in an intricate web that was both infinitely strong and incredibly fragile.

My nights began to give me trouble, so much trouble that I staggered through my days sleep-deprived, brain like cotton wool, barely able to communicate or think or even prepare the simplest of meals. An omelette and oven chips, say, or shop-bought lasagne.

In my sleep my dreams were full of Jonnie, and Ollie, and Ollie's little family, living their utopian dream of self-sufficiency. When I woke, my mind became overwhelmed by nightmare scenarios of plagues and zombies and total global destruction from some unnamed horror.

I was already teetering on the fine line between insanity and everything else, but I was too close to see it. The wonder is that nobody else saw it either.

Lying awake at night, rigid beside Hugo's softly snoring form, I worried for my as yet unthought-of grandchildren. The boys, I thought, would never have families. I couldn't imagine them even talking to girls, let alone getting to the point of settling down. But Flora, she would have children, several of them. She adored children and was good with them, even preferring to babysit in the daytime so she could play with them, rather than at night when they were asleep.

Perhaps I should warn her not to have babies? I considered how that conversation would go. Not well.

I wondered how high above sea level we were in St Albans,

how long we had before the ground water turned brackish and undrinkable. I thought about lower parts of the country, the Fens, the Somerset Levels, Lincolnshire, flooded and uninhabitable. Ely Cathedral, the ship of the Fens, sailing once again through choppy waters on its rocky island. The M5 a causeway through the Levels. People in gondolas in the streets of Cambridge.

My imagination became lurid and wildly out of control in the watches of the night. I'm not sure I even wanted to control it.

I saw villages on hills surrounded by fishing boats. I saw London submerged, the Houses of Parliament no longer alongside the Thames but in it, Big Ben a landmark for tourists arriving in flotillas. I saw the Lake District and the Highlands of Scotland converted into prime farmland, millions of tons of topsoil deposited by helicopter and then washed away by torrents of rain, creating muddy swamps in the lakes and lochs where alligators and hippos and elephants now wallowed. I saw housing estates on flood plains melting into the rising waters.

I rose early, went to bed late, read books and watched TV half the night until I fell asleep on the sofa, made cakes and jam and walked round and round the block until dawn, in an effort to still my ceaseless imaginings. I ironed Hugo's shirts before they were even dry, and his underpants and socks and all the sheets in the airing cupboard. I polished shoes, sewed buttons on clothes that the children had grown out of years before, knitted scarves and mittens.

I took my compact camera and then Hugo's better one out before sunrise to capture the small awakenings of each new day. I spent hours watching birds build nests and spiders spin webs. I sat quietly in the garden and heard rustlings of mice and rats and hedgehogs. I knew where the vixen had her den and how many cubs she had.

I marvelled at the beauty of this world that we were hell-bent on destroying, biting the hand that feeds us. I sorrowed at the plastic rubbish, the cigarette cartons, the paper coffee cups, the tampons and condoms in the hedgerows of the country park as I roamed further and further afield, and the single socks and shoes and gloves and jumpers abandoned and squashed by vehicles along the sides of the main roads. There were broken toys, plastic bottles, sandwich containers, beer cans, half-eaten burgers in the gutters. I wandered down to the marketplace at night and picked up discarded fruit to bring home.

I smelt the fumes of the motorbikes and cars and lorries as the rush hour began, ran my finger over the soot-blackened buildings in the centre of town, raised my eyes on sunny mornings to the haze over London.

And all along, Jonnie was always just out of sight, just behind the next building or the other side of a hedge or meandering through the trees in the woods or cresting a hill, but I felt he was there, guiding me to see with new eyes, to understand with my heart and not just my head. *Love it,* he'd said, *Feel it.*

'Where've you been?' Hugo would ask when he came downstairs. I was already on my third mug of tea.

'Just for a walk,' or 'Out in the garden,' I would reply. The minimum.

Some nights I didn't sleep at all.

TWELVE

The urgency of our emergency

Well, things began speeding up. No longer ambivalent about what Jonnie had stood for, no longer siding with Hugo as we regretfully considered the foolishness of our son's firebrand fanaticism – it was like a conversion. And, naturally, I had the convert's enthusiasm, and the convert's lack of tact.

I decided that normal rules no longer applied. I began to approach people deliberately and intentionally, people who were blissfully unaware of my true objectives as I admired their dogs in the park or commiserated about the weather in the queue in the post office, before launching into desperate monologues about the end of the world as they edged away from me, even fled. In the supermarket I used my time at the checkout attempting to convince the cashiers that they'd sold their souls to some capitalist anti-environmental devil. The younger ones looked alarmed as they passed my recycled toilet paper and tinned sardines and low-energy lightbulbs over the scanner, and then I was sorry to scare them, but not sorry about my message; the older women looked weary and asked if I wanted any cashback and did I have a car park token? One older man surprised me by converting my monologue into conversation, telling me about the store's Fairtrade bananas and sugar, his allotment, his children in Manchester and London, his grandchildren, and the special offer on *Patak's* Indian sauces. I nodded along, hoping to steer the conversation back to my agenda, realising as I left that I had been very charmingly deflected and neutralised.

But what was I really hoping for? At this distance, now, I see that of course they couldn't just throw in their jobs, these people, and turn their gardens into allotments. At the time, though, nothing was clear. All I knew was that nothing was sustainable, not food, not energy, nothing. And without sustainability there was no future.

Hugo rolled his eyes if I ever mentioned any of this. I even caught him one day rolling his eyes when I said that Jonnie had said – actually I can't remember what I intended to tell him. I was so outraged at his reaction that that's all I remember now, his reaction, and mine.

And Hugo telling me that Jonnie wasn't perfect. Not perfect, Hugo repeated. Jonnie was untidy, messy even, and a bit of a know-all, and he and Hugo had had numerous run-ins about his overdraft and spending too much on partying.

You can talk, I thought, staring at the glass in Hugo's hand.

'He's become a bit of saint, hasn't he?' Hugo observed. 'He can't answer back, can't be argued with. Don't forget, Roly, he was just a kid. He didn't know the real world. He was an idealist. Rather like you, I suppose.'

He pursed his lips. 'I hadn't seen it till today,' he said. 'You're more similar than I realised.' He put the glass down on the kitchen counter, and gently took hold of my shoulders, turning me so he could look me in the eyes. I glanced up at him, and then down. I didn't want to be vulnerable, not to Hugo, not to anyone. I might start crying. 'You can't bring him back, darling.'

'I'm not trying to bring him back,' I said indignantly. 'That'd be crazy. I can't imagine what you're talking about. I can't imagine what you think you mean.'

'You can't be him. You can't do what he did. And you can't make him love you any more than he always did.'

For a moment I was breathless with the shock of hearing such an assessment. Hugo had no right to say such weird and cruel things, to say things that made me sound insane. What did he know, anyway? What did he understand about the state of the planet?

Hugo pulled me into a hug. I resisted, standing stiff and still, my arms down by my sides.

'You know how much Jonnie loved you, don't you?' Hugo kissed the top of my head and laid his cheek briefly on my hair. 'How much we all love you?' When I didn't respond he said, 'Roly?'

'Mmm.'

'I want to support you, but you make it very difficult.'

'I'm not crazy,' I said, and pulled away. 'Don't you forget that, Hugo.' I stepped right back and walked to the other side of the kitchen table. 'I have reasons for thinking the way I do. They're perfectly sound and logical reasons, and we should all be thinking the same way.' I briskly shuffled the table mats into a pile and pushed them into the centre of the table. I didn't want to look at him.

'Granted. You're quite right. You know that, of course.'

'Sarcasm won't get you anywhere, Hugo.'

'I wasn't being sarcastic,' he said quietly. 'Roly, listen, just for a minute.'

'Actually I'm quite busy, and when you dismiss Jonnie's life's work as if it's of no consequence –'

'When have I ever done that?'

'Just now, actually.'

'Actually, no,' said Hugo. 'I wasn't dismissing his life's work, as you so grandly call it. All I was saying was that as he grew up, he'd have seen more of the world and perhaps he'd have –'

'Perhaps.'

'What?'

'Perhaps, you said, perhaps he'd have done something else. Perhaps he'd have become an international banker? Or gone off to prospect for oil? Perhaps he'd have changed his mind about global warming, to make life less uncomfortable for his father? Perhaps what?'

Hugo was staring at me with his mouth slightly open. He looked idiotic. I'm ashamed to say I was quite pleased with my goading.

'Have it your own way,' he said, after a moment. 'Just hear me out. I'm concerned that all your anxiety about global warming, together with your grief for Jonnie – absolutely understandable, we're all grieving for Jonnie – well, all this is making life unbearable for you. D'you see? Hmm?'

I didn't want to see, but I was in denial about that, and many other things.

'So you want me to stop worrying about it all.'

'If it preserves your sanity, yes. If that's what it takes.'

'How on earth can I stop worrying about the reality of climate change?'

'A day at a time.'

'And I'm perfectly sane.'

'No doubt.'

'Have you finished?'

He shook his head slightly, staring down at his feet. 'I don't know what else to say.'

'Well, then, don't say it.'

I'd won that little battle. Forced Hugo off my patch. Right, I thought, no more talk. Action. Real action. Activism. Like Ollie and Jonnie. Like Greenpeace. I'd show Hugo. I'd get things done.

ⁿ

The next day in the market I pushed past stalls of cheap clothing, jewellery, fabrics, and watches, all handed over in blue plastic carrier bags. I stopped and looked about me. Horrid thin blue bags, the bags I saw every single day scudding about the roads, caught in trees and blocking drains. Bags we don't really see these days. But this was twenty-odd years ago and I felt strongly – you can't imagine how strongly, I was suddenly passionate, obsessed – that something had to be done. Something needed to be said.

I hung around a bit, strolled past a couple of stalls, and eventually approached one that didn't seem too busy, one of the larger ones, with racks of clothes arranged under a red and white striped awning. The stall holder was a man about my age, short and chunky, with crinkly grey hair swept back from his forehead. I could imagine him dandling a grandchild on his knee and caring for their future.

'Help you?' he grunted, his eyes seemingly everywhere except on me.

I leapt straight in. 'Have you ever considered using paper carrier bags instead of plastic?'

'No,' he said, looking past me at a couple of young women, each with a toddler in a pushchair, who were examining the skirts. He raised his voice. 'Your kids get anything on the merchandise you'll be paying for it.'

The girls took no notice, didn't move, carried on rifling through the skirts, pulling them out quickly and shoving them roughly back in.

'I'm talking to you.' He pushed closer to them through the racks of clothing. 'I mean it. I told you before. Don't let your kids get their sticky mitts on my merchandise.'

'It's OK,' said one of the girls, without looking up. 'We're going anyhow.' They turned and wheeled their children away.

The man came back to me. 'How can I help you?'

'I was wondering if you'd ever thought of using paper carrier bags instead of plastic?'

'Can't say I have.'

I drew a breath, feeling a nervous fluttering in my stomach. But it was easier than I'd thought, opening up a conversation. He seemed interested, or, at least, polite. 'Would you be interested in paper bags?'

'What have you got?'

'I'm sorry?'

'You're selling, I take it?'

'Paper bags?'

'Yeah.'

'Er, no. I wondered if it was something you'd consider?'

'I thought you had some to sell.' He glanced behind me. 'Paper's not cheap. I've got a margin to think about.'

'Oh, I understand. But paper's a lot more environmentally friendly than plastic. It'd be great if all you traders could use paper. Or get people to bring their own bags,' I exclaimed, struck by this bright idea. Strong sturdy carrier bags, made of jute or canvas. I could see it quite easily.

He didn't reply immediately, but looked me up and down, his eyes narrowed.

'You're joking.'

'No,' I said, surprised. 'I'm perfectly serious.'

'Listen. You think people bringing their own bags is a good idea?'

'Yes, I do,' I said.

'You any idea how much stock I'd lose?'

'Lose?'

'Yeah, lose. Light fingers, lady, light fingers. Like them two just now.' He nodded in the direction the two young women had gone.

'Really?' I turned to look in the same direction.

'Really.' He gazed at me thoughtfully. 'Get them to use their own bags, and their mates, wouldn't have a lot of stock left at the end of the day. Know what I mean?'

I tried again. 'But paper?'

'I've got a roof to keep over my head. I've got a family. My youngest, now, he wants to go to college. Even if he gets a loan, we'll be supporting him. Trouble is, paper's pricey. Often as not it's raining, paper gets soggy, it's ruined. Money down the drain.'

It was in fact beginning to rain now, big, isolated drops splashing on the awning and on my bare head, the kind of rain that would quickly turn into a downpour.

'You could keep it under here.'

'And it's bulky and bloody heavy. Pardon my French.'

We were still being polite, but I sensed his patience was being tried. His eyes flickered around watching shoppers beginning to scurry homeward.

'But environmentally it's so much better.'

'Yeah. Thanks for your time.'

'No, I haven't finished what I want to say.'

'I've finished, lady.'

We stood three feet apart, staring at each other, like a couple of boxers in the ring.

'But –'

'I've got work to do.'

'There's no one here!' I said incredulously. Foolishly, I admit now. I realise now that you can't convince people by hammering on about things. They have to come to it in their own way.

He sighed, shook his head slightly, pursing his lips in the most infuriating way, like Hugo at his most all-knowing. 'Go home now, lady.'

'You can't make me,' I said. Why, I have no idea. I knew the conversation was over, I knew he'd stopped listening.

'You don't want to leave?'

'No.'

He gave me another second's hard stare, then walked away. He had his back to me and seemed to be fiddling with his phone. I stood without moving among the racks of cheap thin clothing – all bad seams, colours that would run, fabrics that would shrink – and then said loudly, to his back: 'This clothing is made in sweat shops that exploit children in places like India. They work in appalling conditions, sixteen hours a day! How do you feel about that? Excuse me? How do you feel about exploiting tiny children?'

He turned, briefly, to ask: 'Are you leaving now?'

'No,' I said loudly, firmly.

'Sure?'

'Absolutely.' I put my bags down and edged right in under the awning.

'You're harassing me, madam. I'm going about my work in

a lawful way. I don't want to have to call the police.'

'Police? The police will be the least of your problems! They'll back me up!'

A monstrous comment, unfounded, but I suddenly realised that the police – if they arrived – might back him up, rather than me, so I turned to leave, and found that we'd gathered an audience. Half a dozen people, sheltering under umbrellas, stood a few feet away, gawping at me.

For a few seconds I didn't know what to do. I was feeling a little shaky – lack of breakfast, my own fault, I'd been proving something to Hugo about not needing to eat animal protein at every single damn meal, but he didn't bloody well notice as he scarfed his eggs and bacon, and I'd not even bothered with toast that day, and now I was feeling slightly peculiar, like I wasn't really there, that I might become untethered and float off over everyone's heads above the rainclouds. But despite my low blood sugar I did realise this was an opportunity too good to miss. I raised my voice.

'This clothing is made by children as young as five!' I pointed at the racks of shoddy garments. 'It's called bonded servitude. It's slavery! These clothes were made by slaves! Children! Tiny little children!' I was beginning to shake with rage and excitement and fear. And low blood sugar.

'How do you know that?' asked a woman near me. This was encouraging. I stepped out further into the rain, ignoring the torrent that tipped down my collar from the awning.

'It's well-documented,' I said. 'It's all on the internet. Look it up! Lots of charities campaign against it. People are so poor they have to sell themselves and their children to factory owners, and they hardly get paid at all. It's modern-day slavery. It's like chocolate. If it's not fair trade you don't know where it's come from, and it's most likely produced by slaves.'

'So Mick's stuff is made by slaves?'

'Of course it is! Look at the quality,' I said, and walked back under the awning. I pulled out an armful of blouses and began tossing them one by one to the little crowd, who didn't react, didn't reach out to grab the clothing and examine it as I'd intended. Most of the garments fell onto the wet and grimy tarmac. I heard a yell behind me.

'Fuck! What the fuck are you doing?'

I carried on dragging things out, ignoring the stall holder behind me, ignoring the shocked laughter from those in front of me, like a kind of wild cheerleader. I was seeking a reaction and hoping to get it by means of my frenzy, as I tossed the clothing into the rain. I turned and grabbed one of the stands and hauled on it, pulling it towards the opposite stall and blocking the path.

'It's rubbish! Look at it! Think of those tiny children working in dark, airless factories, not allowed to have toilet breaks or eat or drink all day. They sleep in hovels or on the streets, among open sewers and rubbish tips. I've seen pictures!' I exclaimed. 'There's no education, they can't go to school. They never get free, never! Don't buy this rubbish, don't support the slave drivers, don't exploit children, don't –'

'What about Mick?' said the woman. 'What about us? What about our incomes?'

'Mick's got a choice,' I said firmly. 'You've got a choice.'

She was less supportive than I'd assumed. I had to stamp on this attitude. I pointed at her, at all the people in the crowd, waving my forefinger around righteously like a Victorian preacher. 'You, madam, have a choice about where your stock comes from. These people haven't. Write to your MP, write –'

A hand landed heavily on my shoulder. I turned, surprised to be interrupted, and found two uniformed police officers, a man and a woman, one on either side of me. They gave me a lift home. I went quietly, surprised into silence. As we turned the corner to get into the waiting police car, I caught sight of myself in a plate-glass shop window: tall, thin, my long once-blonde hair now turned to straggling grey rat's tails. I was wearing Jonnie's old camouflage parka and baggy jeans and gardening shoes, carrying my shopping in a couple of mismatched canvas bags and an orange rucksack. I gave myself a shock and thought 'Who is that?' before realising with a second shock that it was who I had become.

கூ

Hugo arranged for compensation for the ruined clothing to be sent to Mick via the police – they wouldn't, naturally, give out his home address – and it all went quiet. Hugo promised, on my behalf – and without my permission, I'll have you know – that I wouldn't shop in or walk through that section of the market.

That man thinks he can fix anything.

I suppose I should have been grateful. But I wasn't, not in the least. For now I'd gained a local reputation for being slightly unhinged and I resented it. I wanted, I told him fiercely, to be taken on my own merits, for my arguments to be taken seriously, to be listened to as an educated person who knew her facts.

'There is nothing I would like better, Roly,' he said wearily, swishing the ice around in his whiskey. 'There are ways and means of being taken seriously, that's all. I just hope we've kept this little escapade of yours out of the papers. That would be too embarrassing.'

'So that's why you sorted it out! Too embarrassing! You care more about your career than poor exploited children in sweat shops.'

'It's not that simple, Roly, and you know it.'

'It's pretty simple. We live a comfortable life while –'

'There are ways and means, as I said.' He rubbed his eyes. 'Join a campaign, do it properly, for God's sake. You can't just go around insulting people.'

'I didn't insult people.'

Hugo finished his drink and placed the glass on the table. 'It's been a long day, Roly, I'm off to bed.' He stood. 'My suggestion to you is that you think over your actions very carefully.'

I felt as if I'd been socked in the stomach. These were the words he'd always used when speaking to our children about their behaviour. As he left the room I shouted after him, futilely, 'And you think over yours!'

He paused, just for a moment, then straightened his broad merino-clad shoulders and walked out of sight. I heard him go into his study, turning off lights, opening and shutting drawers. Then he locked the front door and climbed the stairs.

છ

I sat a long time at the kitchen table that night, my mind looping round and round in a kind of figure of eight, replaying first the market episode, and then at some point crossing over to the state of our marriage and how it was that Hugo or I or both of us had changed so much over the years that things now came between us, forcing us apart rather than bringing us together. And that would bring me back to that half hour at the market stall.

It was too confusing. Plastic bags were a bad idea, everyone said so, and yet they could cause me to be moved on by the police. Or maybe it was the child slavery. Either way, it seemed that speaking out was dangerous. But surely it was better to speak out and retain whatever integrity I was beginning to scrabble together for myself? Surely that was what had driven Jonnie to the Antarctic?

My mind swerved away before I could dwell on Jonnie's dead body. I thought of people I could talk to, people who'd understand. I could join groups, as Hugo had said, and yet I wasn't sure he meant it. I couldn't see him being happy with me under placards on demonstrations, lobbying politicians, staging sit-ins outside government buildings, chaining myself to railings as I'd seen some young people do on the news a few days before.

I would go and see Anne, my oldest and wisest friend, the person who had comforted me most in my comfortless childhood, the girl who'd told me to marry Hugo, the woman I'd asked to be godmother to all my children. I'd get Anne's advice.

⁂

At some point I got into bed in the spare bedroom. I woke a few minutes after seven to find Hugo sitting beside me, dressed in suit and tie, holding my hand.

'I would've let you sleep longer,' he said, 'but I wanted to make sure you're all right.'

'Oh.'

He smiled. 'I've brought you some tea and toast.'

'Oh. Thank you.' This was a surprise. He hadn't done this for a long time. I shuffled upright against the headboard.

'And I've found some clean clothes for you.' He gestured to a pile on the chair by the window.

'Thank you, Hugo, that's very kind.' Unexpected and much

more like the Hugo I remembered.

'Well, I think things have got on top of you recently. Take it easy today, hmm?'

'OK.' I felt exhausted, but I smiled at him. It wasn't his fault he didn't understand. Not his fault he always wanted to fix things. He squeezed my hand.

'We could have a short break, a long weekend, just us?'

'That would be nice. But no planes.' Another reminder. Drip, drip, drip. He'd get there eventually, I was sure.

He shook his head and smiled again. 'No planes. I know how you feel about that. Cotswolds, maybe?' He leaned forward and kissed me gently on the lips. 'Try not to let things get to you, OK, Roly? It'll be all right, I promise.'

I nodded.

'Better dash, I'm catching the seven fifty-five.' He kissed me again. I heard him let himself out of the house. I sipped my tea and wondered. Lovely to be pampered, lovely to be talked to without things erupting into a row, but how on earth could he promise that everything would be all right?

THIRTEEN

Other People Have Problems Too

I went to visit Anne the week after the market incident, as I'd so often done when I'd needed to talk something through – when I'd argued with my mother, when I was trying to handle the twins, and after Jonnie's death, of course. She'd been the best of friends, had patiently listened to my grief-stricken confessions about Jonnie's last Christmas and to my working out that all this eco stuff wasn't nonsense after all. At one point I was popping in two or three times a week.

We'd been inseparable when young; chalk and cheese, everyone said, but somehow our friendship worked. I missed her achingly when we left school – she was all I wasn't: loud, confident, extrovert, sporty, good at maths.

She was brusque on the phone, almost as if she was putting me off. I ignored that. I wouldn't get anywhere in life if I was over-sensitive to other people's moods, I thought. I spent my life running around sensitive people at home, I told myself. Quite likely Anne would have got over whatever it was by the time I showed up.

She greeted me at the door with a frown, even though I'd made an effort with my clothes and hair and looked quite smart, for a change.

'Hi Anne!'

'Hi. Come in.'

I started before I'd even got my coat off and slung over the banister. 'I've got something to show you, Anne, it's brilliant!'

She raised one eyebrow.

'The thing is, I'm really into green stuff now, you know, since... anyway –'

'So you said last time.'

This threw me for a second, but I ploughed on. 'Well, it's important.'

'OK.' She sounded weary. 'I know, Roly. We've got to save the planet. Like Jonnie.'

I flinched.

'Sorry,' she said. 'Tactless of me. Forget I said that.'

'OK.'

She held out her arms and after a moment's hesitation I stepped towards her for a hug. I squeezed my eyes shut and breathed in deeply, thinking of anything except Jonnie – the stained glass in Anne's front door, the mating frogs I'd seen in the garden that morning, the suit trousers that Hugo wanted dry-cleaned and that I was wondering if I could wash – and squeezing back the tears that pricked my eyelids.

She let go. 'OK now?'

I nodded.

'So what is it, this new thing?'

'Um, it's about local food.'

'We talked about this last time.'

'No... well, maybe we did. Did we?'

'Yes, Roly.'

We were standing in the hall. I looked at her properly. There were thin, tired lines round her eyes and her mouth. She didn't look herself. She hadn't smiled once since I'd arrived.

'Can I give you this leaflet, Anne? You can look at it later if you want.' I don't think I meant that. I wanted her to look at it straightaway so we could talk about it.

She took the leaflet with ill-disguised impatience, stuffing it into her back jeans pocket without even glancing at it.

'Come in.'

I followed her down the passage to the kitchen, my eyes fixed on the corner of white paper I could see sticking out of her pocket. I had to fight the urge to pull it out.

'It's about local food,' I said to her back. 'I thought you'd be interested.'

She said something I couldn't hear above the sound of the kettle being filled.

'It's part of the Transition movement,' I said. 'You know, incredible edible?'

She shook her head, gathering milk, supermarket biscuits which she tipped onto a plate, and mugs, clattering around the kitchen as if she were in a percussion band.

'It's more sustainable,' I said. I couldn't think of much more to say.

'Coffee?'

'Yes, please.' Instant coffee. 'You know, Anne, you seem busy. Maybe I should leave you to it.'

She turned and glared at me. 'I've made you some coffee, Roly.' Then she sighed. 'I'm tired and stressed and you've come at a bad time. Sorry.' She sneezed and reached for a box of scented tissues on the dresser.

'No. I'm sorry. Look.' I pulled out a pack of biscuits I'd bought at the farmers' market. 'Let's treat ourselves.'

Anne took the packet and read the label. 'Five quid for six biscuits, Roly? Have you gone mad?'

I winced. Hugo was saying similar things, most days.

'I'm just trying to do my bit.'

'You're bonkers, Roly.' She looked at me almost defiantly. 'Let me see. One egg, four ounces of flour, sugar, a pinch of salt, some butter, baking powder – what's this, coconut? – OK, a bit of that, what do you think? Maybe a pound's worth of ingredients? That would make, let's say, fourteen or fifteen biscuits. So this little lot has set the baker back about forty pence.' She rubbed her eyes, swept her fringe back. 'I don't know how you can justify buying these, Roly. Someone's having a laugh. Even if they are organic. You could have made them for far less and had some spare at home.'

She pushed the *Tesco* digestives towards me. 'Have one of these.'

I took one.

We sat in silence for a minute or two. I glanced around the kitchen. Everything was so familiar, like a second home, warm and welcoming. The green and white plates and mugs on the pine dresser, the salmon-pink geraniums on the windowsill, the wild animal magnets on the fridge. If anyone understood me, Anne did. Better than Hugo, I often thought.

'Roly. I'm not sure how to say this.'

I suddenly couldn't swallow my mouthful of digestive biscuit. I chewed some more and sipped the disgusting instant coffee.

'You're – we – sometimes you don't show a lot of common sense,' she began.

I goggled at her. Who was it who had invested in a start-up company against all my advice and lost thousands?

'I mean, the biscuits are just a symptom. I've got nothing

against organic biscuits, but the cost of these!' She pushed them impatiently away. 'You're showing no sense at all!'

'I'm just trying to do my bit,' I said again.

'Your bit for what, exactly?' Anne had a glint in her eye I didn't like the look of. I'd seen it before, when we were in the sixth form and she faced down our headmistress about home clothes for revision, and won.

'Well, the planet.'

'How, exactly, does five quid for six biscuits help the planet?' She clamped her mouth shut and I saw, suddenly, that she had no lips at all, rather like Hugo, in fact. I didn't know why I'd never noticed it before, and it seemed to me extremely significant, but for what reason I wasn't sure.

Perhaps it was this that drew me into the danger zone. I was hypnotised by her lips and didn't notice where she was leading me.

'Well, organic is better,' I began.

'Hmm?'

I took this as encouragement and carried on, recklessly. 'And recycling is good too, because of all the energy that's saved.'

She nodded, her lips still invisible. I expected her to say, at this point, as she'd done in the past, 'Oh, Roly, you're so good, I don't know how you manage it,' but she remained silent.

'There's so much we can do,' I said. 'Lavender's good for the bees, and they pollinate food plants, so we should all have some lavender in the garden.' I wondered briefly if I was making any sense, if I wasn't rambling, but I was too excited to stop. I felt like I was on a raft rushing down the Yukon, white water bumping and swooshing me into dangerous eddies and missing the rocks by a whisker.

'Did you know that if we lost all the bees, human beings

would die out within five years?'

She raised her eyebrows.

'We're doing this massive experiment with the planet,' I continued. 'We're heating up the planet like there's no tomorrow, in fact there won't be a tomorrow if we don't stop it right now. People around the world depend on glaciers for their water supply and they're melting away too fast and within a few years whole countries will be bone dry. Bone dead. You see?'

Anne had pushed back from the table. She nodded.

'Did you know that Everest is no longer a pristine wilderness, it's a rubbish tip?'

She shrugged in a kind of no-I-didn't-know-but-does-it-really-matter kind of way.

'And there's a great swirling pool of plastic rubbish in the middle of the Pacific Ocean that's a thousand kilometres across. Think of it! A thousand kilometres!'

'OK.' She looked away from me and took a sip from her coffee.

'That's why we must all do our bit; we must recycle our plastics and glass and cardboard and stuff. I love recycling. And composting, Anne. Composting! It saves masses of carbon if we compost our food waste and grass cuttings. I even try to do it on holiday. It drives Hugo mad when I ask in hotels if they compost their food waste, and they look at me as if they don't know what I'm talking about, so I educate them.'

'I bet you do,' she murmured.

I stopped then, just for a second, and looked at her, but I was on a roll. She'd picked up her phone and was fiddling with it, staring at the screen, so I continued. I had nothing to lose. I needed her to be on my side, I needed to convince her.

'I mean, not that we've been on holiday very much recently. Just a couple of weekends away. Hugo went by himself the last couple of times. You know, work events.'

'Mmm.'

'Education's the thing,' I said. 'It's criminal the way it's not taught properly in schools, looking after the planet. Most school kids don't even know where eggs come from –'

'I don't think that's true,' she interrupted.

'Or how to grow food to eat. Or how to cook from scratch, rather than buying all that stuff in packets and not recycling the packaging!'

'You're obsessed with recycling, Roly.'

'I don't think so.'

'Don't you?'

'No, it's – it's – well, it's everything. It's all connected. It's like that domino game where they're all stacked up. You push one over and they all fall over.'

'Or a house of cards,' she said.

'Exactly. What we do in our homes has a real impact on the planet.'

'I'm one person,' she said slowly, 'one person out of seven billion. I honestly don't think that what little old me does in my daily life has any impact at all, when there are a couple of billion Chinese and Indians consuming to their hearts' content. Coal-fired power stations. Am I right?'

'Yes, but –'

'How can what you and I do balance out what all of them do? Supposing you're right anyway. Supposing this global warming or climate change or whatever you want to call it –'

'It's not quite the same thing –'

'– is actually caused by human activity?'

I was stunned.

'Well it is, Anne. Of course it is.'

Was she a denialist? Was she like Hugo – a sceptic? Even though they knew how Jonnie had died, what he believed, didn't that have any weight? I gaped at her, stunned into silence.

'You see, that doesn't happen for me,' she said.

'What doesn't?'

'That recycling thing you were talking about. Composting. It doesn't happen. I don't feel remotely guilty about chucking stuff in the bin on holiday. It doesn't occur to me to even think about it. I mean,' she added, with a sideways look, 'who does think about it on holiday? On our well-earned rests? On sunny beaches when we've been trying to keep it together, keep our lives from falling apart, when we're so stressed that we don't know which way is up? Who the hell thinks about bloody recycling in a Greek villa? Or composting? Apart from deep greenies. Like you.'

I felt the familiar tightness in my chest, a sense that at any minute I would burst apart with grief, my atoms scattered across the universe and crying out in protest, to infinity and beyond.

'Not just deep greenies. And me.' My voice was trembling. I took a deep breath and a swallow of my coffee, tried again. 'I'm not that deep-dyed, you know –'

But she was talking over me.

'You're like a stick of rock, Roly. Cut you open and you'd be deep green all the way through. You wouldn't even have that bit of white in the middle. You're deep green with the faintest tinge of pink on the outside. God, you're annoying.' And she smiled. Perhaps she meant it for a joke, but it was said in a tough, hard little voice, tight like her smile, and tight like my chest.

'I –'

'You know, Roly, people like you make the rest of us feel

terrible. Guilt doesn't even begin to describe it. When I'm in the same room as you, even in the same house, I can feel your eyes boring into me every time I switch on a light, or throw a teabag in the bin, or break open a pack of lettuce leaves.'

'They don't bore into you –'

'Oh yes, they do. They bore. You bore. You bore for England, you really do. I know the planet's in crisis. I know we're all going to hell in a handbasket next week or whenever you think it is, but my God, just shut up. I don't want to know. Any more.'

'But I don't set out to make you feel guilty, Anne, I –'

'I bloody well don't care what you set out to do, Roly, I've had enough, I don't want to know any more. Oh God, don't cry, I can't bear it.' She strode across the room and grabbed the fragrant tissues and thrust them onto my lap.

She stood above me while I fumbled in the box. Somewhere I had a handkerchief, but I couldn't think where, and anyway I didn't want to annoy her with it. That was the last thing I wanted, to annoy my best friend. I sniffed and pulled myself together.

'Sorry, Anne. I expect you've got a lot on.' I blew my nose. 'I'm taking up your morning.'

She didn't disagree, she didn't say, 'Oh no, Roly, stay as long as you like, it's fine, I'm not busy.'

I glanced up. She was staring down at me, frowning.

'You've always been a bit unbalanced, Roly, but I have to say –'

I gasped. 'Unbalanced?'

'Highly strung, then, but I must say this eco-warrior thing you've got going at the moment – don't get me wrong, being environmentally friendly is all very worthy and important – but you're taking it to extremes, like you do with everything.'

'What do you mean?' I could barely get the words out. I had no idea who she was talking about. It couldn't be me, her best friend.

'It's not surprising, really.' She leaned back against the countertop. 'With your background. I mean, Hugo and I –'

'Hugo?'

'We've been worried about you for quite a long time.'

'Worried?'

Anne pursed her lips and frowned again. 'You're repeating everything I say. What is it you don't understand?'

'I…' I couldn't speak. I stared at her, willing her to make some sense. 'Hugo…?'

'Yes?' she said impatiently.

'I'm your best friend!' I rushed the words through while I had breath, like a steam engine.

'Hmm. Yes, well, about that.' She shook her head. 'I can't, Roly. Sorry and all that. It's too much at the moment. I've got a lot on.'

I could hear her words, but they weren't making sense. Or they made sense, but I didn't believe them.

'We went on holiday,' I whispered.

'I know. Hard work it was too.'

'But we had lots of holidays, lovely holidays. You've always been my best friend, Anne, always.'

'Your only friend, more like.' She pursed her lips again, shook her head. 'I'm fond of you, Roly, don't get me wrong, but I can't be your only friend. You need more friends; you need a wider circle. I can't be your only support network. I mean, every time we meet, it's Jonnie this, Jonnie that, Jonnie was so wonderful, so marvellous. I can't do it, Roly. I'm not a grief counsellor. When do you ever ask me about my life, my children, my marriage, my work? When have you ever tried to support me in all the things I've gone through – redundancy and endometriosis and my mum's cancer? When –'

I found my voice just long enough to shriek at her. I screamed, a full-throated screech, and yelled: 'How many of your children have died?'

She started yelling back, but by then I was finding it difficult to breathe, my throat seemed to be closing up and there was a kind of roaring in my ears. Her mouth was opening and closing like a fish. I couldn't hear her; the roaring was so loud. I wept with the pain of it, the two sides of the coin of our relationship. And what did Hugo have to do with it? What had they been saying behind my back?

I began crying silently. I wasn't elegantly sniffing with refined tears trickling slowly down my face. It was more of a silent howl, my mouth wide open, eyes screwed shut, the pain in my chest not allowing me to breathe except in huge rasping intakes, water flowing from between my squeezed-shut eyelids, armpits, chest, groin, back, my face and head hot, my hands clammy and cold. Somewhere in the distance I could hear Anne's voice, ebbing and flowing through the noise in my head.

Let me die, let me die, I want to die, I thought. That desire that I constantly suppress but which has broken through with a life of its own at the most inconvenient moments – it's what I've wanted all along. There is no place for me here, on this planet. I am a parasite on the face of the Earth, like every other human being. Better for me to die, return to the soil and do no more harm.

∽

Hugo collected me an hour or so later. It was extremely inconvenient, he said, and he had a dinner to go to, or had I forgotten?

I had.

He was leading me down Anne's front steps to the pavement, his hand under my elbow, as if he were an orderly in a psychiatric ward and I, his patient. I asked him if he'd come by bus.

He shot a sideways look at me and gave one of his short laughs, the one without humour.

'Bloody hell, you are off your head,' he said.

'I came by train,' I said.

'Good for you.'

The drive home took half an hour. My public transport journey to North London – train, Tube, bus – had taken three times as long. Time is money, to Hugo. Time is a luxury he has to do without. For me, time is a necessity, for our healing, our mending, the healing of the planet. We may not have enough time left.

Hugo somehow got me into the GP's surgery that same day. I never could get an appointment when I needed one. I expect he used the words 'emergency' and 'urgent'. He may even have invoked Jonnie's name.

I was prescribed medication for my anxiety, and sleeping pills, and six sessions with a grief counsellor. Hugo drove me straight to the pharmacy to get the medicines, and at home stood over me while I obediently pretended to swallow the first dose. He supervised my undressing, brought me a sandwich and a cup of tea in bed, and placed the blister packs of capsules reverently in my bedside cabinet before he went off for his dinner.

∽

I suppose Anne felt guilty. I'm not sure I did. I was, in Hugo's words, a bit off my rocker at this point. She came for coffee a couple of times and I showed her the garden, and we talked about how our children were doing, but it was a long while after that before I saw her again.

It was like another bereavement. Hugo said I had pushed her away with all my irrational talk about the end of the world. I said that she was my best friend. He said that people change, and he seemed to look at me in a meaningful way.

'But she's always been the same! Anne hasn't changed! You've not changed!'

'Quite so,' said Hugo.

I rang Roberto, my stepfather, on his birthday, and ended up sobbing down the phone to him about Anne. The poor man was trying to have a family dinner. But he soothed me as he always had when I'd cried over some petty thoughtlessness of my mother's, and he kept his promise and came to visit me when I was not yet feeling strong enough to go anywhere on my own. He brought me roses from his garden and a chocolate cake and admired photos of the twins and Flora – such handsome children, he said – and took me out to a garden centre where we had lunch and walked round the little animal zoo, full of geese and rabbits and miniature goats and zebra finches and even a pair of tamarind monkeys. I'd swallowed one of the anti-anxiety pills before lunch and so it cheered me to see the young mums out with their toddlers, the children running from cage to cage, a free outing on a sunny day. I resolutely ignored the effect of all these people on the planet, all the carbon emissions from their cars and clothes and food, televisions and video games, toys and jewellery and shoes. And the pollution. And the waste. And everything else.

Don't think about it, whatever you do, I thought. *Just don't.*

Roberto and I strolled arm in arm during that happy

afternoon. I remember wondering what he and my mother had ever seen in each other. He'd been too nice for her, I thought, and, seeing him shuffle a bit and looking so much older, I thanked him for being a wonderful father. He patted my hand.

These things are important. Acknowledging the love you have for someone is important. I'm glad I told him. I was frightened that I would lose him too, that he was old and wouldn't last much longer. I needn't have worried. He lived another fifteen years. I wish I'd told Anne when we were young how much I loved and admired her, how much a part of me she was, the sister I never had. It might not have made any difference – she'd probably have laughed and told me not to be silly – but she would have known.

She sent a note in her next Christmas card saying that she was getting divorced and would soon be moving down to Cornwall permanently, and if I ever fancied a short break to let her know.

'An olive branch,' said Hugo. 'Very good of her.'

'Maybe I should go down? Support her?'

He glanced at me and shook his head slightly. 'She's moved on, Roly. The time for support was a couple of years ago.'

'Did you know, Hugo? That their marriage was in trouble?'

'Of course. It was obvious.'

It hadn't been obvious to me. I'd been so self-absorbed that I'd not even realised that her sadness and irritability was not about me or Jonnie.

∽

Hugo told me one day not to try people's patience too much, that people would run out of tolerance. He said I needn't dress like a bag lady, that there was nothing wrong in occasionally buying new clothes. That if it meant so much to me, he would hire a dressmaker to make sure that all my clothes were made locally and for a fair price. That we could source ethical fabrics, genuine Scottish tweed for the winter, organic cotton for the summer. Anything, Roly, he said, tell me what we need to do.

We were in our bedroom, the wardrobe doors open. Hugo had been rifling through my clothes, pulling them out, laying them on the bed for me to look at. I was no longer interested in those smart skirts and dresses, the pretty blouses, the high-heeled shoes. I felt, back then, that my clothing should be practical, sensible, that there was no need for pretty or beautiful or luxurious, that I should get rid of stuff that didn't fit my ideals. If Indian farmers' wives had only one change of clothes, then so should the rest of us.

Hugo held up a pale cream cashmere cardigan adorned with tiny seed pearls, which I'd often worn at Christmas.

I shook my head, said that using up what we already had was greener than buying new things, and that Jonnie's trousers fitted me quite well.

Look, Hugo! The length is really very good, even if they are baggy around the waist, but a belt helps with that. Or I could use braces. Ha! Belt and braces, get it?'

Hugo took a breath, closed his eyes, and let out a sigh. He nodded very slightly.

'I get it,' he said, before quietly leaving the room.

FOURTEEN

The Good Life

When it was properly dark this evening, so dark that I could see stars between the scudding clouds, I spent another hour or so signalling an SOS with my wind-up torch. There's a big container ship anchored out there in the bay. I can see its lights, so someone looking in my direction might see mine.

I thought of something else today. My beautiful red shawl. It's the brightest, most vibrant thing I have in this hole in the cliff. This afternoon I spread it out on the rocks and weighed it down with shingle. Somebody might see it. A heart-breaking waste if it blows away or gets swept off by the sea, but it's a sacrifice worth making.

I shine the torch on my thigh. It's sore and hot and aching, and when I peel back the edge of the rip in my jeans I can see quite clearly the wound's going a funny colour. Difficult to tell in this light, but it looks a bit greenish, a bit yellowy, a bit weepy.

Midnight, maybe. Or three a.m., possibly. No moon, no stars – the clouds are too heavy. I am utterly alone. Terrified. Sick at heart.

Earlier this evening I heard a dog barking. It seemed quite far off, but it may have been directly above me. This cave's pretty sound-proof. It's like I'm buried in the cliff under all this heavy rock. I can hear nothing except the wind and the waves and the gulls.

It might have been a rescue party out looking for me. Perhaps Flora has told the police, and they've put a photo on the news, and people have remembered seeing me on the coast path. I called out, I yelled, I screamed, but the wind whipped my voice away. Even so, there's a glimmer of hope that people are aware I'm missing, that they may be searching.

The moon breaks through a gap in the clouds. The sea suddenly gleams bright silver, striped dark between the waves. It's calmer tonight, but heavy and still, as if thunder's on the way.

I sit quietly, conserving my energy, and gaze out at the sea. Unlike land, there's no barrier between seas and oceans. Six thousand miles away, in this water, Jonnie came to his end.

I wonder if I may see him again tonight. But Jonnie, in life and in death, is not to be commanded. He will come when he wishes.

I take a deep breath.

I wait.

༞

'What about a dog?' Hugo suggested one evening.

'A dog?'

'You're at a loose end. At the moment.'

I like dogs, but I didn't want one. I knew who'd end up looking after it. It would be like extended childcare, walks and vets and feeding and doggy chats with dog owners in the park, comparing doggy habits as parents compare their offspring at a toddler group.

'Or join a club with like-minded people?' he added.

'I'm perfectly happy,' I said.

Hugo said nothing, just stirred his coffee. He reached for the gingerbread.

'Perfectly happy,' I said again.

Hugo sipped from his mug.

'What did you have in mind?' I asked, after a long pause.

'There's the local Wildlife Trust,' he went on enthusiastically.

'We support them already.'

'There you are,' he said.

'No,' I said firmly. 'I don't want to be shaking a collecting box in the town centre on a Saturday morning.'

'Is that what they do?' Hugo furrowed his brow.

'Yes,' I said robustly, although in truth I had no idea what the supporters did.

'OK. There's also Friends of the Earth, and the Sustainable St Albans Week in a couple of months. Lots of things going on that week. It would do you good, Roly.'

I shrugged. He hadn't mentioned Greenpeace.

Later I looked these things up on the computer. Guided walks, community gardening, artworks, a trip to the recycling centre, films, talks, coffee mornings, fair trade events, events for schools, sustainable food, thermal imaging. I peered at the photos. There were some people I knew. I wouldn't be alone or lonely. And I needed that, Hugo was right; I needed to be part of something, to feel I was part of a movement, that there was strength in numbers. It would have done me good. I would have felt less alone.

But I also felt too raw, still, to face the sympathy of strangers, their well-meaning questions, their whispering in corners. 'That's Jonnie Danborough's mother. You know, Jonnie Danborough, the young activist who was swept away on a Greenpeace mission a few years back...'

Instead, I told Hugo that I wanted to remodel the garden, to grow vegetables and fruit and to keep chickens. He seemed quite pleased.

'Yes! Great idea! Use the bottom of the garden,' he said.

I just looked at him. Why is it that people seem to think that proper gardening – growing food – needs to be kept out of sight?

Then he frowned. 'You won't take out the roses, will you?'

'No,' I said drily, 'I won't take out the roses.'

He must have noticed my tone, for he paused in the act of putting on his jacket and glanced at me before flinging his jacket back onto a chair and striding to the kitchen door.

He opened the door and walked out onto the patio, pointing further down the garden. 'If you put the chickens under the trees –'

'So you don't mind about chickens?'

'No, except you can't have a cockerel and don't forget about foxes –'

'No cockerel?'

He turned to me. 'We don't want to annoy the neighbours, Roly.'

'Of course.' He'd been brought up with livestock, as a child. I readjusted my brain to take account of his slightly more extensive experience and tried to picture him on a farm.

'OK. Chickens, minus cockerel, under the trees. You can create an enclosure there, and they'll have shelter similar to their natural habitat. Don't forget a little house for them. I would suggest three or four, to start with. Rhode Island Reds are a decent breed, or Buff Orpingtons.'

'I was thinking of bantams.'

'Tiny eggs,' he said dismissively.

'I don't mind.'

There was a slight pause. He put his arm around my shoulders, hugged me close. 'No, of course you don't. You have what you like, Roly. Sorry. Your idea.'

'Thanks.'

'It'll be fun,' he said, and smiled at me. 'We'll both enjoy it. Fresh eggs for breakfast, eh?'

'And lots of fruit and veg.'

'Fantastic!' His tone was slightly too hearty. 'I'm looking forward to it already!'

ɔ⌣

I got busy as soon as Hugo left the house. What madness. I didn't draw up plans, didn't design anything, didn't think of the twins or Flora. My sole motive was to show Hugo – what, exactly? That I resented being patronised, and that I could run things my own way for once?

If I regret anything, I regret this.

It was an extremely pretty garden. Outside the back door was a patio, with herb planters and geraniums in tubs, and a table and chairs for al fresco meals; then a rose garden with heritage roses, spiny and thorny but strongly scented of honey and citrus; below this a lawn with the children's swing – which had to go as they'd grown out of it years before – then a sort of spinney of flowering shrubs – and then another lawn. Plenty of room for playing, for camping out on summer nights, for dens and make-believe.

We'd had such fun in that garden, and I'd loved it. Hugo really did understand plants and he'd worked hard at creating a lovely space for all of us. On long summer evenings, when Jonnie and Flora were small, he got back from work early and did a spot of gardening while the children ate tea outside before bedtime, and then more often than not he and I sat till sunset with a glass of wine, and we would just chat and laugh. As I remember this my heart is filling up with all sorts of emotion – all the emotions I work so hard to suppress because what on earth is the point now of feeling love, and desire, and the joy of being attuned to the one man I ever loved?

I really don't know what I was thinking when I got on the phone as soon as Hugo left for work and hired a man with a digger to come the following week, when Hugo would be away, and a local odd-job man to build eight large raised beds from timber, about two feet high. I ordered a couple of tons of topsoil and fifty bags of good compost to fill the beds. I checked our garden tools and replaced the fork and trowel at the garden centre. I bought seeds and small vegetable plants, fruit bushes and a grape vine, trellis and wire, bark chippings and edging stones.

My mistake was in not discussing any of this with Hugo, but I was beginning to feel that if I didn't do something huge, something dramatic, then I might as well not do anything at all. And Jonnie would undoubtedly approve.

By the time Hugo came back from his conference, the top of the back garden had been transformed into a rather bare-looking smallholding, with paths of beaten earth between the timber beds, which looked like unfilled graves when I stared down at them from our bedroom window. I'd decided against bantams, thinking it better to take rescued hens from a battery farm, half-bald on their rumps and backs from self-mutilation. Two had been de-beaked, to my dismay, but they seemed to manage food all right. Now ensconced in the new run, the five of them huddled disconsolately under their henhouse, too scared to venture out. I decided to name them, give them dignity, allow them to be individuals: Saskia, Bertie, Jilly, Tatty, and Gloria.

The men and I worked solidly for a week, but as the week wore on my enthusiasm waned and my panic grew. I couldn't imagine how Hugo was going to react. It had been naïve of me to think he wouldn't be shocked by the scale of the transformation. And the roses, the roses… I left them where they were and they looked ridiculous, squashed up between the raised beds and the fences.

Then I waited for Hugo to return, more and more panicky, my stomach cartwheeling with anxiety, unable to eat, unable to even finish a cup of tea.

I have never seen Hugo look so appalled.

✂

'No,' he said later, slightly drunk. 'No, it's your thing, Roly, it's fine, it's absholutely fine. Whatever makes you happy, whatever… rocks your boat.' He waved his glass vaguely at me, at the garden. I stood by the window waiting for this little storm to pass. I was already regretting my impulsiveness, my lack of planning, those things that Hugo had always criticised so that I did nothing without consulting him first.

'Looking forward to the produce, Roly, all those eggs and tomatoes and – and – and things.' He took a gulp of whiskey. The ice chinked against his teeth. 'Pigs? Hmm? We could have bacon… Eggs and bacon for breakfast. Every day. Fatten up a pig for Christmas. Gammon. Pork chops. Apple sauce from our own apples. I can see it now. A hog roast out on the lawn, inviting all the neighbours, some Morris dancing, a maypole, the May queen up at dawn, washing her face in the dew. A bit of merrie England right here.'

He drained his glass.

'Let's bring back the good old days, hey, Roly?' he said, sloshing more whiskey into his glass. 'That's what you're after, isn't it? You, my girl, are running away from modern life. You, darling –' he pointed both fingers at me like a gun '– you don't like the twenty-first century one little bit. I've always known that, and now I've been proved right. Don't – don't you shake your head at me like that.'

'Hugo, please –'

'Hugo, pleeease,' he mimicked.

The room began to rock around me. I caught hold of the nearest chair.

'Bloody hell, Roly, breathe!'

But I couldn't. My throat had seized up.

'God, your lips are turning blue.' He lunged towards me and slapped me, once, twice, around the face.

I sucked in one breath, then another, then began panting, as if I'd been running very fast.

'Admit it, you don't like modern life at all.'

I shook my head, unable to speak.

He raised his eyebrows, took another slurp of his drink.

'It's not modern life, it's the future.' I gulped in some air.

'Even better,' he said. 'You're scared of the future, so you go back to the past.' He turned away, pulled out a kitchen chair. 'Some mythical perfect past, no nasty gadgets or computers or cars. Lots of lovely nature worship. Some imagined Eden. Walking some wild path where no one in their right mind would want to go.'

'No, it's not like that!'

'No? Well, let me tell you something. I don't bloody care.'

He sat at the table, plonking his glass down so the ice clinked, and the whiskey slopped over the rim. 'I'm bored of it, Roly. You've just dug up a rather lovely garden that it's taken me twenty years to create, for no good reason that I can see. I don't care what your reasons are, they mean nothing to me. But it's yours now – that – that – those – those trenches, that World War One battleground. I never want to set foot in it again.' He rocked his chair back on two legs, staring at me.

'I'll make it lovely again, I promise.'

He looked incredulous, then slowly shook his head, smiling as if dealing with a simpleton. 'Not possible, Roly. It's simply. Not. Possible.'

'Just listen, Hugo. One minute.' My breathing was nearly normal now. 'Please.'

'One minute.' He raised his wrist and glanced at his watch.

'We're running out of food and water and –'

'We?'

'The world –'

'That's not new.'

'But it is! There are seven billion people on the planet, and in forty years' time there may be ten billion –'

'May be.'

'Probably will be.'

Hugo raised one eyebrow, made a little moue with his mouth like a sceptical Frenchman.

'Seriously, the world is running out of resources, Hugo.'

He nodded, wearily, and tipped the chair forward again. He leaned his head into his left hand, elbow on the table, and swirled the ice around in his drink.

'And it's not only food, but everything. We're using stuff up and not replenishing it.'

'And this affects my garden how, exactly?'

'We all need to live more lightly on the planet, we need –'

'Lightly.' He folded his arms. 'You call that lightly.' He nodded towards the window.

'It will be, it will, I promise. I'm not explaining myself very well.'

'No.'

'And there's climate change. The more oil we burn, the more the atmosphere heats up and causes disasters and –'

'Roly, Roly, Roly.' He shook his head sorrowfully.

'No, seriously, Hugo. You have to listen to this, it's important. The carbon dioxide –'

'One minute is up, and I'm going to bed.'

'Hugo!'

He stood and walked to the kitchen door.

More, there's so much more you can do. Remember food miles. Grow local, eat local.

'Hugo, don't.'

He turned. 'No, Rosalie, you don't. I've been remarkably patient, listening to your ramblings after you've ruined my garden. I don't know what the hell is going on – don't even think of interrupting – I don't know if you're on the verge of a breakdown, but I don't like it one little bit. If you want to do your gardening experiment, by all means go ahead, but don't expect me to be interested. I'll thank you to inform me the next time you plan on making any major changes to our lives. Good night.'

∽

I stood by the sink, listening to his uneven footsteps stumbling up the stairs, my cheeks stinging where he'd slapped me. I supposed we were even. It struck me that we had somehow become adversaries, when we had started as allies. I was thankful all the children were away, and then I remembered that one was never coming home.

FIFTEEN

The Better Life

A few days later I bought a rail ticket to Penzance with cash. I couldn't relax at home. I'd find Hugo staring at me thoughtfully as I fed the hens or chopped herbs or laced up my walking boots. It was unnerving. But perhaps I unnerved him too.

Just before I left, I wrote Hugo a note:

H.
Please feed hens.
R.

I found the studio where I remembered it, at the bottom of Anne's garden, hidden by a thick stand of bamboo. The main house was empty, and I was sure I'd been unobserved as I walked up the lane, the stone and earth banks on either side higher than my head, the bracken towering above. The lane became narrower the higher I walked. The house was right at the end of the lane, and it was obvious that no cars had driven this way for weeks, bracken and gorse and brambles tumbling over each other in their eagerness to meet in the middle. I pushed my way through, sustaining only minor scratches, wondering which of them was going to have this house now, after their divorce, or whether it was to be sold. The code on the key safe was the same as ever – 1912, the year of the *Titanic*.

There was just enough light from the sickle moon hanging low over the slate roof to see the grey granite cottage, when I arrived at dusk. I pushed the wicket gate open. It creaked. I paused and listened, staring at the house. Lights were on, but I remembered the security lights on timers that we set whenever we left. There were no vehicles in the drive, and when I approached the front door, I saw there was ivy twining across it at the top. I took the house keys out of the key safe and took the key to the studio off the ring, returning the others to the safe.

The studio smelt old and unused, mildewy and damp. Beggars can't be choosers, I thought.

I'd take it now, though. An open door, a pretty garden, a camp bed, sleeping bag and pillow. Two spare blankets. A sink with running water, and a gas camping stove for making tea. A table and a couple of basket chairs. Books on a shelf above the door. A door that locked. A door I could unlock and walk through any time I pleased.

കൗ

The days fell easily into the pattern I'd imagined. I rose at dawn, washed in the little stream that ran past the studio, gasping with pleasure at the coldness of the water, the tingling glow of skin slowly warming up after a dunking. There was a deep pool that had been a particular joy for the children, Anne's three kids with Jonnie and Flora taking turns to leap in and emerge screeching from the cold, laughing and pushing each other in. Fergus and Dugald sat and watched, enjoying the outdoor life in their own way, armed with insect-identifying books and small pocket microscopes. Our two families got on so well, the two couples like siblings. Hugo and I were still in love, and had no inkling of how much our lives would change within a few years. I had everything I needed – money, children, handsome husband, nothing to worry me.

I bathed naked, towelled myself dry, my senses hyper-aware of the small movements and tiny noises of living creatures in the bushes around me, industrious lives living for the moment, seeking food and shelter, incuriously accepting my unclothed presence as I sat in the watery rays of the rising sun. It was chilly, sitting in that basket chair on the studio veranda. I felt like Dorcas, a part of nature, not separated from it by layers of clothing and footwear. I wore no watch, noted the passing of the hours by the shadows of the trees which shortened and lengthened with the movement of the sun. My nipples hardened in the cold air and the little hairs on my arms and legs – and the tinier hairs on my stomach, hairs I had never really noticed – stood erect. Every part of me took hours to feel truly warm in the late autumn sunlight.

But I could breathe. I breathed deeply, filling my lungs with the moist scented air. My chest seemed to expand; my muscles ached as I let go of the tension I had been holding – for how long? Since before Jonnie died. Then they stopped aching, and I slept. I slept for hours at a time, whole afternoons drifting into night; ten, twelve, fourteen hours of deep dreamless sleep rested me. I began to feel at peace.

I lay for hours on a rug in the garden most afternoons, warm in the low October sun, watching the busy life in the long grasses, ants and tiny beetles and little colourful flying insects, iridescent wings catching rainbows. Dragonflies and damselflies and late butterflies flitted through the shrubs. Blackbirds tugged worms from the lawn, thrushes smashed snails on the path, wrens hopped mouse-like through the overgrown herbaceous borders. I sat and dozed in a garden chair under the honey-scented buddleia. I crushed lavender between my fingers and inhaled, feeling the strains of my recent life flow out of me.

It was perfect, an Eden, a garden where no harm could befall me, where I had the illusion of perfect safety.

In the twilight one evening I had what I can only describe as a mystic experience. I was filled with a sense that there was nothing that wasn't alive, crying out with the deepest joy at being part of the universe. Those leaves, that flowing water, the stars beginning to come out, the insects, birds, mice and frogs, the toads, the slugs and snails, the rabbits and foxes, the very stones – all imbued with life. And it was love holding it together. The love of the creator.

I didn't sleep that night. I wandered around the garden, wondering at my blindness. How could I have not seen this before? How could I have been so mechanistic about the world? How had I missed the spiritual, the divine, the eternal?

You may think I'd completely lost the plot at that point, but it was a St Francis of Assisi moment. I got it. I got what he was about. I was St Roly of Anne's Cottage, late of St Albans. Brother Sun, Sister Moon, and all that.

The world is full of people, only some of whom are human.

It's never left me, that sense that all is alive and held together by love.

Love. The simplest and most complicated thing of all. God and Jonnie had given me a mission to save the world.

How could I fail?

೧

Anne's cottage rested halfway up a steep slope, with the garden and stream below and wild shrubby rocks above. Beyond the stream were brambles and fuchsias and hazel bushes, with fields of nettles and bracken rising steeply towards the crest of the hill. Years back, there had been a hamlet on this site, a few scattered houses, but now the property was secluded, granite buildings dismantled, and the stones carted away long ago for building elsewhere.

Some days I spent hours gazing into the clear depths of the stream. It bubbled and sparkled over large boulders and shallow beds of shale and pebbles; it eddied around mossy logs and outcrops; it trickled and flowed. It had a name, that little watercourse. I've long forgotten it. Strange that it should be named since it was so small, but I suppose when there were farmhouses and mills and cottages in every part of the countryside people named not only the roads and hamlets and hills, but also the rivers and brooks, for travellers and locals alike. We must know where we are going.

Sometimes I saw a fish in the stream, but I didn't attempt to catch it. In the golden olden days I might have tried. I'd sent my children as teenagers on bushcraft camps where they had to skin rabbits and eat wild garlic. It sounded delicious and exciting, and part of me envied them. But the only one of my four who ever enjoyed it was Jonnie. Flora was squeamish and afraid of insects crawling into her sleeping bag and getting into her hair, and I was impatient. I may have called her a sissy. The twins were sent home after only one day. I don't know what happened. The course leader was so politically correct that he simply said that he didn't think it was their thing. Fergus and Dugald had refused to talk about it.

In the field over Anne's garden hedge I could see a ring of mushrooms. They grew fast in the mild wet weather. They looked like edible field mushrooms, but I wasn't keen to risk it. I stared at them in the dawn light, suddenly hungry for mushrooms fried in butter, new-laid eggs, ripe sweet tomatoes, potatoes, fried bread, fat pork and apple sausages – all the things I had not eaten at breakfast for years. Perhaps it was a sense memory, a bodily reliving of happier breakfasts from long ago, but I could no longer merely stare at the fairy ring, I had to know, and knowing, I felt, would help me control my longing for Hugo.

There. I had said it, if only to myself.

I let myself into the main house to look for Anne's book on fungi. It had been somewhere in the kitchen, I recalled, where we had once eaten a massive puffball, the book – full of illustrations and descriptions and recipes – propped against the enormous red spotted teapot that I'd bought her as a present.

The house smelt stale and musty. It was clean but had an air of neglect. There were fewer knick-knacks than I remembered. The large clock in the kitchen had been removed, leaving a circular grey stain on the wall. I picked up the three envelopes that had come through the door, none addressed by name, just junk mail. They were floppy and cold with the damp. I shivered. I hadn't expected this. In my memory the house had always been warm and cosy in the winter months, or cool and sunny in the summer, but always, always, filled with light and noise and bustle and fun and laughter. Now it was graveyard quiet. A slug trail snaked from the back door across the kitchen tiles and under the fridge.

The fridge door was open, and the fridge was off, cavernous and dark. There was no warmth from the Rayburn. I'd never known it to be turned off.

I stood uncertain by the large, scrubbed pine table. I couldn't quite remember what I had come for. I felt like an intruder.

When I opened the door that led into the dining room, I could hear a high-pitched beep about every three seconds. It came from the answer phone in the sitting room beyond. Ignoring that, I went through to the stairs which, quaintly, were hidden behind a door – endless fun for the children when they were little – and up. So empty and still, so full of memories. I was drawn as if by some invisible thread – call it love – to the guest bedroom.

We'd slept there many times, Hugo and I. A perfect bedroom. A wide soft bed, a huge square bay window which caught the sun all day, views of garden, trees, moorland and on some days a blue haze which I argued could be the sea, although he said not. Comfortable armchairs, shallow wardrobes built into the thick walls, a fireplace that in the winter, at Christmas, held a fire that cast shadows and flickering lights in the darkness while we made love.

I stood in the doorway. This room, this sanctuary, where Hugo and I had felt so at one, was bleak and empty. The bed had been stripped, the armchairs and curtains removed, dead flies and moths littered the windowsill.

Turning abruptly before tears overwhelmed me, I went to the bathroom where I sat on the small white chair and sobbed, blowing my nose on lavatory paper. Then I used the facilities. Then I went downstairs.

On a whim I played the answer phone messages. They had to be several months old. There were three about mis-sold PPI, one from a window cleaner, and the final one, the one that caused me to gasp and sit down heavily on the sofa, was from Hugo.

It was unsettling, to say the least.

'Roly, it's Hugo,' he began. 'I think you're there. I'd appreciate it if you'd call me.'

There was a pause. He cleared his throat.

'Thanks. Bye,' he ended.

❧

I sat a long time on that sofa. In the late afternoon, when the light was beginning to fade, I let myself out of the house, locked up, deposited the key in the safe box and crept down to the studio. I'd spent the whole day inside, staring at the phone on its little table or gazing out of the window at the trees and clouds. Once I turned on the television to check the weather forecast, but the volume and stridency of the voices and music was such a shock that I turned it off within a minute.

What a waste of a beautiful day. I didn't even have the book on fungi, but I climbed over the gate and picked some mushrooms anyway, cooking them by candlelight on the camping stove, with fresh marjoram from the garden and sunflower oil filched from Anne's larder, and gorged myself silly on those and a box of stale chocolate biscuits I found and a bottle of red wine from the racks in the cupboard under the stairs. I crawled into Jonnie's sleeping bag fully clothed and woke far too early with a thumping head and desperately needing to pee, and the realisation that I had not got very far at all.

❧

Hugo tracked me down a few days later, quicker than I hoped, but not as swiftly as he'd have liked. I'd been at the cottage about a month. It was inevitable. He had guessed where I would end up. He said later that he'd wanted to give me time – time to myself, time to think about things, time to decide whether to come home. I had plenty of money, at least for a winter, but he was worried for me. He didn't realise I'd secreted cash in dribs and drabs over the months, thirty pounds here, twenty there. He just knew I'd left my phone and all my credit and debit and store cards at home.

Poor Hugo. Today I see it so clearly from his perspective. He must have been worried sick. Flora, too. And I was lucky, wasn't I? To have money I hadn't earned, and the freedom to do whatever I liked. To run away. To go missing. To cause heartache.

I heard the sound of a car as it approached the house up the lane. I knew it had to be Hugo. My first impulse was to flee, to climb the hill behind the house, to watch from behind one of the stumpy trees. But it would have been useless. My stuff was in the studio, the door was open, and all Hugo would have to do would be to wait for me to return. It was nearly November, and even I wasn't so stupid as to leave everything in the studio and live rough with no food, clothing or money.

I stood under the bamboo, my heart beating a little faster, my throat dry, my breathing shallow. I took a deeper breath, placed my left hand on a strong bamboo cane, and waited.

Hugo's car came slowly round the last corner of the lane and stopped. The engine shut off. In the silence I could hear the ticking of the engine as it cooled, the trickle of the stream over the rocks, and the dry rustle of the bamboo in the breeze.

The driver's door opened and Hugo clambered out rather stiffly. I watched as he stretched, then leaned into the car to get his phone. He dialled, and waited by the gate, the phone to his ear, looking around vaguely. When he appeared to look through me and glanced back towards the house, I realised that he couldn't see me. I was wearing dark clothing, and it was a sunless morning, leaden clouds gathering overhead, ready to break in thunder and torrents.

Faintly, from the house, I could hear the phone ringing.

When it rang off, Hugo tried again. Then a third time.

He looked so anxious that I took pity on him. As he was putting his phone into his pocket I stepped forward and said, 'Hugo.'

He turned quickly, his hand on the latch, ready to push the gate open and walk along the path to the house.

'Roly.' He put his hand to his chest and took a breath. 'You're all right.'

I nodded.

'I didn't know...' He glanced at the house. 'I tried ringing.'

'I know.'

Hugo gazed at me for a few moments. I waited to see what would happen next.

'Can I come in?'

'Of course.'

He unlatched the gate and let it swing open, stepping through, holding the top bar so it didn't bash against the wall. He pushed it shut before asking: 'Didn't you think of calling me, Roly?'

I shook my head. Quite honestly, it hadn't even occurred to me. 'I got drunk,' I said. 'When I heard your message.'

'Really?' He sounded surprised.

I nodded.

Hugo nodded too. We stood there for a couple of minutes, both nodding like puppets, looking, not looking at each other, not smiling, half-smiling. So much to say. So little understanding of how to start saying it.

'Will you come home with me, Rosalie?'

At that point I wanted to run to him and fling myself into his arms, and to kiss him, hold him passionately, but I just nodded. I was being careful. I didn't know really how things stood between us. We were on shaky ground.

I nodded again. Yes, I'd go home with him. I wanted to mend things between us, and perhaps it would be easier at home. No guarantees, though.

I took my time saying goodbye to my friends in the garden. I kissed the trees on their trunks and leaves. I brushed the tops of the herbaceous plants with my fingertips as I walked up and down the lawn, murmuring farewells and blessings under my breath. I knelt by the stream and trailed my fingers in the flowing water. I asked for 'a moment' to wander up the hill behind the house and look at the view for the last time. I took two hours and twenty-seven minutes to say my goodbyes.

We didn't talk much in the car. Hugo turned on the radio and fiddled around with the settings to get a clearer reception along the deep Cornish lanes. This always makes me nervous, him driving with only one hand on the wheel, but I'm proud of myself. I said not a word.

☙

I had plenty of time to think on the long journey home. I wasn't in the mood to talk. In fact, I didn't know how to start a conversation, after everything I'd done, and Hugo was unnaturally silent. He's always been able to talk with anyone about anything at any time. Airports, restaurants, parks, the doctor's surgery. 'I've just had a nice little chat,' he'd say, and he'd tell me all about it – someone's grandmother's funeral, or someone else's house move, another person's holiday disaster. Blackspot on roses, hip replacements, school fundraisers, children's hamsters. Anything at all. Never bored, unless on his own with no one to talk to. Perhaps that was part of our trouble. We'd stopped talking, and listening.

Hugo led me inside our house and helped me out of my coat, which he hung on the hooks by the front door. Then he took my hand and brought me into the kitchen, where he fussed around with kettle and tea and mugs. I sat at one end of the table, which was covered with unwashed dishes, newspapers and unopened mail. The peace lily by the sink was dying, its long leaves drooping into the washing up bowl.

'My darling, my darling,' he said as he placed the mugs on the table. 'Oh, Roly.' He was shaking his head. 'Oh, Roly.'

It was as if coming home had released him to speak. Familiar ground. Beyond him the garden looked bleak and empty, the raised beds a reproach.

He sat next to me and took both my hands in his. 'I've been so worried. I've missed you so much, haven't slept, you know. It's been hell, not knowing if you were, well…' and he leaned forward and kissed me, tenderly, on my lips. When he leaned back, I saw that there was a small tear running down his cheek near his nose. I reached up and wiped it gently away with my thumb.

We sat a long time, our foreheads touching, his hands gripping mine. After a while he began to weep. After some time, he sat back, rather shakily. 'Phew. Didn't expect that. Thought we'd have a blazing row.'

That's what I'd thought too. I'd worked out what he was going to say and what I would say in return. I'd imagined him slamming doors in frustration and me doing my icy thing, the thing I do when I don't know what to say, the thing that infuriates him most because I refuse to argue. But here we were, most unexpectedly, wobbly with the emotion of being lost and found.

'I didn't know, Roly, if you'd want to come back to me. Even when I came down to Cornwall, I wasn't sure that you'd come back with me.' He glanced at me out of the corner of his eye. 'But I had to see you. Had to know.'

I spoke for the first time since returning home. 'I didn't know if you'd want me.'

'Oh Roly, I love you, of course I want you. You're the most desirable woman I know. I want you; I need you; I love you. I love you.' He kissed me hard on the mouth. 'I love you! How can you say such a thing?'

'It's how it seemed to me.'

'Oh no, Roly, never, never.' He kissed me again. 'Never think that. I love you. We'll grow old together, tend your garden, travel on the Orient Express, visit galleries and museums, all the things we've not had time for. We'll do them together, Roly. You and me.'

'You slapped me.'

'I – I – that was to get you breathing, Roly.' He leaned back, pushed right back into the chair, frowning at me. 'That's all that was. You'd stopped breathing. Seriously. That's all it was.'

'OK,' I said, after a pause. That's what it had looked like to him, although he'd never slapped me before. I wasn't sure what to make of this. Not appropriate treatment for a panic attack, after all. 'Don't do it again.'

'No, no. I'm sorry. I won't. It was just instinctive, I suppose. It worked, though, didn't it?'

'Mmm.'

Hugo squeezed my hands. I looked down at our hands, his big and square, mine long and thin, tucked between his. Jonnie had inherited my bone structure. His hands had been like mine. But today, this was all about Hugo and me. 'You've got to promise me something, Roly.'

'What?'

'Promise me that when it all gets too much, if you ever –' he took a breath '– if you ever want to get away from it all, you know, you need a break, a rest, whatever, just promise me you won't disappear. Please. Just tell me. You can go wherever you want, for as long as you like, it's fine, seriously, it is, Roly, believe me.' He squeezed my hands again.

'Quite honestly,' he continued, 'I didn't realise quite how

much things had got to you. Completely understandable. Tell me, next time, hmm?'

I nodded.

'Promise?' he said.

'Yes, all right.' I nodded again. 'It's not really about you, Hugo.'

'Pleased to hear it!' He squeezed my hands again.

No, it wasn't Hugo. It was everything he represented; all the people like him. Consuming without a thought for tomorrow, without a care in the world. Using up the planet.

I was probably being unfair.

He sent me upstairs for a bath while he prepared dinner – simple stuff, smoked salmon and salad from a bag and new potatoes and rolls. It was almost too rich for me, but I passed over what I couldn't eat to him, and he ate it without comment.

We slept together that night. He hadn't presumed or assumed, but it was a comfort to lie in his arms again and remember what it was that we had.

Our fragile peace lasted a week or so, and then I ventured into Jonnie's room. It had been tidied up – I detected Flora's hand; the neatness was not Hugo's – but I didn't mind that. I noticed instantly that the laptop was not on the desk where I'd left it. I turned to the shelves – it wasn't there. The desk drawers held nothing more than old bits of stationery – half-used notebooks, old biros, broken pencils, postcards and receipts. Under the bed were large plastic containers of Lego and his Warhammer models. The wardrobe held clothes and shoes, nothing else.

I was becoming frantic. I climbed up onto the desk chair to search the top of the wardrobe, I ran to the cupboard on the landing, I hurtled downstairs to Hugo's study, pulled open drawers and cupboards, stood panting and dizzy in the hall, paralysed by the panic that was engulfing me. I fought it, I'm proud to say, I fought it with everything I had. I found my phone and with trembling hands texted Hugo at work, asking him where Jonnie's laptop was. Waiting for his reply I paced up and down in a long loop that took me through the kitchen and conservatory, out round the garden via the hen house, through the rose garden and back to the hall.

He replied about an hour later.

'Flora's got it.'

Oh, thank God. I dropped to the floor in relief. Flora was keeping it safe. She would look after it. I couldn't bear it if anything had happened to that computer, my one last and so tenuous link with Jonnie. My research, all the documents I'd saved. All the emails sent to him after his death.

❧

What Hugo hadn't mentioned was that he had taken the laptop into work and got it cleaned up. Strangers, handling Jonnie's laptop. They'd transferred everything onto a hard drive – Hugo had at least remembered that – but they'd also upgraded it, new software, new hardware, new battery. A better charger that someone had left in a cupboard. To all intents a new computer. And then he'd given it to Flora.

To give him his due, he looked stricken when I told him.

'I had no idea you'd been using it,' he kept saying. 'I had no idea.'

'It's been my one link with him, my one way of –' A sob caught in my throat. I fought back the tears.

'I'm surprised you didn't take it with you then, to Anne's.'

'That's a mean thing to say, Hugo. Why would I have taken it to Anne's? Tell me that!'

'You tell me,' he said quietly. There was bewilderment in his eyes, and a kind of pain, and even, I think, pity. He stood before me, his hands half-held out towards me, his shoulders slumped. For a few moments he looked old and worn out.

'It's typical of you, barging in without a moment's thought about it.'

'I did think about it. I was trying to do something nice for Flora. She's missed him so much, Roly. You're not the only one, you know.' He ran his fingers through his hair. 'My God, Roly, I'm sorry. Why didn't you tell me you were using it?'

'Because not in a million years did I think you'd do anything so stupid!'

'Stupid?! Who was being stupid when they ran away and disappeared, Roly? Tell me that!'

'That,' I said icily, 'was different.'

'Not so different, Roly, not so different. We were desperate! We thought you were dead, that your body would be found in a field or a ditch somewhere. It was the least I could do to cheer Flora up. First Jonnie, and then you. We thought you were dead, Roly!'

I said nothing.

'You do not have a monopoly on grief, Roly.'

I bit my lip.

'Remember that,' he said. He walked out, out of the kitchen, down the corridor, out of the front door. I heard him snatch up his keys from the hall table as he passed.

SIXTEEN

Of Course I Love You

And it's dawn. Tuesday, I'm pretty sure. A new day. Roberto used to say that every day can be a new beginning. I'd love that to be true, today.

Last night, when I was somewhere between waking and sleeping, Jonnie sat beside me on the shingle, hugging his knees, his bare feet in the water, watching the waves. I could see him so clearly, as if he were lit up, although there was no moon. His profile, his straight nose with the tiny bump where he broke it, his firm chin, the curve of his lips, his tousled fringe. After a while he looked at his watch. Then he looked down at me and smiled.

What shall I do, Jonnie?

He shook his head slightly, still smiling, placed his warm hand on mine. *Be patient.*

Then I realised his clothes were wet, dripping, his curls damp with salt water. I felt so sorry that he was so wet. I know how that feels. I turned briefly to push myself up so we could sit together, side by side, and gaze at the ocean. But when I turned back, he was gone.

I could have wept, then, for loneliness and hopelessness. But the feel of his hand on mine remained.

❧

Weather's atrocious, once again. A high wind has whipped the waves into a frenzy of white breakers and foam. I suppose it's not surprising, it being January. A winter's day on the north Cornish coast.

I crawl dizzily over to the entrance to check the landslide once more, thinking I might have been mistaken, that there might be something I've missed – handholds and footholds that I could grasp as I clamber my way up to the top. But I was right the first time, and all the other times I've looked. The tiny path, a narrow track almost like a rabbit path – it's gone, vanished.

My red shawl's still there. Hopefully someone will see it, will want to investigate, contact the coast guard.

The fingers on my right hand where the bird stabbed me are like fat sausages, pink and stiff. I'm aching all over. My thigh's swollen up and I can't bend my knee. My head feels as if it'll fall off if I move it. And I'm cold, so cold...

Don't know if the bird's awake. Not that it matters. I don't need an audience.

I watch the sea. The waves roll incessantly towards the rocks below. Hypnotic. Entrancing. Seductive. It would be so easy to let go, to slip under the surface and let the current take me. I am – almost – tempted. All I'd have to do would be to crawl out there to that rock, green and slippery with weed, and just... lose my balance.

I am so very tired.

❧

One could say that Hugo and I co-existed from then on, after my return from Cornwall. We went through the motions of being husband and wife, and, when the children were home from university, of being a proper family, although that had sometimes been rather notional where the twins were concerned. I made the effort to tell them that they were expected to attend evening meals and Sunday lunches, and that if we had people to dinner, they should appear for half an hour and drink a *Coke* –

'A *Coke?*' asked Fergus.

– or any drink they wanted, and to tell people about what they were studying, in the most general of terms, because most people just didn't get the finer points of physics, and to ask people about their lives, which meant *How are you?*, nothing more complicated than that, and remembering just one or two facts about each person, and if all else failed to ask them about their last holiday.

Flora was splendid with small talk. She had Hugo's gift of making each person feel that they were important and necessary to the whole occasion, that it somehow would be less fulfilling if they weren't there. I watched them both, the way people smiled with pleasure as they approached, the way they never had for me. At the time I thought it was simply technique, but looking back now I believe people were responding to genuine interest. Hugo and Flora loved being with people, the more the merrier. The twins and I didn't. Jonnie had had the same gift, and perhaps I had loved him because of it.

Our coexistence was a compromise. Neither Hugo nor I wanted to upset things any more than we had already, neither of us wanted conflict. I quietly got on with changing my life – all our lives, as far as anyone would let me – and Hugo quietly carried on as normal. This went on for several years, three or four at the least. We got older, perhaps a little wiser, and all the children graduated; and Flora got a job in a good legal firm and the boys started their doctorates and took to cycling home from Cambridge about twice a year for a short break. They never seemed to take holidays.

We entered a kind of truce. I concentrated on the garden, began to think about becoming self-sufficient in fruit and vegetables and eggs, about how foraging for wild foods could supplement our diet. I bought a chest freezer and installed it in the garage, subscribed to the newsletter of a permaculture association, and occasionally went to local Greenpeace meetings, where I listened to plans and campaigns but always politely declined to be physically involved. I planted vines and apple trees, replaced our privet hedge with hazel and plum, tried to have edible plants growing all year round, easier than I'd thought. We ate a lot of leeks and kale in the winters. More and more often Hugo came home late and said he'd already eaten, or sniffing the aroma of vegetable soup as he came in said that he was going to the pub. He never invited me.

౭౩

Just before one Christmas Hugo surprised me with an expensive gift of glamorous shoes, extravagant even for him. It was the third week in December, and he'd bought them for me to wear at his office party. I stared at them. He was holding one in each hand, and I wondered why he'd bought me shoes, of all things.

'Try them on, Rosalie, do,' he urged. It was a Saturday morning, and I'd just come in from feeding the hens. I was wearing old jeans and a filthy jumper, wellies that one of the twins had grown out of, and mismatched walking socks.

I felt unready – it was too much of a surprise – and was aware that I was quite grubby. My feet, I knew, were not up to being seen in designer footwear – rough heels and untended nails – and my legs hadn't been waxed for months.

I stood uncertainly as he held them out before me, like a child. I could see he wanted to please me. He was smiling eagerly, as if he had brought me the most wonderful treat.

'Go on Roly! Do.'

'I'm not dressed –'

'Go and change, then! Try them on with what you're going to wear next Friday. You'll look fantastic.'

I took the shoes from him. 'Give me half an hour,' I said. 'I'll have a quick shower.'

His smile grew broader. 'I knew you'd love them,' he said. 'I told Flora you would. I said if there's anything that'll get you out of your civvies and get you dressing up, it's these.' He tapped me on the bottom as I passed. 'Go on, I can't wait.'

I showered quickly, used his spare razor to shave my lower legs and under my arms, searched through my and Flora's drawers for new tights, hurriedly applied lipstick and mascara, and tottered down the stairs in my new heels and a long dress I'd last worn about ten years before.

He was waiting at the bottom of the staircase with two glasses of champagne.

'Gorgeous, gorgeous, gorgeous! Give us a twirl, Roly!'

Despite myself I laughed.

He placed the champagne on the hall table. 'You'll knock 'em senseless, darling, you always do.' He kissed me. 'God, you're wonderful.'

We ended up in bed, the champagne forgotten till later.

☙

What a day that was. We laughed together as we hadn't in years. I felt safe and warm and happy for the first time since I didn't know when: validated as a woman, as Hugo's lover, as the love of his life. I felt we had some hope at last, some way of moving on into a future where we were all in all to each other, as we'd been at the beginning.

I began to imagine a life in which tragedy was just one of the many strands of the tapestry of our lives, one of the deeper and richer colours among the lighter and shinier threads. I would try to meet him halfway. I wouldn't blame too much.

And he always, always said he loved me. I didn't always reply. Maybe that was my mistake.

&

Hugo's office parties were hard work, the same conversational ground covered every year – holidays, house prices, children, bonuses – with one or two retirements and one or two new faces. Tedious in the extreme. I used to get stuck with Hugo's secretary's husband, a man whose obsessive conversation about traffic flow in central London made the twins seem positively scintillating. I spent that particular evening watching for him out of the corner of my eye and moving away every time he seemed about to approach.

I'd extracted a promise from Hugo in the taxi about not leaving me on my own too long and rescuing me from both bores and creeps. Hugo had been surprised but then seemed amused.

'That's more like it,' he said, and patted me on the knee. 'More like a spark of the old Roly.'

'What do you mean?'

'You were always very feisty at Oxford, weren't you? About male chauvinists and people who droned on and didn't contribute anything interesting to life.'

'Was I?'

'Were you!' He chuckled. 'Of course you were. You were terrifying! That's one of the sparky things I've always loved about you, darling.' He took my hand and gently squeezed it. 'Thought I'd lost you, for a bit, Roly,' he said quietly.

'What?'

'You know, the shock, after… you know.' He squeezed my hand again.

This was new, this idea that I'd changed somehow. I mulled it over for few minutes, watching the traffic and the back of the driver's head. After a while, I said: 'Hugo… I'm sorry if I've not been myself. I –'

He cut me short. 'Entirely understandable.' He turned to me and kissed me swiftly on the cheek. 'We're here.'

❧

I couldn't imagine where Hugo had got to, and looked everywhere for him, clutching my glass of champagne, wobbling on my heels, too high for balance and bloody uncomfortable. I wanted to kick them off, but this wouldn't have gone down well with Hugo.

A soft-footed waiter brought canapés, small swirls of savoury things with a good deal of cheese and bacon and smoked salmon. I realised that I was hungry and took three, stuffing one immediately into my mouth and balancing the others in my right hand, a tiny Christmassy paper napkin gripped between my first and second fingers. To his credit the boy didn't flicker, merely waited a few seconds to see if I would take more, then moved on.

I finally spotted Hugo by the door, where he hadn't been two minutes before. He was standing chest-to-chest with a young woman, smiling down at her, crinkling his eyes. She fiddled with his clothes in a superficial but possessive sort of way. There was a bit of tie-straightening, a bit of imaginary dust brushed from his shoulder, a tidying up of the silk handkerchief in his breast pocket. He bent and kissed her on the cheek.

I am no fool. I can read the signs as well as the next person. Maybe they felt invisible. Or maybe it was common knowledge in the office.

He bent his head and spoke quietly into her ear, then straightened up, smiling. She gazed up into his eyes and laughed. I turned away.

But the shame of it – I was being watched too. I saw three women, heads together, glancing in my direction. They didn't look like colleagues, they looked like wives, and I could bear it no longer, to be the object of their pity or derision. I slipped out of the Jimmy Choos and walked to the window, which fortuitously was open a crack to let in air, and threw them out. Size six, new season, Hugo's Christmas present, out they went. My feet thanked me.

❧

'What the hell was that about?' he asked coldly, in the taxi.

'What?' I sounded innocent, indifferent, bored even.

'You know bloody well what. The shoes. For God's sake, Roly, if you didn't like them, we could have changed them. We could have got you something different. A bag, maybe. A coat. You didn't have to make a scene.'

'Neither did you.'

'What?'

'You didn't have to make a scene either.'

'What are you talking about?'

'That girl. The one with the lovely blonde hair, curly. Very pretty. I liked her dress.' It was true, I did.

I turned to him, watching his face in the flickering amber light of the streetlamps we passed. We were almost out of London.

'Christina,' he said. 'She's not a girl, she's a mature woman and an international lawyer. Been with us now, oh, I dunno, about three years.'

'You kissed her.'

'A Christmas greeting. Look,' he said loudly, 'her husband was there. There's nothing going on.'

'I didn't say there was.'

'But you implied it.'

I remained silent.

'What is it you want, Roly? What is it I'm not understanding?'

'I want you.'

He frowned at me. 'You've got me, Roly, you've always had me, and you always will. That's never going to change.'

'Do you love me?'

He glanced irritably towards the driver. The glass window was closed.

'Of course I love you, Roly,' he said impatiently. 'I just don't know what you want anymore.'

'More time with you.'

He shook his head. 'It's too busy at work. It's impossible. You know, with my level of responsibility –'

'It's all right.' I said. 'Let's forget I said anything.'

'We'll have a holiday, go skiing in the new year, just you and me? What do you think?'

'Mmm.'

'And another break, the Caribbean perhaps, maybe June?'

'Not flying.'

'Of course, sorry. Well, a train to Italy, why don't we? I'll look into it.' He laid his hand on my knee, sought my hand, squeezed it, while I was thinking, *no, you won't look into it. If you remember, you'll get someone else to look into it, just as someone else bought my Christmas shoes.*

℃

I wore my scarlet shawl at that Christmas party. No one seemed to notice it. No one complimented me on it. No one has noticed it here either, and now it's gone. The wind and the water have taken it; I saw it go, lifting off like an exotic bird, and it's now floating somewhere in the murky sea, or trapped in a rocky crevice, or sailing over the cliffs to land in a hedgerow, and no one will ever connect it with me or with this cave where this beautiful broken bird and I will, I believe, breathe our last.

SEVENTEEN

A Different Sort of Question

What have I achieved in my life? I really couldn't say. So while I wait here, I'll keep talking, see if I can make any sense of the whole mad course of my life, and the wildness that surged up within me and changed everything. Apart from anything else it'll keep my mind off the weather.

Thinking aloud is really purely for my benefit. The bird has made clear it's not interested, and Jonnie, well, I don't know where Jonnie has got to. I catch glimpses of him, from the corner of my eye, from time to time. He was here earlier, standing against the cave wall, little rock pools between us, hands in pockets, his feet crossed at the ankles. I stayed very still until I had to move because of cramp, and when I looked across he had gone. But I think he's listening.

What I believe about the last twenty years is only my point of view, of course. Hugo might have very different things to say about the way things went, how they turned out, what part I played in it all. What part he played. I like to think I did my best.

☙

'Tell me,' said Hugo. He leaned forward, across Peter's mother. He was already slightly drunk. 'Justin, tell me. How do you care for someone who's mentally ill?'

There were nine of us at dinner, our daughter Flora and her fiancé Peter, and Peter's parents – Justin and Clare – and Hugo and me, together with our twin sons, Fergus and Dugald, and my mother. It was just after Flora and Peter had announced their engagement, getting on for fourteen years ago now.

My mother had been so appalled by what I proposed to cook that she'd rung up *Waitrose* and ordered dinner: salmon terrine, chicken in tarragon, cheesecake and fruit salad. Not particularly environmentally friendly, buying ready-made food, which is why I'd planned to cook my own produce for everyone. But that wasn't good enough, apparently, and I'd been overruled by Hugo, my mother, and Flora. So while they tucked in, I was eating green beans from the garden with a couple of my own hens' eggs, lightly poached, to be followed by blackberries from the hedgerows.

There was a silence. I looked up. To give him his due, Justin didn't look in my direction. He regarded Hugo who was grinning manically, almost wolfishly.

'Well, Hugo, it would depend on the nature of the illness,' said Justin.

'Yes, yes,' said Hugo, impatiently. 'I know all that. What I mean is, how do you love them, how do you continue to love someone who's mentally ill? When they've changed out of all recognition? When they're not the person you married anymore? You're the psychiatrist, you tell me. How do I do it?'

Justin cleared his throat. 'That's a different sort of question.'

'Damn right it is,' said Hugo. 'Damn right.' He pointed his fork at me. 'I mean, look at Roly, just look at her.'

Justin turned towards me. Clare looked at her plate.

'I mean, this isn't normal behaviour, is it? Those beans and eggs. Nothing else. I swear she'll eat nothing else tonight. She's all skin and bones, practically anorexic these days.'

'I'm not anorexic, Hugo,' I said. 'I just don't like eating meat.'

'You don't like much these days, darling.'

'I like to eat food I have produced myself.'

He knew nothing about it. I ate well: handfuls of herbs, parsley, wild garlic, sorrel, lettuce and spinach, my own carrots, parsnips and beetroot, radish pods by the dozen. I offered him healthy salads every day, but he obdurately refused. It was a war of attrition, on both sides.

'She doesn't even cook for me these days, except stewed apple.'

'I offer to cook for you, but you don't want it.' I was proud of myself for remaining calm under extreme provocation. I seemed to go into an icy place where nothing could harm me.

There was movement around the table, some shifting of chairs as people leaned backwards or forwards. The clink of cutlery stopped. I ignored it. This conversation was too important to be deflected by social niceties.

'Well, I certainly don't want nettle soup or steamed cow parsley. You know, Justin, that's what she likes to eat. She goes out in the mornings and gathers food from the fields like some Russian peasant. One of these days she'll poison herself.'

'I can see that might make you anxious,' remarked Justin, conversationally. His eyes flickered quickly in my direction. Clare passed the wine down the table to Peter, away from Hugo. 'What foods do you especially enjoy, Roly?'

'Hostas are tasty, if I can get to them before the slugs, and Solomon's Seal. I adore broad bean leaves – they're surprisingly scented, a really delicate flavour, quite different from the beans or pods. And the flowers have an extraordinary perfume too, and are quite delicious, although of course I wouldn't eat them.' I looked round the table and chuckled slightly. 'I mean, if you eat the flowers, you don't get any beans! Anyway, that was last year. I'm concentrating more on root crops this year. Carrot leaves go nicely in soup.'

'Carrot leaves?' asked Clare.

'Mmm. Lovely with garlic and herbs and potato and carrot root to thicken it up.'

'Really? I should try it!' She laughed. She seemed to think I was joking. 'Have you ever heard of these people who try living for free off the land?'

'Oh yes,' I said. *I'm going to be one of them,* I thought. 'Oh yes.'

'Rosalie…' said my mother. I ignored her.

'A lot of people,' I said – and here is where I made my first mistake that evening – 'a lot of people believe that we're about to experience runaway climate change, and within fifty years this planet will be uninhabitable.'

'Oh God,' said Hugo. I ignored him too.

I rose from my chair and stepped back to address my audience (my second mistake). 'Those of us who *really* care, we're experimenting with living lightly on the land. That means going back to basics, in the hope that somehow we can show the way to the world –'

'The way?' asked my mother, with a light laugh. 'It sounds like some religious cult, darling.' I continued to ignore her.

'A way of stopping the massive consumption of fossil fuels so that global temperatures don't go up by more than, say, one more degree centigrade. Higher than that – then we're stuffed.'

I'd begun pacing round the table, round and round. Justin and Clare swivelled in their seats to watch me. My mother toyed with her food. Hugo stared morosely into his wine glass. I couldn't blame him. He'd heard all this before.

'More than two degrees,' I continued, 'means runaway climate change. Without the shadow of a doubt.' I stopped pacing. 'I've got the figures upstairs. I'll just go up and –'

'Mummy,' said Flora. 'You promised. Remember? You promised.'

She was blinking. I remember thinking that it looked like her hay fever had come on again, and wondering, briefly, where the eye drops were.

'You *promised,*' she said again, louder, more firmly.

'The United Nations –' I began.

'No, Mummy,' said Flora. 'Not *now.*'

'In fact,' I said, 'most people don't realise –'

'No, Mummy, NO!'

'This is precisely my point,' I said, loudly. 'It's inconvenient – impolite – to talk about these things at dinner parties or anywhere, really, people don't want to know.'

'People may want to know, darling,' said my mother, 'but not here, not now. We're celebrating Flora and Peter's engagement.'

'Well,' I said, from my icy stronghold, 'Flora and Peter aren't going to have much of a life together. They won't reach your grand old age, Mother. They'll be scrabbling around for food, it'll be dog-eat-dog, every man for himself – anarchy, no water, no medicine, nothing.'

'Oh God,' said Hugo. 'Shut up. You're upsetting Flora.'

She was crying, it was true, but I needed to say it, I'd been quiet for over a week. It used to build up in me, the need to talk about it all, the need to persuade people to live their lives differently. I suppose I may have come across as rather fanatical, humourless. Not the easiest of dinner companions, in fact.

'If you won't hear it, I won't be responsible for what happens to you all,' I said, and with dignity I picked up my plate of beans and left the room. Fergus and Dugald followed me and went upstairs with their dinners.

I went into the garden to eat, parking myself on the bench under the dining room window. Through the open window I could hear Flora crying and Peter murmuring to her and everyone else talking. Hugo's voice rose and fell like a double bass, my mother's twittered like a piccolo. Justin and Clare were the violin continuo. Around me the night insects were flitting about, and I could smell the evening primroses.

ↄ

After a while it went quiet inside. I imagined they were drinking coffee in the sitting room. I was in no hurry to join them. In fact I was wondering whether to try and get some sleep in the summer house rather than brave the wrath of Hugo, Flora and my mother combined, when I heard the dining room door open – its distinctive creak and click – and footsteps on the parquet floor.

'She was flying tonight, wasn't she?' said my mother.

That would be me, then. I decided to stay where I was, hidden by the wisteria. If I moved someone might spot me and there'd be hell to pay.

'Most nights, Janet,' said Hugo. There was a clink of glass, the sound of a cork being pulled, and wine being poured.

Peter and his parents must have gone home. Perhaps they hadn't stayed for coffee. Perhaps they felt embarrassed by a family row. I began to wish I'd kept my mouth shut, just for a couple of hours. I could have sounded off to the twins the next morning. They'd have agreed with me, and we'd have had a civilised conversation.

Sometimes they told me I'd said it all before, and then they'd put on their noise-cancelling headphones and I'd just talk and talk, and they'd get on with whatever it was they were doing on their computers.

Flora spoke, so quietly I could hardly hear the words. 'I'm worried about her at the moment, Daddy.'

Poor Flora. An evening which was meant to be about her and Peter, and I'd made it all about me.

'Oh God, don't be worried about Rosalie!' exclaimed my mother. 'She's always been oversensitive. Honestly. She was a nightmare as a teenager.'

'I met her as a teenager,' said Hugo. His voice sounded faraway, as if he was musing on our shared youth.

'Well, yes, but that was university. A bit different.'

'She was eighteen. That makes her a teenager, in my book.' Hugo sounded firmer now.

'As were you.'

'Well, of course I was. I was nineteen. That's how it works. People go to university in their late teens. And legally they're adults.'

'Daddy –'

'Just a minute, darling. So, we were adults.'

'I'm not disputing that, Hugo. I'm simply saying that she was oversensitive. Rather like the twins.'

'The twins? What have they got to do with it?'

'I mean, dear Flora here, she's the only sensible one of the lot of them. You're such a darling, Flora. So steady, so... so sensible.'

'Flora's wonderful,' said Hugo heartily. 'Aren't you, darling? Completely wonderful. I couldn't wish for a more wonderful daughter.'

'Of course,' said my mother. 'And really, nothing like her mother. Perhaps she takes after me?'

'Um,' said Flora doubtfully.

'I mean, I suppose you look a bit like Hugo,' continued my mother. 'You've got his dark hair, although of course, Hugo, there's quite a bit of grey in there now, isn't there? And Rosalie's so blonde. Or was. She should dye it.'

'Janet, it's getting late –'

'Eyebrows are a problem, of course. They often don't match. But I was lucky, mine are quite pale.'

'Right,' said Flora. I could – almost – guess what she was thinking.

'Jonnie had the best hair, of course.'

There was a stunned silence. My heart seemed to stop, then it sped up – thumpthump thumpthump.

'Dark and curly, gorgeous. What a good-looking boy he was, with those eyes. Such an amazing dark blue. Like Elizabeth Taylor.'

'Well,' said Hugo. He sounded hesitant. I couldn't tell from his tone whether he was going to agree with her or try to change the subject, but she was off again.

'I miss him so much. Such a wonderful, handsome, kind boy. Such a marvellous sense of humour.' She sighed. 'If only he hadn't gone off on that Greenship thing and got himself –'

'Janet!'

'I'm only saying what everybody knows, Hugo. Anyway, if he hadn't, we'd have had an entirely different kind of celebration tonight, wouldn't we? Roly would never have –'

'Janet, I need you to stop this right now.'

'Stop what?'

'This whole conversation. It's been difficult enough this

evening, let's not make it worse.'

Nobody said anything for several long seconds. I held my breath, literally, held my whole body stiff and still, waiting.

'Anyway, it's late and I'm tired. I'm off to bed,' my mother announced. 'Don't wake me early, will you.'

Her heels clacked on the floor.

There was a silence. I strained to hear any movement. A soft drizzle began to fall, and I thought again of the summer house, wished I hadn't sounded off at dinner, wondered how the next day would be.

'Unbelievable,' said Hugo.

'Poor Mummy,' murmured Flora.

I heard Hugo sigh.

'It was just the wrong time and place,' he said.

They didn't say anything for a little while. I watched a pair of white moths fluttering around the wisteria.

'I should have had a chat with her earlier,' he added. 'Let her talk about the planet if she wanted to. Let her get it out of her system before dinner.'

There was another silence. The white moths had disappeared and I was feeling a little damp and chilly on my garden bench.

'Are you all right, Flo?'

'I'm fine.' I heard her breathe in deeply and let the breath out slowly, as if releasing all the tension I had brought to the evening. 'Do you think Mummy's all right?'

'I'm sure she's fine.' Beneath his heartiness I detected something else. 'I'll leave the kitchen door open for her. I think it's raining.'

They were talking so quietly I had to strain to hear them. There was a sniff, from Flora, I presumed.

'We'll make sure your wedding's everything you want. It'll be perfect.'

Flora gave a little laugh. 'Had better be.'

EIGHTEEN

Our Balance of Payments

'Just listen to that weather... Are you well enough to lift your head? Can you open your eyes?'

I can see the mist of my breath this morning. It floats above my face for a few seconds before it disperses in the cold air.

The cormorant opens one eye, appearing to assess my ability to move. The pain in my thigh keeps me pinned on the shingle.

I munch, very slowly, my last apple, and my last three walnuts. I make them last, savour them, the flavours reminding me of better times. No more peanut butter or cheese. The last bagel has gone mouldy. I look at the use-by date on the packet. It was already out-of-date when I bought it.

It feels like it's been one continuous storm, barring a few hours here and there, a glimmer of sunshine or moonlight, a sunrise or sunset. How long now? Five days, I think. And the few hours of calm have always been at high tide. Before that, the Winter Anomaly, as the Met Office calls it, the snow and ice that have blanketed the whole country for weeks. The coldest winter since 1948, apparently. We'll know if that's true once the statistics are collated later this year. If we get that far.

Winter Anomaly. Ridiculous. The anomaly is calling it that.

The north wind doth blow and we shall have snow, and what shall poor Robin do then, poor thing?

Anyone with half a brain cell could see this coming. The end is hitting us hard and fast, punching like a professional boxer, *left right left right bam wham bang.*

Torrential rain and floods, storms and cyclones and super tornadoes, heat and drought, crop failures, dead forests, dead seas, anoxia, methane fires over the tundra, forest fires in the Med and Australia and California and the Amazon, the growth of the Gobi and the Sahara by miles every year, refugees drowning off the North African Coast and New Guinea and China and every bloody place.

This is only what I saw in the news, before I turned to DVDs and CDs and good old-fashioned books. That was after Hugo found me screaming at the radio – there'd been some patronising nonsense about the benefits of a warming planet. He quietly turned the radio off and put the kettle on for tea, and held me and kissed me, and let me rant and rage for a few minutes, and somehow then I calmed down.

Jonnie's well out of it. My mother too. We last heard from her about ten years ago, a couple of postcards claiming she'd found love at last. I don't know why she stopped being in touch. My fear is that one of the Florida hurricanes finished her off. I can't bear imagining her last few seconds. Hugo made some enquiries, but got nowhere.

Hugo used to help me in the garden at weekends. We worked companionably together – he even asked for instruct-ions – and then we'd go inside to have a warm drink and watch a favourite movie. His way, I suppose, of keeping me on an even keel. We both noticed the changes in the seasons: warm and wet in the winter, cool and wet in the summer.

More wind most of the time.

Late at night, sometimes, I would imagine Jonnie married, bringing his children to visit; that trip to the South Atlantic put aside; his degree completed, a doctorate under his belt and his work on climate change honoured for its breadth of vision and originality.

Every now and then, particularly on quiet moonlit nights, I would see Jonnie in the garden, just sitting, waiting. Sometimes I went out to talk to him, but he always disappeared before I got there. Other times I just watched him from a window, until he began to fade in the early morning light.

Jonnie turned up to chat one December day, when I least expected him. The days were short of course, that time of year, dark at four, but mild, almost warm. No frost. I'd been watching that autumn as trees both dropped their leaves and grew new buds, as flowers bloomed both too late and too early, as insects forgot to hibernate. The monstrous orange and brown slugs munching their way through my garden became even larger, almost the length of my foot, and I went out at night with my head torch and a spade, slicing them in half and throwing the bits into the woodpile for the toads. Not native slugs, invaders from Spain, twice as big, twice as fertile. They eat anything – plants, dead animals, dog poo. I've always hated killing anything, but the alternative is worse – everything consumed, and the garden reduced to stalks, like some ghastly plague.

It was soon after breakfast and I was digging up parsnips for soup. As I dropped one into my basket, I looked up and saw Jonnie standing the other side of the bed. He was wearing a blue anorak in the drizzle, and it struck me how very practical that was. I hadn't seen him to talk to for years, although I'd glimpsed him during my countryside rambles, as well as out in the garden, in all weathers and all times of day and night, and now here he was, ready to talk. We stood and gazed at each other.

You look well.

Thanks, so do you.

Jonnie did look well. His few freckles stood out against his pale skin, which seemed almost luminous under the low grey cloud. There was a dusting of tiny raindrops, like those on autumn cobwebs, on his hair and on the shoulders of his blue anorak, and the tip of his nose was pink with the chill. He was so handsome, no longer a boy but a man.

You're wearing my old parka. It looks a bit battered.

Do you mind?

He shook his head and smiled. *It's yours now, Mum.* He stepped back a pace, half-turned, looked around. *What does Dad make of all this?*

He's come round to it… I think he quite enjoys it now. Our own produce.

Jonnie nodded. *Great idea. I didn't think you had it in you.*

No, this was all wrong – surely it was Jonnie who'd put the idea into my head?

Your idea, Mum. All yours. I had nothing to do with it.

I stared at him. He took another pace away, began walking down to the chickens.

Have you noticed the weather?

I can't not notice it, it's been havoc.

Jonnie nodded.

The media had been full of the unusual weather, people obsessing about global warming when the time for talk was long past. *Head for the hills* would have been my advice, but who could I have given it to?

Jonnie listened, calm and serious. *So now what?*

I closed my eyes. Decision time, again? No, I couldn't. I

was barely keeping it together, my anxiety threatening to overwhelm me, day by day, night by night, moment by moment. As long as I could occupy myself in the garden, I could keep everything at bay. But when things went wrong in the garden, I could no longer ignore what was happening in the rest of the world.

I didn't open my eyes for a few seconds, convinced that Jonnie would have disappeared. But he was still there. He walked forward until we were within touching distance. I could smell coconut, I could see the flecks of green in his blue eyes, I could count his eyelashes, almost.

Be brave, Mum. Tell the truth. Hold tight, it's going to be a bumpy ride.

Jonnie laid his hand lightly on my arm. I looked down at the long fingers, the beautiful nails, a tiny cut on his thumb. Closing my eyes, I could feel the weight of his hand, but this time I knew he'd gone.

After a few moments I walked back into the house. Hugo was in the kitchen making three mugs of tea. 'One for the gardener chappie,' he said. 'Does he want sugar?'

I stared.

He looked up. 'Roly, sit down. You don't look too good. A bit pale. Bet you were up half the night. Sit down, and I'll take this out to him.'

'He's gone,' I said.

'Shame. You could do with some help. The garden's gone to pot this year.'

'It wasn't a gardener. It was Jonnie.'

Hugo stopped in the act of sitting at the table, half-stooped, half-crouched over his chair. Then he stood, pushing himself upright with his palms on the table.

'No, Roly. It wasn't Jonnie.'

'It was. You saw him.'

'I saw you talking to someone, in the rain.'

'It was Jonnie. Hugo, I've been seeing Jonnie for years. Sometimes we have conversations. Like today.'

Hugo didn't say anything, just looked at me. It was one of those times I couldn't tell what he was thinking. More and more that seemed to happen.

'I see him at night, in the garden. He likes it there.' *Tell the truth.* Hugo might not like it, but it was the truth.

'I think you need a good rest,' he said, kindly.

I nodded. I did. I was surprised he'd noticed.

Hugo seemed to be thinking, didn't speak for a few seconds. Then he came round to my side of the table and gathered me into a bear hug, his arms squeezing tight, his cheek on my hair. 'Darling,' he said, and held me so tight that it felt like he would never let go.

NINETEEN

To Have and To Hold

It pains me now to think about Flora's wedding, because of what came after. Ten years after Jonnie died. Twelve years ago.

The wedding itself was a huge success, all Flora's dreams come true – the ceremony in the cathedral, six bridesmaids, white lilies and roses everywhere. Flora was radiant and beautiful – my mother said that, my mother who had called me gawky at my own wedding – on the arm of Hugo, the proud paterfamilias who cut a very fine figure as he walked her down the aisle. She smiled deliriously as she walked out with Peter to the finale from Vierne's first symphony (she was very particular about that, no Mendelssohn for her). Fergus and Dugald looked extremely handsome in their hired morning suits, and I spotted them making polite conversation with old ladies, relatives of Peter's. Good for them.

At home we had a marquee on the lawn. Guests picked their way through my raised vegetable beds to reach it, the women teetering in high heels across the bark chippings. The caterers set up a field kitchen in a separate tent at the bottom of the garden, with their own gas cookers and access to the garden tap. No invasion necessary, except for toilets.

It was all, in its way, remarkably relaxed. Half of it had been organised by Hugo's assistant. The other half – dress, flowers, shoes, little gifts for the guests – by Flora. Dear Flora, so practical and efficient. I had needed to do nothing. Literally nothing at all. No input to my only daughter's wedding. She even chose my outfit for me, gave me three options from which to make the final choice, hovering behind me as I stared at the images on her laptop.

You'll be wondering – was I hurt? Did I feel resentful? Or angry?

Well, I can let you into a secret. I was, in fact, indifferent. I had been cultivating the art of detachment, and it was a matter of profound indifference to me at the time whether I was involved at all. Other mothers might immerse themselves in preparations, talk of sleepless nights, dress fittings, anxiety about the weather, the scurrying around to get everything perfect, but I slept like a baby and wished for nothing. There was nothing I worried about. I even forgot one day that there was a family wedding to attend and double-booked myself with a coach trip to Ryton Organic Gardens, which I immediately cancelled once I realised. Of course I did.

ᔕ

There was a kind of frenzy about Flora before her wedding which even Hugo became infected by. The boys, away at Cambridge, were oblivious, turning up the night before the wedding, eating huge quantities at the reception, and disappearing early on the Sunday morning. Back to the lab. I hadn't talked to them properly, assuming that they would stay longer, and we'd have time to catch up over the following day or so. I wondered briefly how Cambridge coped with this two-for-the-price-of-one physicist duo, identical in all respects apart from their favourite flavours of ice cream, and then thought well, it didn't matter, really, at all, how Cambridge coped. What mattered was their happiness, and they seemed happy enough.

I was quite clear that I was not going to be frenzied about anything. I would not eat, drink or talk too much. I would hold myself serene and aloof from all expressions of emotion of any kind. I had decided by this point that all emotion was toxic. Don't get involved, Roly, I told myself, and you won't get hurt.

So it was a success, and for a week afterwards, with Flora away on her honeymoon, the tents dismantled, everything tidied up, the house quiet, Hugo and I had a rest. He went into the office for short days; at home we were deferential around each other, eating solitary suppers in separate rooms. I caught him watching me sometimes, his thin lips pursed, his eyebrows drawn together in a slight frown. He quickly looked away if he saw I'd noticed.

He asked me one day where we should go on our holiday. I was mildly surprised and took a few moments to reply. We were standing in the kitchen, brewing coffee, a gentle habit we'd fallen into around elevenses time.

I took down the cups for our coffee, and told him I didn't want a holiday, I was content to be at home. I was practising the art of mindfulness. I said this calmly, as if I were a long-suffering personal assistant.

Hugo's eyebrows shot up, making his eyes appear to bulge.

'Is that what it is?'

He stepped back, shook his head, and clapped both hands to his forehead in what seemed to me an overly melodramatic gesture.

'Christ, Roly, I thought you'd got dementia! I was really worried. I thought there was something seriously wrong with you.'

I gazed calmly at him. He burbled on.

'Flora and I have been frantic! You've been so – so – indifferent to everything – so –'

'That's the idea, to be detached.'

'Detached! My God, have you any idea what it's looked like? It's looked like you've lost your mind! You walk around with that blank look on your face, you don't seem to care about food or clothing –'

'Wedding outfits,' I said coolly.

'Precisely! You didn't care what you wore at your own daughter's wedding! You didn't care about the food, or the flowers! You didn't care about Flora's dress, even! I've had her –'

'It's a matter of rising above the anxieties –'

'Don't interrupt, Rosalie.' He stepped towards me and waved his hands about in a most un-Hugo-like fashion.

'I've had her sobbing down the phone to me about you. I've had her in the office crying her heart out about you. I've had her hysterical, Roly, in a wine bar in Covent Garden, about you and your bloody mindfulness. I nearly got thrown out – they accused me of molesting her! I had to explain she was my daughter, and I said, God help me, that her mother was terminally ill, to explain why Flora was beside herself and inconsolable in a bloody wine bar in Covent Garden. Have you any idea what you've been like, Roly? Have you any idea?'

He'd been shouting, and my detachment was beginning to come unstuck. I concentrated on my breathing. *Out... in... out... in...*

'You're doing it again! That blank face! What the fuck's got into you, Roly?'

He had never sworn at me, never. I was, despite my careful breathing, shocked.

'This was Flora's wedding, Roly. Her wedding. Her wedding!' He stepped towards me and grasped me by the shoulders and started to shake me. 'Her wedding!' he bellowed into my face. 'What kind of a mother are you? It was her wedding!'

I tried to pull myself away, but I was backed against the cooker and couldn't move. Hugo's strong, and his grip on me was beginning to hurt. I wriggled, and he let go, but stood there inches away, breathing heavily, his face red, a sheen of perspiration on his forehead and his upper lip. I gazed at his lips. A memory jumped unbidden into my mind, a memory of our first kiss, when we had stood just so, inches apart, under a streetlamp on that frosty November night on our way back from the party. I had a sudden desire to kiss him now, and the juxtaposition of our row and my desire was so bizarre that I giggled.

He took a step back.

'What's so funny?'

I shook my head. 'Nothing.' I swallowed down my laughter and became still and solemn.

'You – you're – you're becoming extremely odd, Roly. I don't know if you know this. I don't know where you've gone.' He stared into my eyes. 'Where's the real Roly, hey? Where is she?'

I shook my head again. It was no use even beginning to explain. He wouldn't get it.

'Please, Roly. Give me a clue. What's going on?'

I closed my eyes. This was heavier than I could cope with. I didn't want to explain myself to Hugo.

He placed his hands on my upper arms, stroked my arms gently, pulled me towards him, hugged me. I had a sudden desire to cry.

We stood for several long minutes, me enfolded in his embrace, him gently stroking my back, my hair, holding me very tight but carefully, as though I might break. I breathed in his scent, felt the slow and comforting beat of his heart, and nestled into his neck. I closed my eyes and began to let go of the tension I hadn't realised I was holding. Perhaps I wasn't as detached as I believed. Perhaps I was just about holding myself together. Maybe we could make a go of things.

'Roly,' he whispered. 'I've got an idea.'

He waited for me to nod, then continued.

'Why don't you have a chat to someone?'

I didn't reply.

I heard him sigh. 'I think you may need some help. You know, it's a difficult time for you, at the moment. Empty nest, and all that.'

He paused again. I had a sudden lurch in my heart. Surely, he wasn't about to say –

'And of course, you're in your fifties. Tricky time of life, for a woman.'

I wrenched myself out of his embrace. 'Don't you think you've got something to do with my stress levels?'

'Me?' He seemed genuinely hurt and surprised. His eyes were wide, his eyebrows up.

'Yes, you, Hugo. You. Did you not think I might find out about your girlfriends?'

'Girlfriends?'

'How many now, six, is it, over the years? All these women you've worked with – I've seen how you've looked at each other at the Christmas parties. Let me think, now. Stephanie, Lucy, Plain Jane – anything but – Caroline, Mary, and Christina.'

'I've never –' he began, but I was determined to beat him down.

'Have I missed any?'

'Roly, I have never, ever, cheated on you.'

'Really?' I used my most sceptical tone of voice, raised one eyebrow, and smiled slightly, which I knew would infuriate him. At this point I didn't care whether he was telling the truth or not. I was breaking free, breaking free of all his masculine superiority, as I saw it.

'Never,' he said firmly. His jaw was set, his mouth compressed in a thin line. 'I like the company of women. I like your company, God knows why, these days. I mean –' He gestured at my jeans and old sweatshirt.

This stung. I ploughed on, determined to hurt him.

'You just can't keep it in your trousers, Hugo, can you? Whatever happened to our vows – to death us do part? Forsaking all others? You're such a great lawyer, Hugo, such a clever-clever man, you thought you could have your cake and eat it. You thought you could keep to the letter of the law and not the spirit – yes, we're still married, yes, we'll be together till our dying day, but not without some little adventure on the side. Poor old Roly, she doesn't matter, she'll never notice. Too busy with the family and her chickens, a bit unhinged –'

Hugo shook his head vigorously. 'I never said –'

'Let me finish, Hugo. Let me finish, for once. Let me have the last word, for a change.'

He bowed his head and stared at his tartan slippers, the ones Flora had bought him as a nod to his ancestry.

'How about all those deals, Hugo? Strictly legal, are they? What about those Arnolfini brothers from Naples that I had to be extra nice to? What were they really after? Those men from Beijing? That Russian, all designer suits and gold teeth?'

Hugo was shaking his head, raising both hands in a plea of innocence.

'I don't want any more to do with all of this, with you,

anything at all,' I continued.

'What?'

'I've had enough.'

'What do you mean?'

'I need to live. For too long I've serviced you and your career, I haven't lived at all. I haven't lived the way I want to. What I've learnt since Jonnie died –'

'Is this all about Jonnie?' he said with disbelief.

'What Jonnie stood for, that's what I live for now,' I added. 'You've never cared about nature or climate change or anything environmental. I can't live with you any longer. I don't want you any more, Hugo. You can go.'

'Go?'

'Leave.'

'Yes, go!' I crowed. 'Pack your bags tonight if you want! I don't care!'

There was a resounding silence. Hugo stared at me with his mouth open, and I heard what I had just said, as if it was being replayed on some scratchy old record audible to my ears only. The euphoria began to subside.

His cheeks had a high colour, as if I'd slapped him, and I wished I could snatch the words back and fling them into the kitchen bin. They hung quivering in the air between us.

'If that's how you feel,' said Hugo heavily after a few moments, not looking at me, staring at his slippers.

I didn't answer. Nausea swept over me, and I sagged back against the cooker. We stood a second or two more in silence, then he gave a kind of low wave, almost like a farewell, and shuffled out of the kitchen. My knees gave way, and I slid to the floor. I remembered to breathe.

He slept on the sofa in his study that night, wrapped fully

clothed in an old picnic blanket from the cupboard under the stairs. I saw it the next morning crumpled in a heap to one side of his desk. I didn't pick it up.

I hadn't slept. I sat in the kitchen, drinking cup after cup of weak tea, drawing faces in the sugar bowl with my fingers.

Soon after dawn we passed each other on the stairs, both wobbling with exhaustion like old people. I glanced up into his face, but he didn't look at me, just said quietly, so quietly that I almost didn't hear him: 'I've never cheated on you.'

I didn't really want a divorce. I just, I don't know, I just wanted things to change. I wanted to be taken seriously, my concerns to be listened to. I'd been trying to force some sort of change by behaving differently myself, but Hugo, and Flora too, wanted everything to remain the same.

Later that day I took Hugo a cup of coffee, which he accepted without a word. He'd been crying. He looked simply terrible.

I said I was sorry, he said he was sorry, and I can't quite remember how it happened, but I found that I was offering to go and talk to Justin.

'Just a little chat, over a cup of tea,' said Hugo, as if it was something I did all the time, as if Justin was a girlfriend with whom I could go shopping. Shopping was to be avoided, in my opinion, and I had nobody that I would drop in to have tea with. But I agreed, and having wondered why, I spent the next few days trying to get out of it.

TWENTY

Just A Little Chat

It's Thursday. Or Wednesday. Or Friday...?

I'm desperate for water. That trickle at the back of the cave has dried up. My only supply.

I feel grim. Nausea sweeps over me in waves and there's an odd distortion at the edge of my vision, a kind of shimmering. I've been retching into the rock pools. But the warmish breeze and the sunlight sparkling on the waves means, I hope, that the storm's finally over. If I wasn't so dizzy and sick, I'd sit outside and attempt to attract attention... Tomorrow... I'll do it tomorrow...

I glance up at the bird. It's stretched out on its shelf, not moving. Slumped against the wall, like me. Reflected light from the sea dances across the cave, dazzles me as it flashes across the pools. There are even more colours in the rock than I realised: mahogany, russet, coffee, orange, ochre, deep mulberry. Jonnie would be able to tell me what happened here millions of years ago to make this cave so colourful, why there is even a cave here in the first place.

And here's Jonnie now, stepping carefully around the pools,

his bare toes flexing as they grip the uneven floor. It's as if I have conjured him into being.

Careful. Don't cut yourself. We haven't got plasters or antiseptic cream.

I'm OK, Mum. Don't worry about me.

Jonnie sits on a boulder opposite me. *Beautiful, isn't it?*

I nod, my throat so dry it's impossible to speak. *Stunning.*

Do you see why I love it?

I nod again. Yes, I do see. It's impossible not to be impressed, now that I have time to examine the details.

It'll survive, Mum. All this. He sweeps his arm around, indicating the cave, the sea, the sky.

I'm confused. Then I realise. Bare rock, water, atmosphere.

I close my eyes.

Not long now.

⁊

Hugo dropped me at off Justin's house the following Saturday. Quick work, I thought, and wondered what sort of conversation they'd had, a conversation that had catapulted Justin into the urgency of giving up a Saturday afternoon. Clare was out, said Justin. She was helping Peter and Flora with curtains or blinds or something. News to me. But Flora doubtless knew I wasn't that interested in home furnishings. I was glad I didn't have to hang around in department stores and pore over fabric books.

We'd been to Justin and Clare's for dinner, once or twice, but now I was in the uncomfortable position of being a relative by marriage and also a specimen, it seemed to me, to be examined. We did the usual – how are you, fine, fine – and he made a pot of tea and placed it on the coffee table in his sitting room next to the biscuits already laid out on a flowery plate. Chocolate chip cookies and shortbread. It was straight after lunch, so I wasn't hungry.

'I suppose,' I began, 'Hugo has briefed you.'

'Briefed? That's an interesting word.' He smiled as if this was just a neighbourly visit, and I'd said something amusing.

I allowed two seconds before replying. 'It's the sort of word Hugo uses all the time.'

'Well, no, Hugo hasn't briefed me. It would be unethical of me to listen to his opinion, when he's so close to you. It's best if we start from a clean slate, and you tell me what's bothering you.'

'Hugo's worried because I haven't been myself since Jonnie died.'

'Are you able to tell me why that is?'

'You tell me,' I said coolly.

'I'm afraid I don't know how Jonnie died. Your son, I believe?'

So I told him. I watched him throughout. I spared no detail, not the slow-motion dance on the water-washed deck, not his sudden disappearance, not the difficulty they had in getting him out of the water – dead already – not the look of surprise and shock on his poor dead face.

Justin slowly registered that he did know about this case, of course he did, but that somehow he hadn't connected it with Flora. She can't ever have told him; I don't know why. Surely Peter knew? Surely she'd talked about it?

Surely the whole bloody world knew about Jonnie Danborough?

Justin's face was a study in professional detachment by the time I finished, with Jonnie's funeral, and Hugo saying to me at bedtime that he could never forgive Jonnie for what he had done to our family. I had left the house at that point and walked all night in the driving April rain, through fields, along the side of the motorway, struggling through hedges and falling into ditches. The police picked me up on the outskirts of Hemel.

There was a long silence. We listened to the grandfather clock, ticking.

'That was a lot to cope with,' he said.

I nodded.

After a little while, he said, 'I am truly very sorry.'

'Thank you.'

There was another long pause, a longueur during which I closed my eyes and listened. I could hear, somehow behind the ticking of the clock, small rustlings and creakings, and above it the song of a blackbird, melodious and liquid, the notes falling like raindrops from a clear sky.

He cleared his throat. 'Rosalie…or do you prefer Roly?'

I shrugged. It wasn't important.

'How would you like to proceed?'

I opened my eyes. He looked different now, somehow, as if a layer of skin had been sloughed off. His eyes no longer seemed hooded, no longer hid the person looking out at me. They were less careful, but seemed to hold more care.

'What's the usual form?' I sounded like Hugo, and mentally kicked myself for it.

'Well, Rosalie, I don't know that there is a usual. Everyone's different.'

'You must have a sort of pattern, the usual way of going about things.'

'Just tell me what you'd like from these sessions.'

'It's what Hugo would like. Isn't it? After all, he's paying.'

'It's what you would like. Let's leave Hugo out of this, shall we? And don't worry about payment, we're friends. We'll just work out what's best for you today.'

'But can we?' I said. 'Can we really leave Hugo out of this? I mean he wants me to get better, whatever that means. If it means forgetting Jonnie, then I don't want to get better. If it means forgetting that this planet is hurtling towards disaster, well, then, maybe it would be better to forget, for my sanity, but in fact I can't and I won't. How responsible is it to say, oh yes, well, seven billion people, or eight or nine or ten, we're all going to fry, or be destroyed by wars over water and food and oil, whichever comes soonest? Hugo wants me back as I was, before I ever found out about it, before Jonnie died, and it's impossible. It'd be like a doctor saying he was happier before he went to medical school and found out about diseases and so he'll just forget it all again. How can I forget, how can I?'

'It's more a matter of keeping your anxiety in check, so you can function in normal life.'

'Function? I am not a robot, Justin.'

'Function is short-hand, Rosalie. But –' he waved his hand at me, a kind of just-a-minute gesture to stop me interrupting, 'Let's talk about that. Grief.'

'No.'

He raised his eyebrows.

'It's private. You wouldn't understand.'

'I can try.'

I shook my head. 'I can't,' I said. 'I can't. Even Hugo doesn't know how much I hurt.'

'Do you really think he doesn't?'

There was a pain in my chest, like a rock pressing into my lungs. I shook my head.

'It's physical,' I wheezed. 'In here.' I thumped my chest. 'In here, and here –' I grasped my head in both hands – 'and here.' And I hugged my arms around myself. 'You have no idea. It's like losing a part of me.' I made no attempt to stop the tears which were now streaming down my cheeks.

'I'm so sorry,' I heard Justin say.

I rocked forward in the armchair, my face pressed to my knees, my arms wrapped tight around me, gently-gently back and forth, like a mother rocking her child on her lap. Slowly I stilled myself. At length I pulled myself upright, eyes closed, head tilted forward. I didn't want him to look at my face, didn't want to be that vulnerable.

'Here.'

A box of tissues appeared on my knee. I pulled a tissue out of the box, a good manly tissue, big and white, and mopped my eyes.

'Roly. I would like to help you.'

I sighed. 'You can't. No one can.'

'I don't think that's true.'

'And it's not ethical. Your son is married to my daughter. Too close.'

'That may be true.' I could hear amusement in his voice. I looked up. There was the faintest smile crinkling his eyes.

I closed my eyes. 'My life… my life is like a tangled ball of wool that a kitten's been playing with, and I can no longer find a straight bit to knit with, if that makes any sense.'

'And you'd like to straighten it out.'

'Yes.' I nodded. I thought about the ball of wool, how long the thread would be once unravelled, miles and miles of it. I saw it stretching out before me, straight and purposeful. 'To infinity and beyond.'

'I'm sorry?'

'Buzz Lightyear. Jonnie's favourite.'

He nodded. There wasn't much he could say to that, after all, nothing that wouldn't sound trite and shallow.

'How do you sleep at night?'

'Not well.'

'We can give you something for that.'

'No, thank you.'

'Sure?'

'I keep a vigil.'

'For Jonnie.'

I had to explain that I didn't just keep vigil for Jonnie, but for the world, for the dying of the planet, as if my prayers, my watches of the night could rescue one polar bear, keep safe one acre of rainforest, reverse one degree of warming. He shook his head when I told him that half of the world's animals had gone – dead, extinct – in the last forty years. He paused and didn't answer immediately when I asked him if it wasn't logical to grieve for what has been lost forever, just as we grieve for those who have died. Then he said, yes, of course it was logical, but we know that life has to go on, that we work through the cycle of grief, from denial and anger to acceptance and hope for the future.

'Ah,' I said. 'That's just it.'

And he asked, 'What was *it?*'

And I said, 'How can we accept the death of the planet, and look forward with hope to the future?'

And to that, he had no answer.

TWENTY-ONE

Taking the Long View

'So how did you get on?' asked Hugo when he picked me up. We'd been going barely ten seconds in the car.

I didn't answer.

'Roly? Hmm?' He placed his hand on my knee, only letting go to change gear. 'How was it?'

I sighed. 'It's private, Hugo.'

I felt rather than saw him glance swiftly at me. 'But do you feel a little better, darling? That's what I mean. You don't have to tell me anything, erm, confidential, of course.'

We stopped at lights, and he turned to look at me properly. 'I mean,' he continued, 'as long as you start feeling more yourself. That's the important thing.' He put the car into first and we moved forward. 'When's the next session?'

I shook my head. 'There isn't going to be another one.'

'What?' Hugo said, as if he didn't understand.

'There isn't going to be another session, Hugo.'

'Roly, if it's the money, it doesn't matter, I –'

'No charge, he said. We're friends, apparently.'

'Of course we're friends! We're relatives now!'

'By marriage.'

Hugo pulled the car over into a leafy residential street and stopped the engine.

'Sorry, Roly. I can't drive and absorb all this at the same time.' He turned towards me, one hand on the steering wheel, and frowned. 'You're telling me that you're not going back.'

'That's right.'

'Is this what Justin recommends?'

'It's got nothing to do with him.'

Hugo's eyebrows shot up. 'Excuse me, Roly, but I think it has. He's the professional, he's assessed you.'

'Yes, and the professional doesn't think I'm mentally ill.'

'That's a relief. But –'

'He suggested I could find support elsewhere.'

'Ah. Right,' said Hugo, relieved now to have something tangible to discuss. 'A support group.'

'In a manner of speaking.'

'I see,' said Hugo, although he clearly didn't. 'Bereaved Anonymous?' He smiled at his joke.

I shook my head. Whatever way I put it I knew Hugo wouldn't like it. 'It's not really about Jonnie so much, anymore.'

'No?' Hugo put his head on one side and frowned again. 'Us? Roly? Is it us? Me?'

I shook my head again and briefly placed my hand on his. 'No, it's not you. It's all right. You're you and I'm me. We're oil and water, Hugo. I've got used to it.'

Hugo shook his head. 'We're not going to end like this, Roly.'

We sat in silence for a few moments.

'Hugo, it's so much more important than us, or Jonnie, or anything.' I glanced over at him. He was frowning in consternation.

'Are you ill?' he whispered.

'No, no, nothing like that.' I paused, counted to ten, tried to calm myself. I knew he wouldn't like it.

'Hugo… It's the planet.'

He contemplated me for a few seconds, then said, quietly, 'Bloody hell,' and started the engine. A couple of streets away from home he said, 'And Justin doesn't think you're mentally ill.'

We got into the house, and he said then, 'So now what?'

'I don't know, Hugo.'

'For crying out loud,' he said and went into his study.

ↁ

'What sort of support was he talking about?' Hugo asked later.

'I suppose finding people who feel the same way.'

He nodded, sloshing red wine into a large glass. He held the bottle up, inviting me to have a glass with him. I shook my head, and he shook his, as if saying that he hadn't expected me to anyway.

'I suggested that before,' he said. 'And you decided not to do anything about it.'

'I wasn't ready.'

He raised his eyebrows and shook his head again, not looking at me. 'I despair, Roly,' he said and took a mouthful of wine, swilling it around in his mouth before swallowing. 'Needs to breathe,' he said, and put the glass down on the kitchen table next to the bottle. He took a bottle of white out of the fridge and held it up to the window to see how much was left.

'I despair,' he said again, pouring white wine into an equally large glass. 'I mean, what gives you the special insight into the planet that the rest of us don't have? You and the other lunatics.'

'I suppose I take the long view.'

'And other people don't?' He had his back to me. I could hear his anger, barely suppressed, his voice tight, his words clipped.

'Maybe not,' I said. 'I take a really long view. Along with the other lunatics. Hundreds of years. Thousands.'

'Well,' said Hugo. 'You may be right. I don't know. I'll have to think about it.' He held up his hand. 'No more. Please. I've had enough of the whole bloody thing. I want to eat without feeling guilty, drive without feeling guilty – bloody hell – fly without feeling guilty. I want to have a bath if I feel like it, rather than four minutes in the shower. I want to top my bath up with lots of hot water and bubbles and stay in it for hours if I want to. I want to eat exotic imported food that reminds me of exotic foreign holidays. I don't want to look at the labels on my clothes to see where they've been made. I don't want to not buy stuff and live on a shoestring when I've worked bloody hard to earn enough money to keep us all very comfortable, all because it might be bad for the planet. Roly,' he said wearily. 'Just leave it.'

I let him go. He shut himself in his study with the bottle of red and a tray of cheese and biscuits and watched television all evening.

So he had been listening all along.

✌

Perhaps it was at this point, after my meeting with Justin, that Hugo began following me, in a sense, not knowing where I was heading, trying somehow to pin me back down to his day-to-day and his here-and-now. And when he couldn't catch me up, when I began accelerating, speeding off mentally and emotionally to some place he couldn't even see, that's when he stopped trying. I imagine him now, standing by a road, his hand shading his eyes, watching me as I run, run, run.

TWENTY-TWO

Walking Free

It wouldn't be seemly, said Hugo, for us to split up when Flora was recently married. This begged the question of when exactly seemly came in the calendar of our lives. Surely Christmas or New Year was no better, or near our anniversary, or Valentine's Day, or Easter, or any of the children's birthdays. So he took his time, moving into the spare room, sifting through his belongings, choosing what he might need for what he called a trial separation. I watched, made no comment, began a new way of life in our family home.

He watched me and also made no comment, except – twice – to ask me if I was sure, was this really what I wanted?

I didn't reply. I was so unsure I thought it best to let matters take their course.

'So what are your plans?' he asked.

We were standing in the kitchen, both too on edge to sit at the table over our coffee and cereal and toast, so we stood, moving slowly from station to station – kettle, toaster, cupboard, fridge – circling round without looking at each other, three feet apart. It was like some anti-courtship ritual.

I shrugged.

'Much the same,' I said.

'Ah.'

'I mean, it can't be right, can it, this trashing of the planet.'

'No.' He gave a kind of heavy sigh. 'It's not right, Roly. I don't think we disagree about that.'

'And I wonder what God thinks about it.'

'God?'

'Well, God made it all.'

Hugo took his bowl and mug to the sink and placed them in the washing up bowl.

'Not my expertise, old girl,' he said. 'Good luck with it all.'

That was the last thing he said to me. *Good luck.* As if the future of the planet was a matter of chance, depending on a throw of the dice or a casting of the runes, as if one day our luck would change, and we would win at the roulette wheel. Earth and the environmentalists in the green corner versus everyone else.

I watched him drive off, a little after eight o'clock on a misty October morning. He waved once and was gone. The smell of exhaust lingered in the damp air. I went to the garden to feed the hens and pick the last of the beans, the leaves grown large with the autumn warmth and brittle with the chilly nights. Inside I sat at the kitchen table and let the tears roll down my cheeks. I'd expected to feel relieved that at last things had been resolved between us, that the shilly-shallying that had gone on for months was over. Instead I felt so very empty and sad.

As I'd told Hugo it would, my life carried on much as before. I gardened and tended my chickens and went on foraging trips for mushrooms with a local expert. There were five of us, as I recall, turning up at six-thirty in the morning to tramp the fields and beech woods a few miles away. We paid for this privilege, of course. It was a kind of early-morning evening class.

I went to church a few times, starting with a harvest festival. I'd asked Hugo what God thought; it was time to work that out for myself. I was pleased to hear that the Almighty cared deeply for the world, for his creation, for every one of us, for all the animals. I was pleased to see the church was raising money for people already affected by climate change in less privileged parts of the world. I was happy enough with the collection of tinned and boxed foods – I'd brought a bag of apples from my garden – as they would keep longer than fresh foods after being distributed to local shelters and charities. I was taken aback by the family sitting near me who told me afterwards that they were jetting off to Tenerife for half-term.

I wrote to the vicar. I asked him how people who were raising money for those affected by climate change could also *at one and the same time* (I underlined this) be happy to contribute to global warming by flying away on holiday, *perhaps several times a year?* Was this not hypocrisy, I wanted to know? It took him a while to respond. He thanked me for my letter and said that while he couldn't comment on an individual family's decisions, I had given him food for thought. He hoped to see me in church again soon. And perhaps I would be interested in the enclosed leaflets from Christian environmental charities.

This wasn't good enough, I felt. I went back a few weeks later, for a carol service. They served mulled wine after the service in disposable plastic beakers. Were they recycled after use, I asked. The woman serving the wine said that they went in the bin, right there beside the table. 'I expect so,' she said. It didn't look like it to me. The bin held a large black plastic sack. People could bring their own glass or cup, I suggested. 'Well, I don't know,' she said, looking confused. She turned away from me, greeting a friend.

I bumped into the vicar outside *Holland & Barrett* a few days later.

'There's no Planet B,' I said, pointing to his *Marks & Spencer's* carrier bag. It was a feeble joke. 'Thank you for your letter. I appreciate it.'

'Ah,' he said, straightening up a little – he has quite a stoop – 'Not at all. I hope it was helpful?'

'Not exactly,' I said. 'I know you mean well, and you've got to balance all sorts of demands on your time and listen to all sorts of people going on about all sorts of things, but I don't think you understand the seriousness of the situation.'

'No?' He looked concerned; his eyebrows rumpled in a half-frown.

'Rapid climate change is upon us.'

'Do you think so?'

It was rainy and cold, it's true, a typical December day. He may have been in thrall to the Mediterranean temperatures' myth as I had been, once.

'I know so,' I said. 'By the time you've fixed the church tower, it'll be all over. Actually, don't bother to fix the tower, there's no point. No point at all. You may as well let it collapse. Have you any idea what rapid climate change will do to us all? You won't be worrying about ancient buildings – it'll be food and clean water.'

'Oh, now, I don't think –'

'But that's just the trouble. You, none of you, think! Rapid climate change,' I said. 'It's more serious than you know. Once we reach two degrees of warming, there's no hope at all.'

I was losing him, I was sure. He glanced at his watch.

'You know, I often have a coffee this time of day. Would you like to join me?'

I wasn't quick enough to think of an excuse not to.

We sat opposite each other in the window of a nearby café. I insisted on paying for my chamomile tea. We talked about this and that, the weather, his summer holiday in Norfolk, Christmas. I clammed up a bit at that. Christmas was always difficult, I said, and he just nodded and said it often was.

That surprised me. No judgment. No expectation that I should come to church. I had always been an irregular attender, but he didn't appear to hold that against me.

We'd nearly finished our drinks. He glanced at his watch. I bent to pick up my bag from between my feet.

'Now, the environment,' he said. 'Climate change. Knotty.'

I stared at him as if the understatement was blazoned across his forehead. 'More than knotty,' I said, pretty calmly, all things considered, although I was immediately aware of my chest tightening up, my heartbeat increasing. 'More than merely knotty, James.' The first time I'd used his name.

He nodded.

'I'd like to know why people in church don't take climate change seriously.'

'Some do. Others aren't there yet. We're all at different stages of faith and understanding. But God does care. God cares very much.'

'So tell me, if God cares so much about the planet, why doesn't God do something about it? I mean, I'm seriously thinking of becoming an atheist. There can't *be* a God if all this is allowed to happen.'

'Mmm.' He nodded again. 'The old problem of suffering. *How can a loving, all-powerful God allow suffering?* War, famine, natural disasters. Climate change.'

'Exactly!' Here was something I could pin him down on. 'Why doesn't God stop it all?'

'I don't think we want God to break the laws of physics.'

'I'm not talking about that. Why doesn't God make people care about the planet? Stop them flying everywhere, make them recycle things, stop them chopping down rainforests and polluting the sea and the air and flooding everywhere with tiny bits of plastic?'

I stopped for breath, my heart pounding. I was gripping my bag on my lap, its strap twisted round and round my hand.

'It's a good question, one that's been asked many times.'

'And I want an answer!'

'We could talk about this all day, Rosalie, but –'

I pushed my chair back and stood, rocking the table. I'd had enough. There would be no good answer, I felt, nothing that would make sense.

'– how do you feel when someone forces you do something? Or stops you doing something?'

I stared down at him, panting slightly, my bag clutched to my chest. What on earth was he talking about?

'Would you like to sit down, Rosalie?'

I sat, dimly aware of a kind of hush around me. The café chatter resumed slowly.

The vicar continued, unbothered by the attention I'd received. 'If God didn't allow us freedom to make our own decisions, we'd be like puppets, or chess pieces, unable to choose where we live, what jobs we do, who we marry, what to eat or what to wear, even how to organise our days. We wouldn't be fully alive.' He drained the dregs of his coffee. 'A loving God wants us to be autonomous, to have responsibility. And our loving God gives us plenty of guidance.'

'Well then, how do you square it?' I asked. 'A loving God that's also all-powerful, that lets us mess things up, that could step in and make everything better, but doesn't.'

'With a magic wand?'

'Exactly.' But even as I spoke, I knew how ridiculous that sounded.

'This is a huge topic. Lots to think about.'

I nodded.

'I'm afraid I have to go now. I'm visiting a very sick person in hospital in half an hour. We can carry on this conversation, another time, very soon.'

We both stood, then I said: 'But I can't imagine that God doesn't have a plan for this beautiful planet. Surely God doesn't want us to trash it, surely there's a plan?'

He smiled. A nice smile, kind and hopeful. 'I think we're the plan. Communities learning together, working together, working with nature. Kindness and forgiveness go a long way. So does a sense of humour.'

'But climate change isn't funny!'

'No, but we are. Let's not sweat the small stuff.'

The small stuff. Recycling, probably. Well, look where *not* recycling's got us.

He was still talking while shrugging on his coat. 'Forgiving each other, while keeping our sense of humour. None of us is perfect, of course.'

I couldn't resist one last sally, as we left the café together. 'It may be too late.'

He nodded. 'But it's still the right thing to do.' He waved and walked off down the street.

I didn't attend church. His suggestion of communities had left me cold. I didn't want to depend on people who might not see the world the way I did, might not understand the threats lining up to meet us, probably wouldn't take any of my fears seriously.

I learnt to knit on a Sunday morning instead. I joined a knit-and-sew workshop run by girls young enough to be my granddaughters. I paid my fee every week, stayed for two hours, went home with a new skill. I held myself aloof from friendships except of the most necessary and superficial kind, the kind that you have with a pleasant neighbour with whom you trade favours – feeding cats, say, or chickens – the same neighbours whose children had played with ours, with whom we'd shared picnics, and school runs and tips on music teachers. Neighbours we'd once called friends and who'd come to dinner parties.

My life became what I had wanted: calm and empty, devoid of drama, anxiety, or catastrophe. It was calm and I was able to breathe. I walked free. I held myself accountable to no one, not even Flora. But what was I thinking, cutting myself off so completely? It was hardly healthy. They probably thought I was a bit crazy, all the neighbours, and the people at the church, and the mushroom expert and the knitting woman. No doubt they remembered how I'd let myself down in the market. Doubtless they knew about Jonnie, and that Hugo had left me, and that the twins never came home for visits.

∾

For a year or two, I occupied myself with becoming as self-sufficient as possible. I installed solar panels for hot water and electricity, and a wood burner, and I got a man to help me with re-insulating the loft, putting another foot of insulation down on top of the six inches we already had. I'm sure he overcharged me, but Hugo was paying so I didn't care.

Hugo was generous. I never had to worry about money. It popped into my bank account on the fifth of every month, more than I needed, but enough, as Flora pointed out, for a rainy day. I didn't ever want to have to ask him for more, so in many ways that was a blessing that I took every advantage of. For the house and garden.

In terms of my own needs, well, when you reach sixty or so, a lot of stuff isn't important anymore. I'd seen enough theatre shows and visited enough exhibitions and travelled to so many exotic places (I swallowed the guilt down like bile), and I had more than enough clothes and shoes for ten of me, although many of them were not practical for my purposes so most of those I gave away. Flora was horrified. She told me that some of my 'vintage pieces', as she termed them, were worth a lot of money. I told her that I had decided to live outside the normal economic system. She looked at me thoughtfully and said that maybe I didn't need Dad's money, in that case.

We changed the subject.

She visited me quite often, sometimes with Peter at weekends, when they would fly down from Aberdeen and stay with his parents. I suggested the sleeper train a couple of times, but they never took it. I could tell Peter didn't like spending time with me. He looked at his watch a lot and after his first coffee (they brought their own as neither enjoyed my home-grown herb teas) he would start walking around the house, if it was raining, or out in the garden where he peered at the chickens and strolled between the raised beds, occasionally stopping to brush a leaf or some mud from his shoes. It was better once they moved back to Hertfordshire and had their first baby. Flora and Timmy came on their own. Timmy was a superb subject for conversation.

I purposely didn't ask about Hugo. I had put him in a small walled-off room in my heart, like a shed overgrown with ivy to which I had lost the key.

She told me anyway.

She told me, watching me without seeming to, stirring her coffee, glancing slyly out of the corner of her eye, that he had met someone.

He had met someone; he was very happy.

He had met someone called Juliette; he was very happy.

Juliette was much younger. She wanted children.

Juliette wanted children, but he wasn't sure.

Juliette was pregnant.

Juliette had given birth. Hugo was a father again.

They were building a straw-bale house near Ripon, with solar panels and rainwater harvesting and no heating at all. Juliette's very eco-minded, said Flora. A bit like you, Mummy.

It was a lovely house with a huge garden and orchard and a pond.

They were keen on growing their own food. Organically.

They'd got chickens.

It's rather odd, Flora said, having a baby brother. At my age.

At sixty-one, Hugo was a father again.

༄

I don't know why Flora felt she had to tell me all this. Perhaps she thought the information she was drip-feeding me would get me interested, that I'd be jealous and Hugo and I might, just might, patch up our marriage and get back together. Not possible, is what I should have said to her, but never did. Too much water under the bridge, you know how it is, I should have said, we're too different. I'm sorry, darling, it's better this way. And other such platitudes.

I never said a word. I kept my feelings – of love, and loss, and betrayal – to myself. I didn't mention how much I missed him, how he still figured in my dreams, that when waking I turned, sometimes, to his side of the bed to say good morning.

I didn't articulate my deepest suspicion, that perhaps I'd driven him away by being so fundamentalist, that it wasn't a natural parting of the ways and that we hadn't simply grown apart. I didn't even express surprise that he appeared now to have embraced an eco-lifestyle. He'd known all along that we have to look after the planet, everyone knows that, but he was doing it with someone easier to live with than me, that's all.

But another child… that was a shock. Had he needed a lot of persuading? Was this baby Hugo's new start, a way of putting all the grief and anger behind him? Or was it simply Juliette's biological clock driving her on? Her first child, Hugo's fifth. Another strain on the planet.

ॐ

Fergus and Dugald have always rung me without fail at seven o'clock on Sunday evenings. They aren't long calls, none of us given much to chat.

I fool myself. They had never chatted, that had been me, long ago in another life, when I was young and full of optimism; when the sun shone even when it was raining; when my days were warm and cloudless even while I was so exhausted by pregnancy and childcare that I could barely stay awake during meals and once fell asleep on the toilet; when I basked in Hugo's love and approval and my own desirability; when I knew – I knew it – I knew that there was nothing that could possibly go wrong in this world we had constructed together. We were the golden couple.

I don't know if the twins ring Hugo on Sunday evenings too. Perhaps they ring him on another evening. Perhaps they never ring him at all. Our conversations are safe and predictable. First Fergus, then Dugald. Three minutes each. We discuss the weather, mine and theirs; our crop yields and prospects; how the livestock are doing; our health. We say goodbye. I have an address for them but have never visited. It's not that I'm not curious, you understand, or that I don't care or no longer love them. I'd love to see where they live and work, listen to their plans, eat meals that they cook for me. I asked them once – oh, years ago – if I could visit them. I wouldn't be in the way, I said, I would stay in a bed and breakfast. There was a silence before one of them said, 'No, thank you.'

TWENTY-THREE

No Soft Landing

Another dark dawn. The wind's been blowing strongly all night, punctuated by sharp showers of rain and hail. Again.

It must be around eight. At home I would right now be letting the hens out before breakfast. My hen-sitting neighbours are probably annoyed that I'm still away.

The cormorant opens one foggy, bleary eye. It's not well.

'I'm not getting out of here alive. Neither are you, my feathered friend. This is the end, the very end of the world, and I should have seen it coming a week ago when I stumbled into this cave. Earth has brought out the big guns. A final all-out assault on the enemy. That's people. Humans. Me. But there'll be collateral damage. That's you.

'I'm not exaggerating. I mean, it would be great if I'd got it wrong, but is the weather improving? No, it's getting worse all the time. And I'm so hot, despite it being January, and despite all that water, the sea and the rain. I'm sweating in here – the heat, it's tropical.'

What I wouldn't give now for some cold. An ice cube, or a frost, or some snowflakes falling softly onto my upturned face.

Even the inside of a fridge.

I feel so hot, so dry with thirst and heat. My face burns, my arms and legs too, and yet I shiver as cold trickles down my spine. I've managed to pull off my two fleeces and have crawled over the shingle to roll myself in the water in the deepest pool near the cave, to soak my clothes and cool myself down. My right arm and my left leg – my injured limbs – are stiff and swollen, fiery hot. I can barely move them.

'I need to apologise to you, my little cormorant chum. And to all the molluscs and plants attached to the rocks in this cave, the tiny fish and crustaceans in the pools, the sandflies, the invisible plankton and microbes, the grey seals and herring gulls. If I could leave this place, I'd cry out to the trees and forests and orchards, the elephants and rhinos and hippos, mice and shrews and rats, to the household pets that stave off our loneliness and the farm animals that feed so many of us.'

The bird doesn't stir. I strip myself of Jonnie's parka, wipe my wet forehead with my sleeve, and approach. Its feathers move slightly, ruffled by the breeze. It looks dead, almost. Then it opens its eyes, stares right at me with that lucent green gaze.

※

Earth is more alive than we give her credit for. She's a thinking, feeling being. She's injured, hurt, feels betrayed and angry, and now she's on the warpath. The weather's her weapon of choice: freezing, heating, flooding, burning, drought; it's all the same to her. More energy in the system leads to more drama in the weather. It couldn't be clearer.

And cleverly – she's thought this through – weather leads to disease and pestilence. Mosquito-borne malaria in the Fens. Zika, dengue, yellow fever. Plagues of insects. Fungal diseases in our trees and crops. New untreatable infections. Not to mention heatstroke and foul water and pollution.

And mightn't there be the teensiest little bit of civil unrest to go with all this? Such an easy way to get rid of us. We just kill ourselves off as we fight over food and water and energy and land and medicine and fuel. You name it, we'll fight over it.

Earth has decided to kill us before we kill her, and we have carried on as usual, oblivious. We've taken no notice of her increasingly shrill demands to back off, to lay down our weapons of mass destruction – the energy use, the mining, the fracking, the deforestation, the over-fishing – and to parlay. We didn't parlay, we had no idea how serious she was, how heartbroken she is.

Something I have learned: you can still love the person you're at war with. And actions speak louder than words.

⁊

I feel dreadful. I ache all over – my back, my legs, my head, my stomach, even the muscles in my face. My throat feels like knives have slashed it to pieces. And the unbearable heat and the smell, that pungent mix of rotting seaweed and my own body odour, just makes my nausea worse. I don't want to think about the next few days, how terrible it's going to be – I'm desperately trying not to worry about my children and grandchildren, and Hugo.

I drink my last mouthful of water. I'll have to chew my two remaining paracetamol. Disgusting. Paracetamol is so horribly bitter. I have a thumping headache and my thirst is torturing me; my tongue sticks to the roof of my mouth, I can barely swallow. Dehydration. I should collect rainwater in my bottle. I will, when I feel up to it.

I'm so hot I can barely breathe. I slowly peel off my clothing, and drop it piece by piece onto Jonnie's old parka. My fleece, my sweater. My trousers, my shirt. My socks. I stand in my base layers, damp with sweat, feel the breeze from the sea, a blessed relief. I kneel, then lie on my back stretched out on the shingle, my arms by my side, and listen to the waves.

If I had my time again, I'd try and get on with the neighbours, take an interest in the local community, make myself a little network of companionship. I'd go to coffee and invite people back. I'd smile at people in the street, and pass the time of day. I'd enquire after their families, listen to their woes, sympathise when things didn't go well. Live in community, like the vicar said.

The cormorant shifts uneasily on its ledge, its eyes closed now. I don't even know if it's male or female. I wish I did. It would make my time in here a bit more meaningful, somehow. I do know, though, that it's in pain, and I wish I could have helped it. I close my eyes too.

TWENTY-FOUR

Travelling Light

One year, when Flora and Peter still lived in Aberdeen, before they had children, she sent me a plane ticket to visit her. I'd just read an article about the melting tundra, and I'd wept half the night, mourning the consequences of ice melt, the sinking houses and roads and railways, the Northwest Passage open all year round, the fresh water pouring into the oceans, the methane pouring into the atmosphere. The future. She didn't understand when I said I wouldn't be flying, and the train was fine, and honestly, I didn't mind at all and in fact I preferred it, please Flora, I know what I'm doing.

She said, quite nastily, as I recall: 'Oh, get off your bloody moral high ground, Mum.'

We didn't speak for a few weeks. I was wounded. I had tried to point out I was doing it for her and the baby she was expecting, but she put the phone down. When we next spoke, it was to arrange my visit, by train. I offered to pay for the cancelled plane ticket, but Peter wouldn't hear of it. I don't know what to make of that. Perhaps he was claiming the moral high ground for himself.

&

A few years after Hugo moved out, Ollie began sending me young activists who needed a bed for the night or a place to set up a tent before they scaled the Shard or tried to break into Parliament or simply presented a petition. Or friends of friends, on their way somewhere. It was quite fun, having young people around, although their rucksacks contained worryingly large amounts of hardware – chains and padlocks and bits of drainpipe for locking onto railings, or each other – and tubes of superglue. They laid all this out on the sitting room floor the night before they went off, to check it over. Or they bought garden canes and daubed slogans on bits of cardboard in the garden and stuck all these together with parcel tape.

There was a kind of optimism back then, before the conferences got hijacked by oil companies. We were all infected by the possibilities: wonderful public transport, local jobs for all, solar panels on every rooftop, abundant local-grown produce, the lot.

Once I joined the activists for a march in London. I'd assumed it might be quite fun, I don't know why. I certainly thought there would be more people, all gathering at one end of Waterloo Bridge and marching across together to Parliament, chanting slogans, waving flags, making a real impact.

But there were very few of us. Perhaps it was the weather, cold and wet, and the midweek date, or that we were a very small group. Dartmoor Butterfly Conservation had teamed up with Save Our Slow Worms, which I only remember now because of its SOS initials, and I tagged along, knowing no-one except the young woman who had stayed with me the night before.

I felt very exposed, very visible. Part of me hoped that Hugo might see me on TV; another part wanted to slink off and hide. And I hadn't expected that people would want to chat and exchange stories. I got into conversation with the middle-aged woman walking alongside me. We found that we had children of similar ages and that we both feared for our grandchildren and their futures. I mentioned Jonnie only in passing, the fact that he had been passionate about nature and had travelled to the South Atlantic with Greenpeace, and saw in her face the sudden realisation that here was news of significance, here was someone connected to that wonderful young man whose death had flashed all over the world.

She invited me to sit down with her in a café and tell our story. She said she could write something up and give it to her editor and it would probably make the weekend paper. I froze, my heart suddenly beating far too fast. We'd been through all that when Jonnie died. Journalists camping outside for interviews. Speculation in the media. We'd escaped then – to Anne's place in Cornwall – and I would escape now. I told her I would just nip to the loo, left my little banner propped up against the railings like a promise of return, dashed off to the Tube and went home.

I texted Ollie that evening and told him it was just too stressful for me. I couldn't get involved in protests. He replied that there was no pressure, he hadn't expected me to join the activists in London; providing beds was enough. Smiley face and thumbs up.

Flora always worried that I might be taken advantage of, wondered who all these people were who kept turning up, who I was feeding and providing beds for without charge.

But I was capable of looking after myself, as long as Hugo carried on financing the house and the insurance, the council tax and the road tax for the little red Fiat, fifteen years old, garaged five minutes' walk away, which I hardly used but which Flora (Hugo?) insisted I keep 'for emergencies'. *What emergencies? I wanted to know. I never go anywhere; I never do anything. There will be no emergencies.*

Between activist visits I lived my solitary existence, like a masonry bee, darting out to harvest food from my garden – I was so very proud of my year-round productivity: parsnips waiting to be dug up, leeks standing proud like sentinels, long white winter radishes, rainbow chard, red Russian kale. I hummed happily around my plants and hens, living mostly outside, except in the rain. Very bee-like. Bees aren't keen on rain.

Sometimes I made it out to some other kind of activity, or even a social engagement. Tea and scones with the neighbours. Or out with the early-morning foragers. But I usually avoided these occasions, giving in only to the most insistent invitations. The trouble was that people would keep talking about world events, government policy, clashes between statesmen or states, elections, even the weather – things that began to get my heart racing and my imagination churning. They'd talk about holidays in hot, hot places, and people dying in heatwaves, and I'd wonder when that kind of heat would hit us here. Or floods, campsites washed away, people drowned in India, France, Italy, America, and I could imagine that all too clearly. Or about inflation and the price of food and houses and yes, holidays again, or what was happening to the health service.

To save my anxieties from multiplying I avoided most outings, most people, listened only to classical music on my CD player, read books on gardening and cooking or the gentler classics, Jane Austen and lyrical nature poetry. No conflict, no worry, no news. I kept myself together without drugs. And I lived gently on the earth.

Flora once opened the door between the garage and utility room and peeked in, bemused. 'What are you going to do with all this stuff, Mum? Why do you even need it?' I told her, quite fiercely, that she could deal with it when I was dead and gone.

I was protective of my found items, saving them from landfill or careless fly-tipping: pallets (could be useful for the garden), old chairs, casserole dishes, suitcases with broken zips that could and should be mended, although my local handyman said he wasn't going to do it and didn't know anyone who would. I kept my bike in there too, and the lawnmower, and the big chest freezer for my plums and apples and beans, and homemade ice cream for Flora's children.

Once a month or so I stocked up on toilet paper, dried beans and flour, and a few tinned supplies at the supermarket. I'd got it down to an art, my near self-sufficiency. I grew root vegetables and pumpkins, which stored well in my garage. Fresh beans, courgettes and fruit, all frozen. Apples and pears in boxes. Pickles and chutneys. Tomatoes oven-dried or preserved in Kilner jars. Sauerkraut and other brined vegetables. Bunches of dried herbs. Some hardy winter crops which I collected as I needed from the garden. It was a pretty sight, the ruby and saffron stems of the rainbow chard vibrant on the cloudiest days.

But Hugo – I wished he could have seen this. I wished he could have seen for himself how well I was doing, not filtered through Flora's critical eyes.

I admit I was jealous of his new life so I looked up his address on Google Earth. I went north, stayed in a bed and breakfast close to some stately home, drove into his village. I thought about turning up at his love-nest but I lost my nerve. Perhaps it was the idea of Hugo's horrified face when he opened the door to me. Or the idea of his girlfriend in the flesh, saying hello, of shaking the hand that caressed him at night in their bed, smelling the perfume he inhaled as they embraced and made love.

Or catching sight of their little boy, playing in the garden, and knowing he was as dear to Hugo as Jonnie had been.

TWENTY-FIVE

In Two Minds

It snowed heavily the week before Christmas, thick soft flakes falling from a pewter sky, the streets hushed, so I brought the chickens into the conservatory out of the cold, which although it's never exactly warm in the winter does remain a few degrees above zero. I dug out Jonnie's childhood sledge from the garage, his old wooden one with metal runners, to go shopping, and made sure I was well wrapped up against the wind. It felt like I was in Siberia.

These erratic winters, veering from warm days and sunshine and roses still in bloom to snow and ice and all manner of sub-zero disasters – railway tracks freezing, people slipping down their garden paths and banging their heads and dying right there of exposure, supermarkets running out of food, and silly little girls ending up in hospital because they insist on wearing midriff-baring tops – these winters are just the beginning. People still say the climate isn't changing. Or if it is, it's not a problem.

The snow reached the top of my wellies, and I sank into it with every step, the sledge skittering along behind me as I tugged on its string, step by laborious step. At *Sainsbury's* the shelves were already thin, no bread or fruit or veg, but plenty of greetings cards and magazines, cosmetics, household stuff like mops and buckets, and tinned spam, which I'm amazed they still even sell.

It all melted in time for Christmas Day, and Peter picked me up in his enormous car, as he always does, the two older children sitting in the back. They were already overexcited, so I listened to their chatter and occasionally answered, while gazing around at the vehicle's interior, and (now I'm being honest) luxuriating in its warmth at the same time as condemning it, in that way we all have of being able to hold two thoughts in our heads at the same time. The fields we passed were flooded with snow melt, but it was worse in Wales, I heard on his radio, before he turned it off in favour of Christmas music.

And Christmas itself was lovely, of course, with Flora's little family, amid all the noise and laughter and fun. Justin and Clare popped in for tea, which nobody could eat because of being too full from lunch, and we sat together and admired the children and exchanged our bits of news, and were friendly, if not exactly friends. On Christmas Day I was more than happy to overlook the central heating's cost to the planet. In fact, I revelled in its warmth.

I wasn't sure we'd be able to get to Anne's for New Year, what with the snow and all, and I wasn't sure I wanted to, but Flora and Peter were determined: whatever the weather, they said, his big car could cope with it. They're terribly gregarious; they love parties and gatherings of all kinds. I'd have found it a great stress as a young parent, ending the Christmas holidays hundreds of miles away with grumpy tired children, but I'm not Flora. And this was the first time Anne had invited me specifically, not as an add-on to Flora, which made me thrilled but nervous. So I bought some paperbacks and soaps as presents, paracetamol for my hip, a few tins of pears and peaches for my larder, and some cheese which was reduced because it had reached its sell-by date. I planned to use it in a macaroni cheese. Then I rang my neighbours to let them know I'd be away and to ask them to feed the hens. I promised I'd be back in four days, and made a mental note to buy them some clotted cream fudge as a thank you.

The wardrobe in the spare bedroom still held some smart clothes, things I hadn't worn for years. I picked out a couple of decent outfits and a pair of elegant heels, and began looking for a small suitcase, which I couldn't find, even in the loft or under the stairs. I would have to take my things in Jonnie's rucksack to Flora's, squeeze myself into the middle of the car between two of the children, with the dog and the third child in the back row of seats, and resign myself to the very long drive. I would take the precaution, as I always did, of including a few apples and a bag of walnuts, in case the food wasn't to my liking.

I wished Hugo could have been coming to Cornwall with us. But I pushed that thought right to the back of my mind, buried it deep under all the planning and preparation. I'm no better than anyone else, I begin to see that. Maybe it's our capacity for lying that sets humans apart from animals, our ability to see the truth and turn our backs on it. So we might say, *I adore Nature, I love the planet, I'm really green,* while we go on polluting and destroying the planet. I can relish Flora's central heating and hate my own; Hugo said he loved me, yet could flirt outrageously with other women. And I could tell him I hated him, that I wanted to divorce him, yet be so deeply bound to him that daily I miss his voice, his touch, his companionship, his care.

TWENTY-SIX

I Don't Drive Very Often These Days

My old Fiat was cold and faintly smelly, with an odour of unwashed socks and mildew. I rummaged in the glove compartment in case there was anything useful but found only a pair of old grey knitted gloves, a few car park tickets and an open bag of jelly babies, congealed into a sticky lump inside the plastic. On the back seat was a child's green sweatshirt and a road map of Hertfordshire.

The snow had returned overnight, driven by a biting north-easterly wind, and now lay knee-deep over the garden and the streets, banked up in drifts against hedges and walls.

The car actually started on the first try, to my amazement. I cleared the snow from the windscreen and the roof, then drove carefully through town at about ten miles per hour, keeping to the dark track in the middle of the road. It seemed the council had sent a snow plough through. I should think that's a first, for St Albans. In ungritted side streets I glimpsed children playing, and several snowmen of different sizes.

I was on my way to Flora's at last, well prepared, anticipating the giddy whirl of a New Year spent socialising, eating and drinking and staying up far too late. I hoped nobody would upset me with comments like: 'Global warming, we need a bit of that round here!' I felt shaky with excitement and nerves.

Flora wasn't in. The house was quiet, the windows dark at three o'clock in the afternoon. I went back to the car to wait. As I watched, a lamp came on in the sitting-room, and another in the front bedroom. I trudged through the snow to the front door once again, knowing already that these were just security lights. I rang her eventually from the car, beginning to feel very cold despite my many layers.

'Didn't you see my text, Mummy? We're coming back tomorrow.'

They were at Peter's brother's place in London.

'Go home and get warm, Mummy.' I could hear voices and laughter in the background, and suddenly saw myself as others must see me, a lonely old woman who is too frightened to make friends. 'Have a lovely warm bath,' she added. She must have been eating, or in the kitchen, for there were the clinks of cutlery on plates as she spoke, and her voice sounded a little muffled, as if she had food in her mouth.

I wanted, briefly, to cry, sitting in the dark outside her house. I had her key, which I'd never used, and it occurred to me that I could go in and get warm there. The heating would undoubtedly be on, and there'd be food in the fridge. I could make myself a sandwich and have a cup of tea. Then I remembered the security system, and that I didn't know the alarm code. I could have asked. She'd have told me. I could have asked to stay overnight and see them when they returned the next day, but I felt that perhaps that would be pushing it, that Peter might not be best pleased.

I drove out of her cul-de-sac and back towards the main road. The snow had begun falling again, smudging thickly against the windscreen. One of the windscreen wipers was damaged and having a tough time keeping up. I could just about see where I was going, but not well enough to take the right direction back to St Albans, and by the time I realised this I was driving north on the M1, towards Birmingham. Entirely the wrong direction.

Then the wind got up. The snow began hitting my windscreen horizontally, and in it were hard things, pellets of ice which cracked and crashed against the glass. I saw no one else – no other headlights, I mean. I crawled up that motorway and eventually came to a stop on the hard shoulder, the needle of the petrol gauge almost at the bottom of the red, where I stared at the snow drifting across the road, piling up against the central barrier, thickening minute by minute.

I must have drifted off, despite the cold, and woke a few hours later, exhausted and frozen through. The snow had turned to sleet while I slept and again it seemed only a matter of minutes before it was turning again, rain and wind slapping the car, shaking it so violently that it almost seemed that it might be tossed over the embankment and thrown down in a field somewhere with me inside.

This is how the police found me, at the side of the motorway in the dark at four-thirty on a winter's morning, on a day when the whole country had shut down because of the superstorm that was on its way and that I knew nothing about because of my aversion to current affairs.

The Winter Anomaly – the snow which is no anomaly at all when the North Atlantic Current has slowed almost to a standstill – the Winter Anomaly, as I say, was being swept away by a hurricane.

The police escorted me off the motorway to an all-night petrol station. The manager was about to drive home and was disgruntled to have to open up again for me. The wind howled banshee-like around the signage and through the buildings. I could barely stand against it, and the manager and I held the fuel hose together, like firefighters. He signalled to me that I should go while I had the chance; he didn't want payment. I waved goodbye, or tried to, at the police officers sitting in their car a few yards away, but the wind took my arm and lifted me a step backwards. I've never known a wind like it. I've seen things like this on the news, hurricanes in Florida and typhoons in the Philippines, but never in central England.

I drove at a crawl down the road, the car buffeted every few seconds by waves of air crashing down on me. What with the rain and noise of the wind I felt as if I was driving an amphibious vehicle into surf. My phone had no signal, and I suddenly remembered that I'd left the charger at home, not that I could have used it just then.

There was just enough watery light from the streetlamps to spot a thin alleyway between two rows of terraced houses. I turned carefully into it and in the comparative silence stilled the engine in relief. The rain poured down the windscreen as if from a waterfall.

I pushed the door open, gasping with the cold shock of the water that reached my skin in a matter of seconds. I felt along the wall to the end of the car so I could get the rucksack out of the boot. I could barely see. It wasn't sheets of rain; it was blankets, duvets of rain, so dense that I couldn't even see the streetlamps. I kept my head down so I could breathe. Breathing has never seemed as important to me as it did then.

I must be tougher than I think. I didn't get exposure, although I didn't warm up for hours. I clambered into the back to change into dry clothes, twisting my long scrawny frame into the tiny space between the seats, wriggling my damp body into underwear that stuck to my skin. I pulled on two long-sleeved tops and a jumper and my one spare pair of trousers and sat shaking in the little Fiat, while the glass steamed up all around me and the car convulsed in the wind.

After a while I ate some walnuts and an apple. I tried the radio, but there was no signal. Outside there was no indication of the time of day. I guessed it to be around eight o'clock in the morning when the sun should have been rising, but there was only a dark twilight.

TWENTY-SEVEN

Perhaps I Was a Little Over-Confident

The wind dropped eventually, and the rain eased. It was already Wednesday lunchtime, so why not drive down to Anne's myself? It seemed such a good idea. For a start, I'd be independent, not having to squeeze myself into the car with Flora's children. I could leave when I wanted. And as far as carbon emissions went, well, my day-to-day life was almost carbon neutral, so a few hundred miles in a tiny car was probably acceptable. I felt carefree, exhilarated, liberated.

I found my way out of Birmingham and round a sort of roadblock onto the M42, all the red and white barriers and bollards slewed around as if there'd been an earthquake, then over to the M5. Droitwich, Gloucester, Bristol. There were various flashing orange and red signs, but I ignored them. I had it all planned out. I could be with Anne by early evening – there was no point in retracing my route and going home, only to pack up again and drive down with Flora and Peter in a crowded car with squabbling children, and really I was doing them all a favour – but first I would find a service station and coffee, lots of coffee, which would have a marvellous effect and save me from falling asleep at the wheel after my terrible night.

There was nobody on the road. I mean nobody. I saw not one vehicle, apart from a few lorries on their sides which I drove carefully around, an abandoned fire engine on the other carriageway, and a number of cars sitting on the hard shoulder. Mine was the only car on the move, even when I got past the motorway embankments and could see lanes and roads and villages and farms. Everything was still, every vehicle halted.

I began to worry. It felt like the zombie apocalypse that Jonnie had so earnestly desired and feared. The electronic road signs became black and dead, and there was damage to buildings, roofs blown off, windows blown in, chimneys fallen. And trees down, everywhere I looked, great swathes of them lying in the same direction across hillsides and fields, little sticks waiting to be picked up by giants for firewood.

I turned the radio on. I needed company, the sound of human voices. I needed to know what was going on.

The signal was variable. I fiddled around with the dial and found Radio 4. There were two men discussing the 'weather event'. We were in the eye of the storm, they said. What had happened last night was just half of it; there was more to come, predicted to hit within four or five hours. Then a break for a day or so, followed by more strong weather fronts rolling in from the Atlantic. These storms would affect the country for the following five or six days, possibly longer. All motorways were closed; all ferries and aircraft and trains cancelled. People were being advised to stay where they were, and at all costs to avoid travel. There was some worry about food supplies, with the population being urged not to stockpile, and to check on vulnerable neighbours.

This was a national emergency, said the man on the radio. I was passing Bristol at this point and could see three huge black plumes of smoke down by the port.

I ask myself now why I didn't understand, why I couldn't

see what was happening. I've been taking Earth's warnings seriously, preparing for decades for this event, the world's end. I've planned how to live and even how to die – holding off the ravening hordes with an axe, or letting them in and sharing what little I had. For years I've had two scenarios planned out, the heroine of each.

I suppose it took me by surprise, in the end. My shed crammed with tinned food, my plastic box of batteries and spare light bulbs, my extensive medical kit, my firewood – years' worth of firewood stacked in the garage and round the side of the house – my soap, my shortwave radio, all left behind. Perhaps it was the headiness of being on the open road, surviving a night in my car, but I felt confident, truly I did, confident that I was safe and that I knew what I was doing.

I scanned the empty sky above the empty road. There were a couple of narrow shreds of blue between dove-grey tatters of cloud, but not enough to sew a sailor a pair of trousers, as Hugo might have said. He's good at dredging up these old sayings. To my right the sky had darkened to a sullen purplish grey. I could see a wide slate-coloured band of rain blurring the horizon. It was coming my way. I sped up.

By the time I got off the motorway at Tiverton services, the fuel gauge had been hovering around the lowest point of the red for some miles. The small petrol station seemed deserted. I parked alongside a few other cars and scurried into the Burger King. About a dozen people sat inside the café, scattered around the tables in little disconsolate groups of two or three.

It wasn't clear who to ask, so I called out as I got inside: was there any chance, I asked in my politest tones, of filling up my car?

Several shook their heads, and a girl sitting near the door said the manager had gone home after turning off the pumps.

I bought a properly-caffeinated coffee with oat milk and considered my options. I could stay at the Travelodge just across the car park, wait out the next storm, buy fuel when the manager came back, drive to Anne's the next day. I considered this option for all of three seconds before dismissing it. I would get to Anne's under my own steam today, pick up the car next week, enjoy my little adventure. To be quite honest, I was finding this all quite exciting.

I hauled the rucksack out of the car and staggered down the access road and across the vast roundabout over the motorway, buffeted by gusts of wet wind that pushed me back a step or two every few yards. Through the winter-bare trees I could see Tiverton Parkway railway station on my left, miles from Tiverton itself, built in the lee of the motorway on a greenfield site. If there was the remotest chance that a train might come through, I wanted to be there to catch it.

I climbed over the low motorway barrier and slid down the slope, scrambling through dead brambles and wet, yellow grass and saplings. There was a large pond at the bottom, its surface rippling with surprisingly large waves and dimpled with raindrops. I squelched my way round the edge and walked along a path to the station. Still nobody about, so I climbed over the barrier onto the platform. There, I thought. How many people my age could do all this? It just shows that walking and gardening are good at keeping people fit. No, Flora, I thought, I don't need to join a gym or do aqua-aerobics. In fact, I doubted very much whether Flora could have managed to keep up with me, and felt quite smug.

There was a train. It was stationary. The carriages were the old-fashioned type with proper handles, so I opened a door and climbed in. I hadn't seen a carriage this old for years. It looked as if it had come from a museum.

Of course, we always think we're behaving logically. I could have stopped in Cheltenham and found a hotel. Or gone into Bristol and looked up Hugo's sister. Or stayed at the service station with everyone else.

❧

The man who shook me awake wasn't dressed in a guard's uniform. He looked like he'd rolled out of bed in the middle of the night and put on anything that came to hand – a grubby pair of jeans, trainers, a red sweatshirt, a black hoodie. I hadn't meant to fall asleep.

'Care to tell me what you're doing?' he asked. I was sitting at a table, and he sat down opposite me.

I rubbed my eyes. I was cold and aching, and my mouth had a nasty bitter taste. 'What time is it?'

He pushed back his cuff and looked at his watch. 'Ten past three.' He shook his head. 'You've got to get off.'

'I'm trying to get to Cornwall, to my family.'

For the first time, he seemed to look at me properly. He surveyed my clothes, strewn around the nearby seats in a vain effort to dry them.

'I am not running a charity here,' he said. 'In the normal run of things homeless people don't get seats on my trains. In the normal run of things people have to pay.'

'I can pay,' I said quickly, and rummaged in my pockets for my purse. 'And I'm not homeless.'

He shook his head, closed his eyes and rubbed his forehead. 'In the normal run of things,' he repeated.

There was a silence. He leaned back against his seat, his eyes still closed. He wasn't young, in his mid-forties, I guessed, about the age Jonnie would be now. He looked exhausted, his face pale and flabby, his mouth turned down at the corners.

'I'm waiting for a driver,' he said. He opened his eyes. 'If he comes in the next five minutes, we're on our way to Truro, Penzance if possible.'

'Is that him?' There was a man coming out of the station onto the platform, hefting an overnight bag onto his shoulder.

'That's him.' He stood. 'Pack up your stuff,' he said. 'Keep out of sight. I don't know you're here, mind. I've not seen you.'

'Why's this train running?' I called after him as he swung away from me and began to make his way rapidly down the carriage.

He turned at the door. 'It's not running, as such. I've got to get it back to where it needs to be tomorrow morning, or there'll be chaos once everything starts up again.' He stood with his hand on the door. 'You wouldn't believe the trouble we've had this winter. Leaves, snow, floods, and now this. Storm of the century. Four derailments, you'll have seen it on the news, that's why we're using old rolling stock. A pain to drive, I don't mind telling you.' He paused, seeming to think of something. 'Look, you're not meant to be on this train, we're not insured for passengers, it's just me and my driver. It's at your own risk, OK?'

'Fine,' I said. Everything was at my own risk. I felt energised, focused. I wanted to get to Anne's.

Later, he brought me a bottle of *Coke* and a couple of flapjacks. Nothing hot, he said, he couldn't run to that. By then it was dark. The lights were off – no need for lights without any passengers, how very sensible, I thought, how very energy-saving – and the only thing preventing me from sleeping was the hail against the window on the far side. It burst against the glass like shells from a machine gun, fat pieces of ice as big as olives, and each time it hit the train the carriage rocked and swayed so that I had to hold onto the table.

It wasn't quick, this journey. We reached Penzance around supper time, got shunted into a siding, and I was left to think about my next move. I wasn't far from Anne's now. There were no staff around. No trains, no need for staff.

Most of the guesthouses in Penzance appeared to be closed for the winter season, their owners no doubt in the Caribbean or Florida, contributing their greenhouse gases to the hike in world temperatures and the Winter Anomaly. Others – five others in fact – told me they had no vacancies, despite the Vacancies signs in their windows or dangling from chains just inside their front gate.

I felt leprous. No blacks or Irish or dogs. No asylum seekers. No benefits. No witchy women with long straggly hair.

I shamed myself at the last, the sixth, when I told the woman who answered the door that my money was as good as hers. Her husband loomed behind her, a hulking presence in shorts and T-shirt.

'It's you,' I said. 'You people are making it snow, you with your heating on all the time.'

I couldn't help myself.

'No snow here, love,' said the man. 'Off you go, now,' as if talking to a simpleton. 'There's the Queen's Hotel, down on the front.'

It was dark and I had no choice. I didn't want a night in the open. I'm tough, but not that tough.

'Remember,' I said, with an attempt at levity, 'you heard it here first.'

'That's right, love. Let's show you the way.' He stepped outside the door and pointed back down the road.

'We've burnt too much carbon and the world's paying us back.'

'So they tell us, love.' He took my elbow and steered me through his tiny front garden to the gate, closing it behind me. 'Good luck, then. Mind how you go.'

❧

They didn't refuse me at the Queen's Hotel. They were extraordinarily professional, considering my appearance. I caught a glimpse of myself in a mirror I passed on the way to my room. I hadn't realised just how grubby Jonnie's parka was. I've never washed it, couldn't bear to, couldn't bear to get rid of the last traces of his DNA. Hugo offered more than once to buy me a new one, one that fitted better, whose zip worked properly, whose buttons matched. Maybe it was the parka that drove him away. And the rucksack is impossible to wash, too big on its frame to fit inside a washing machine. It was filthy, smeared with grime and tar and black sooty marks.

Before I did anything else, I rang Flora. The answerphone was on.

'Flora, this is Mummy. Just to say I'm all right, you mustn't worry about me. I'm in a hotel in Penzance. I'm on my way to Anne's and I'll ring you when I get there. Can you pick up my charger before you leave? The alarm's not on. If you can't find your key, there's a spare in the third flowerpot to the left of the front door. Thank you. Goodbye darling. Please don't worry. I'm fine. It's all fine. Goodbye.' This seemed to cover everything, and so I felt, at last, that I could begin to relax.

I showered and washed my hair, running my fingers through it to make it less straggly, and ordered a small supper in the restaurant – two fried eggs with baked beans and mushrooms on toast, and a large pot of tea. This wasn't on the evening menu. The girl who came with her little notebook was at pains to point out that this was a breakfast, not a dinner, but

I asked her if it was really a problem, and she said no it probably wasn't, but she'd check with the kitchen first, and then without checking with me she brought me my meal with a tomato on the side.

I agonised over this tomato. It was – of course – imported. An item of food that I could live without. I called the girl over and asked her if she could give it to someone else, but she frowned and said no. What would happen to it, I wanted to know. It would be thrown away, she said. In that case, I said, would she like to eat it? She shook her head, mute.

I ate the tomato. Many grams of carbon had been burnt to bring it to me from wherever it had been grown. This tomato had been refrigerated – more carbon – and packaged in plastic – more carbon – and then transported and refrigerated and transported and refrigerated some more. This tomato was a *sacrifice*.

I felt better after a night in a proper bed. I rose early and made my way to the restaurant to eat a similar meal. A different girl was on duty. She accepted my request for no tomatoes without a flicker. I also ate porridge and an apple and some yoghurt. It was easy to obtain, like magic. All I had to do was pass over a few pieces of finely printed paper. I didn't have to grow it, I didn't do battle with predators, I didn't chop it or grate it or thresh it or harvest it or fry it or boil it. I'd forgotten how the rich do live.

TWENTY-EIGHT

A Kind of Miracle

That dawn was calm and crimson, with salmon streaks across a turquoise sky – a shepherd's warning, if ever there was one. I got the bus driver to drop me at the corner of the lane that led up to Anne's cottage. It was a beautiful morning, despite the blood-red sunrise the day before: the promised lull in the storms. The sun warmed the top of my head, the breeze wafted gently across the hedges. I could smell new grass and hear birds – gulls and blackbirds and thrushes.

I shouldered the pack and began the half mile trek up the lane, working out what to tell Anne. She'd be surprised to see me arriving a day early. I didn't want her thinking I was taking advantage, simply that – how we lie to ourselves – I'd been so looking forward to our weekend together, and I wanted to help with the party.

I would apologise again for putting unbearable pressure on her in the past. I would show her that I'd changed. We could start again. In my pocket was a jar of local honey. A peace offering, however small.

It was a little after eleven as I approached. The two young saplings I'd helped Anne plant either side of the entrance were now tall bushy trees. I couldn't see the house until I got right up to the five-bar gate.

I mentioned before that things never turn out as you expect.

The house wasn't the same.

The front door didn't seem to exist. I peered at the bit of wall where I was sure it had been. I took a few steps to my left and saw a huge glass and wood extension to the cottage, supported on stilts over the slope of the garden. The roof was steep and shingled in blue-grey slate. There was a deck running round the side of the house, and garden furniture – basket-weave chairs and a glass table – and below the deck was slung a hammock.

My first reaction was that Anne and her husband had been spending a lot of money. My second was surprise as a youngish man walked around the side of the extension and up the slope to meet me. He was carrying a bundle of sticks and wearing leather gardening gloves. The gardener, I assumed.

'Can I help you?'

Not the gardener. He sounded too much in charge, a voice that expected answers. A son. A son of the new husband.

'I'm looking for Anne,' I said.

He frowned and shook his head.

'Sorry, you've got the wrong address.'

'Er, no,' I said. 'I haven't.'

He raised his eyebrows.

'I've come here many times, in the past,' I continued.

'Ah. How long ago?' He didn't return my smile. I got the impression I was interrupting his morning. He glanced at my rucksack. I slipped it off my shoulders and let it drop to the ground.

'That's better,' I said, and smiled.

He was waiting for my answer.

'It was quite a long time,' I admitted. 'Maybe twenty years?'

Now he frowned. 'Who did you say you're looking for?'

'Anne. Anne Pettit, I mean Godfrey. I think. Or Geoffrey.' He frowned at me again. 'Sorry,' I said, 'she remarried, and I can't quite —'

'Just a minute.' He walked off and into the new extension, through a door that blended so well into the wood I hadn't noticed it. I remained standing behind the gate. He returned with a young woman.

'Anne Graham?' she asked.

'Yes, that's it! She remarried. We were at school together...' I stopped. The man was looking blank and bored. The woman had her eyebrows raised and was smiling very slightly, politely.

'We bought the house from the Grahams about three years ago,' she said. 'I'm sorry for your wasted journey.'

'Oh!' Now I remembered. Anne had downsized, finding the garden too big to cope with. She sent me the address last spring, but in all the excitement of my journey I had completely forgotten. 'Do you have their new address?'

'Sorry. I don't think I can just give it out. Sorry.'

'Oh.' I couldn't think what to say, aware once again of how I looked. I stared down at my rucksack. 'Oh.' I got out my phone and stared at it. No signal.

There was a silence. I looked up. The man had disappeared, and the woman had come a step or two closer.

'Is that how you're travelling?' she asked.

'Oh yes,' I said. 'I'm a great walker.' I gave a short carefree laugh.

'I'm sorry,' she said. 'I expect you were hoping to catch up with your friend.' Her husband had appeared at the front door. He was holding a mug and sipped from it. 'Would you like a coffee or tea? A glass of water?'

'Oh no, no, I wouldn't presume,' I said. 'I don't want to put you out. I couldn't possibly.'

'It's no trouble,' she said. 'Have you got far to go?'

I hadn't thought beyond this place, this time, this reconciliation. My universe shifted around me once again. One less certainty to hang on to. What do I know now, anyway? I had a husband – no more. I had a son – no more. I never had a real mother, or a father. I never had the twins. I have Flora, perhaps I have Flora.

ᔇᔆ

She gave me a lift into St Ives. A walking holiday, she guessed, in such a beautiful part of the world. Be careful with this treacherous weather, she said. I smiled and agreed, thinking I'd be under cover before long, thinking how I had embarrassed myself, a silly old woman who doesn't know what she's doing.

The sun had given way to a gentle mizzle on the windscreen, the wipers moving back and forth with a slight squeak on the upward stroke; the hills were hidden in a sea mist which came in slow billows across the slopes.

She dropped me at the bottom of the hill in town. Would I be all right? she asked. Of course I would, I said, and gave her my cheeriest and most enthusiastic smile.

I walked along the harbour, staring at the rock-grey waves disappearing into the fog and mulling over my options. There was a café that did vegetarian food, so I went in and was their first lunch customer, choosing after some deliberation an aubergine and chickpea lasagne drizzled with olive oil and accompanied by a mixed salad, avocado and tomato and cucumber and limp lamb's lettuce. I asked the girl if there was any dish they could give me that wasn't full of imported ingredients, because these things can't grow here in the winter, but she looked so blank I felt sorry for her and let it go.

The mist disappeared during lunch and the sun came out, warming the air, and I decided to walk onto the cliffs while the weather was good enough. I nipped into *Boots* and bought athlete's foot cream and cheap reading glasses; into the *Co-op* for walnuts and apples and cheese and bread and peanut butter and carrots; into *Mountain Warehouse* for better walking boots and new socks and a couple of tee shirts, all on special offer. I left my old boots outside the Salvation Army building.

I rang Flora.

Phoebe answered. 'Hello?'

'Hello, darling! It's Granny!'

'Hello.'

'Lovely to hear your voice, Phoebe darling!'

'Yes.'

'Is everyone all right?'

'Yes.'

'Did you have the big storm? Lots of snow?'

'Yes.'

'Is the house all right?'

'The lights went off.'

'Did they?'

'Yes. And the telly.'

'Did it? Phoebe –'

'And the fridge.'

'Gosh. Phoebe –'

'We had lots of snow.'

'Yes, darling, so did I.' I tried another tack. 'Is Mummy there?'

'Yes. But we're going out. Bye.'

She put the phone down before I could get her to fetch Flora. Not bad, I supposed, for a four-year-old. I would try again later.

❧

The streets were empty, clean and rain-washed, the holiday homes shut up until spring, grey granite giving way to bright white fishermen's cottages with sky-blue windowsills. I began to relax. Perhaps I could give myself a little holiday after Anne's party. A bit of walking, visiting the art galleries. I could see the Tate St Ives Gallery ahead of me, its beautiful curved portico standing high beyond the houses. A holiday would do me good, give me energy – a change is as good as a rest, they say – and something lovely to think about as I got back to normal: gardening, tending my hens, writing letters to my MP, making my weekly phone call to the twins, remembering to keep Flora 'in the loop' about my activities, such as they were. I might take up another hobby when I got home, I mused. I could quite fancy watercolours.

I don't know how I managed to get myself into this holiday frame of mind. I was lulled into a sense of security which was utterly false, by the blue sky, the familiar surroundings, the sense of spring in the air, the early primroses.

It was lucky I kept Jonnie's rucksack with me that afternoon or I'd be in a worse state now. I'd half-thought of choosing a guesthouse before lunch and dropping it off, but in the end, I couldn't be bothered. It had seemed too much effort when I was hungry and wanting a hot meal.

Out of the breeze it was warm in the sun. There was nowhere to hide the rucksack on my cliff walk, just bracken, dead and flat and the colour of rust. I remember thinking how fortunate I was not to be in some genuine emergency.

I stopped now and then to gaze at the sea. It had turned that colour you see in postcards, a colour that looks impossible, an intense turquoise which has nothing to do with the sky above, pale and insipid in comparison; further out the colour deepened to sapphire and then indigo. There were people on the path with cameras hoping to catch that elusive quality, beauty. But for me the beauty was in the whole experience, the softness of the air, the sunlight, the blue-grey haze on the horizon, the springiness of the turf behind me and the greys of the rocks on the cliff edge, the sea salt I could taste on my lips.

I passed lots of people, some with dogs, some without. Couples, mainly the retired sort on a cheap mid-week break; small children and harassed mums; a birdwatcher or two. Every now and then a narrow path wound its way up the cliff through the rusty bracken, access to a lane or to someone's house. Lucky someone, with that view. So vulnerable, though, facing the Atlantic.

I forgot, just for that hour or so, that the storms I'd battled through over the past few days weren't over. I'm sure it didn't occur to anyone else up on that cliff either, although they must have heard the weather forecast. Their cheery smiles seemed to say, *Spring at last, thank goodness that's over.*

Sometimes we can be so close to something we can't see it for what it is.

TWENTY-NINE

The Zombies Return

I've had better days than this.

The gash in my leg is throbbing, burning. If I'd brought rope with me, I would never have skidded down those rocks and gouged the hole in my thigh, the skin flapping around like a spare part. At least I didn't fall into the sea and drown. And why would I ever have thought I needed rope?

Get a grip, Roly, get a grip.

This is more reasonable: if I'd brought my medical kit, I would have a bandage and antiseptic cream on my leg, rather than my scarf and sea water.

And if I'd checked into a hotel I would never have run out of water, or food, and there would be people to talk to, and I would have a warm bed and supper.

But I have to wonder, are there any hotels left?

Are there any people?

I gaze up at the ledge on which the bird lies. I have seen no movement for a day or two. While I was still able to stand, I hobbled over to look at it, and it opened its eyes just once, gazed at me for a long moment as if it knew me, could read

269

my heart, then closed them again. I gently laid my hand on its back. The feathers were cold. I stood there for a long time, waiting. There was nothing more.

ↄ

Grey waves crash constantly against the narrow exit, darkening the cave each time. Outside this cave the sea is cobalt, black, midnight blue. As the tide turns, the water rushes in every few seconds, in such a hurry to fill the cave that it meets itself rushing out. It eddies and swirls and churns, forming tiny whirlpools and waterfalls around the rocks. I could watch it for hours. In fact, I do watch it for hours, unable to move, sick with fever and mesmerised by the patterns, almost but not quite identical each time, a semi-circle here, a sinuous curve there, a spiral.

I have nothing else to do, after all. My life has been reduced to this horizontal existence in which I spend days thinking over my unlikely escape, and, in my nights, I'm whisked miraculously back across the ravaged landscape and over the zombie hordes and into my home forty years ago, where the sun shone golden, and we laughed and loved and lived.

I doze off now and then. Everything's the same when I wake. I'm no longer very hungry, but I thirst, I thirst.

I've been so cold in my damp clothing that to be hot now is a relief. The atmosphere must be heating up very fast. Rapid climate change. Rapid sea level rise. I'm sweating, and I pull off first my hat and gloves, then my boots, then my coat and my jumper, and now I am lying here in my torn trousers and socks and thermal vest.

My arms shock me. I've always been thin, but now my limbs are positively skeletal.

I'm cold again. I struggle into my jumper and fleece and jacket; I pull on my hat and gloves. I'm shaking. Everything is difficult. Things stick to me and stick to each other with the salt and the damp and the sand. My leg hurts all the way up to my hip and down to my foot. My arm is swollen and fiery with pain. My head pounds.

There's someone here with me. I see him moving round the cave, jumping from rock to rock, walking on the water. I try to raise my head, but something is holding me down. I can't move. He turns and smiles as if I have spoken, and waves at me, then dives out through the water at the entrance. It was Ollie. I recognised the beard.

The heat's unbearable. I'm burning. I touch my forehead with my icy fingers and it's hot and dry. My cold hands are delightful. I lie with my fingers pressed to my throbbing eyes.

Ollie's back. He's brought Jonnie. They jump around in the waves, laughing and splashing. I want them to splash me, to help cool me down, but they don't seem to notice me. They jump onto the rucksack and paddle it out of the cave like a canoe, laughing.

Flora's looking worried. She tells me to take *Lemsip*. I want her to make me some elderberry tea, but she isn't there when I make a stupendous effort and open my eyes.

My rucksack is propped against the wall where I left it. I contemplate it, wondering when the boys brought it back.

I'm very cold.

Hugo has cut off my leg. It's such a relief. I wave my stump around. It feels so light in comparison with the weight of that mouldering old leg. It always gave me trouble, that leg. I watch Hugo as he props it against the wall next to Jonnie's rucksack. He comes back and gives me a smile.

'Off with the old, on with the new!' he says.

How very true.

I watch with interest as my new leg begins to grow, complete with matching trouser leg and boot.

Excellent. I get up and test it out. I wade into the water which is so cold that it hurts but I take no notice of that. I need to discover what's been going on out there, how our new globally-warmed world looks.

I slip through the narrow cave entrance and find the twins sitting on rocks either side of me, staring out to sea.

'Good evening,' says Fergus.

'Hi,' says Dugald.

We join hands and leap into the waves, letting them curl around our feet and knees and waists. We decide to swim, pulling ourselves forward with long front-crawl strokes. The twins seem to have lost their fear of getting their faces wet. How brilliant.

There are explosions all around us as great bubbles of methane appear without warning. Ahead a huge cargo ship drops into the space created by the gas and sinks as the waters close in above it.

We turn on our backs for a while and float, watching the blue methane flames flicker around us. Above us the sky is a yellowy-grey, a haze that stretches from the horizon behind to the cliffs ahead, which are ablaze not with the sunset as I'd first thought but with real fire, real flames that devour the heath and heather, the stunted windblown trees, the barns and garages and sheds and bus shelters and houses and cottages and hotels. We swim rapidly to the harbour where boats shimmer in the heat of the burning air which is only just breathable.

I'm worried for the harbour frontage, lovely old buildings that at any moment will go up in flame. The wind is getting stronger, fanning sparks into flamelets that flicker along the tops of masts and sails. But I needn't fear. There's a storm on its way and the sea rises up and up, and what with the high tide and the storm surge the harbour and the town are safe from fire, today.

Fergus and Dugald and I ride the waves like a fairground ride. It's exhilarating – up – and down – up – and down – up – and – down… But I hear screaming, and I remember, of course, they never liked fairground rides. Our one trip to Alton Towers was a disaster and a complete waste of money.

'Let's go, boys!' I cry, and we're off, skimming the waves like flying fish and up and over the cliffs.

We leave the screaming behind, and looking back I see the town swamped by massive waves and there are people and cars and bikes being swept out to sea and all the highest windows of the buildings along the front have smashed and all the roofs have caved in, and the church tower sits above the surging waters like a lighthouse.

We hold hands, the boys and I, and I look at each of them in turn, and they are crying. There are tears running down their cheeks and they weep and weep as though their hearts are breaking.

We glide over the cliffs, we brush the tops of trees with our hands, we swoop and soar above villages and churches and farms, we follow the lines of hedges and roads, and all is black with soot and brittle with heat. We go far inland, we find rich farming country rather than thin Cornish soil, and we drop low over the fields to see the young wheat burnt by the heat of the sun, stillborn grains no good for harvest. The apple trees have no fruit for all the bees have died. Cows and horses and sheep stand in the scant shade of the biggest trees, leafless branches giving no rest from the sun to those patiently waiting below, skin stretched tight over protruding ribs. There are pigs with skin cancer, great tumours riding their backs like saddles, blackened ears crisp and frayed, snouts bruised from snuffling into the baked earth that no longer yields soft cooling mud.

Little birds hop among the hedges, dunnocks and wrens and thrushes and blackbirds and robins, and at first my heart is joyful, but then I see that their nests are empty, or their eggs addled by the heat; the birds hop and flutter and find no seeds, no insects, no worms. Sparrows fall one by one to the ground. A fox lying by a hedge, its fur matted and mangy with disease, heaves itself to its feet and furtively approaches the dead birds. It sniffs but does not eat them.

In the distance I see a desert, its biscuit-coloured dunes rising and falling gently to swathes of emerald green surrounded by the dark skeletons of huge trees. The desert is the South Downs, its grassland lifeless and crumbling to dust; the green is a golf course. I look for the sprinklers but there are none; the grass is plastic over dead dry ground. It suffocates the life beneath it, the worms and microbes, centipedes and slugs, seeds and roots. The golf course is a murderer. When I land, I leap immediately into the air for it burns my bare and tender feet.

I see a river and have an overwhelming desire to bathe my hot feet in its clear waters, to sit beside it and picnic as I did as a child, to swing from willow branches over the sparkling pebbles. But the river is a sluggish muddy trickle at the bottom of a deep trench, the sides cracked and fissured with drought. An angler sitting on the bank looks up at me as I hover above him.

'Pointless,' he says, 'no fish here. What's the use of a license?'

We fly on to the twins' place and there they are, my boys, skeletons, dead of starvation, propped up against their caravan, a hoe and fork at their sides.

'As a nation, we import nearly fifty per cent of our food,' says Fergus, beside me.

'That means we grow just over fifty per cent of our food,' says Dugald, on my other side.

I look from one to the other.

'Which thirty-seven million do we not feed?'

And I raise my eyes and see the ravening hordes, women and men and children and babies. They are thin and hollow-cheeked and zombie-eyed, and converge from all directions, along motorways and lanes, streets and bridlepaths, canal sides and alleyways, sniffing out food wherever it may be found. They are not in rags, oh no, they wear designer outfits and expensive shoes, they sport pricey sunglasses and drive their super-polished cars. They walk, they jog, they shuffle, they push their babies in three-in-one buggies, they have the latest electronic gadgets, so they are never not connected.

And on the news, we see that central Africa is a belt of desert, and there is no more snow left anywhere in the world for they have sent out search parties unsuccessfully to find it, and London and New York and Mumbai and Singapore and Sydney and Hong Kong are underwater, and all the rainforests are aflame and can be seen from space.

THIRTY

I Breathe, Still

I have composed myself for death, at last. You could say it's been a long time coming. I've lost count of how many days I have lain here on the damp sand, my body past aching, past thirst or hunger, past even seeing. My eyes closed, I listen to the water, little wavelets caressing the rocks, the sign of high tide. Earlier, this morning, the middle of the night, I no longer know, larger waves crashed against the entrance, making the cave boom around me, leaving my ears ringing. I was afraid, thinking that the water would rush in and drag me out with it, that I would be pushed down by the energy of the tide and drown under tons of water. A death I wouldn't choose. Whereas this, this slow withdrawing from life, this has, I feel, a kind of dignity.

In any case, I no longer have any choice. I have no strength. I cannot even move my hand to brush away the small creatures that occasionally land on my face. I imagine them to be sand flies, making their living among the hanks of dried seaweed washed up at the top of the cave. They tickle me, an exquisite torture that I endure for the sake of them. They have a right to land on my dying body.

I lie here and attempt to pray. My prayers are very simple. I say sorry, again, to the world, and, for the first time, to God. I'm sorry about what's happening, and sorry for my part in it. I ask for safety for my loved ones. That's it. All I can muster. Nothing deep or sophisticated or theological, just heartfelt and genuine, here at the end of everything. I am, finally, at peace.

I can still smell things, although what there is to smell here rarely alters. It is salt and rotting seaweed, a pungent odour that I have to remember to take notice of, so accustomed to it have I become. Some hours or days ago I smelt fuel. It was a shock. I couldn't imagine where it came from, and opened my eyes to see, but there was nothing there. I decided it must be a sensory hallucination, raised up by my subconscious which desires me to be rescued. It was bright, the sunlight on the waves telling me it was early evening and dazzling me.

I sleep, I wake. The casual observer would see no difference between the two.

I wake. I sleep. I am disturbed. Something has disturbed me. I lie listening. The sound of the water at the cave entrance is different somehow.

I listen and listen. I am too tired to open my eyes. There is the suck and whoosh of the sea. There is the sound of gulls. There is a foghorn, a long low mournful sound. There is a knocking sound, a couple of small knocks, then they're gone. Suck and whoosh. Suck and whoosh. Scrape. Suck and whoosh. Scrape. Scrape. Knock, knock, knock. Clank. Suck and whoosh.

A voice.

'Are you sure?' A man.

'Pretty sure.' A second voice, young, teenage, a boy.

My heart leaps, just for a second. Jonnie?

'This one?' Their voices echo in the cave and yet are muffled too by the sound of the waves. I have to concentrate.

'Yeah. I saw the stuff outside on the rocks.'

'When was it again?'

'A few days ago. Monday. Or Tuesday.'

Suck and whoosh. Scrape. Panting, splashing, grunting. Scrape. Suck and whoosh. The sound of wading. A bigger splash.

'Damn.'

'Language, Dad.'

'Shut up.' There's a smile in the voice. 'Pull her up.'

A loud scrape, so loud I jump, the sound of a boat being pulled up over shingle, the sound of it being wedged between rocks.

A light flashes over my closed eyes.

Splashy footsteps. Crunching on the shingle.

A long breath in, then out. His, not mine. I am barely breathing at all, my breath so shallow I doubt he can see my chest move.

'OK. Stand back a minute.'

'Dad...'

'Just a minute.'

I feel rather than hear the man kneel down beside me on the sand. I feel the heat of his body, I smell the smell of him, cigarettes, sweat, waterproofs, deodorant, chips. A finger touches my cheek delicately, traces the line of my jaw down to my neck.

'Dad?'

'Ssshh.'

The finger has found my pulse.

'She's alive.'

Two hands gently cup my face. The light crosses my eyes again. He must be wearing a head torch.

'Rob… Phone the Coastguard.'

THIRTY-ONE

In Our Hands

It was an ordeal, being rescued. I slept and woke many times. Each time things had changed just a little bit.

I slept and woke while the man and his son kept guard over me. They talked sometimes in low voices. They worried about the tide, and the possibility of getting me out either at high or low tide, I forget which. The boy said, several times, that he was glad I was alive, and the man replied gruffly in the affirmative. He was doing what I would have done with my son, not wanting to worry the boy that they might, after all, be too late, that I might die on the way to the hospital, or soon after. But, I thought, he thinks I will not make it.

I was lifted onto a stretcher and strapped in. Someone tried to hold water to my lips, but I couldn't open my mouth. I was mildly interested in what was going on, but it seemed almost as if it was happening to someone else. I couldn't get too excited about the possibility of living; I didn't have the energy. At one point it seemed to me that I was at a fairground being whirled about in the air on one of those huge machines. Then I woke and realised I was being winched on my stretcher up to a helicopter. Jonnie would have loved it, I thought, but I had no liquid left in me and so no tears came for him.

So I was rescued, and hydrated, and whisked to a hospital bed where now I lie in state, and people keep coming in, and they lift my arms and eyelids and blanket and sheet to look at various parts of me. They keep up a running commentary, assuming or guessing or hoping that I can hear and may respond. I don't bother. I'm too tired, and I don't want to start answering questions. There are tubes of various kinds for various purposes going into and coming out of my body, and monitors, and lights, and beeping, constant beeping, and doors being opened and shut and loud voices in the corridor outside my room. I almost have a nostalgia for the quiet of my cave.

I have been here, I think, about three days, and today I will open my eyes, particularly as Flora has arrived. It has taken them this long to work out who I am. I don't know if that is a triumph of policework or not.

∽

Flora is upset. She has been crying. Her eyes are red, her nose is red, her whole face is mottled, her lips swollen.

She edges her way into the room, sits on the chair the nurse has placed by the bed, and bursts into tears. I inch my hand towards her over the white open-weave hospital blanket. She takes it in her right hand and keeps dabbing her eyes and blowing her nose with the other. Her diluted mascara has blotched her cheeks with grey. At length she stops crying.

'Oh Mummy…' It's something between a sob and a sigh. 'What happened to you? What on earth happened? We thought you were dead!'

'Slipped,' I whisper. I can't tell her the truth, not today. It would take too long and I don't have the energy.

She leans forward and I have to say it again. It comes out as a hollow rasp. 'Slipped.'

'Oh Mummy, you poor thing. You poor, poor thing.' She pauses and dabs her eyes. Then she frowns. 'But what were you doing down here?'

I have it prepared. 'Early.'

'Oh, I see. You must have forgotten to mention it.' She squeezes my hand. 'Of course it can be lovely down here in the winter. A few days on your own.'

I give her a small smile.

'It's a lovely route,' she continues.

I gaze at her in bewilderment.

'By train,' she says. 'I came down by train.' She squeezes my hand again. 'I thought of you all the way down.' Her voice is wobbling. She swallows and takes a deep breath. 'Ooh… sorry.' She smiles but her lips are trembling. 'I thought, Mummy'll be pleased I've taken the train. It was a lovely journey. And so quick! I couldn't have driven. I was in such a state. You know…'

Her lips are trembling, tears gathering in her eyelashes. I do know. She's quite right. She couldn't have driven.

'The boys rang me when they couldn't get hold of you. You upset their routine, apparently.' I think this is meant to be a joke, but she has tears in her eyes again and her voice wobbles. 'And mine,' she adds. She smiles briefly and squeezes my hand. 'You left such an odd message on the answerphone. And you didn't arrive at Anne's. I thought – I thought –' Flora begins to sob.

I close my eyes to allow her to compose herself.

My designated nurse, Maggie – short and plump, Irish and red-haired – chats when she comes in to check my vital signs. She runs through them quickly: temperature, pulse, oxygen levels, liquids in and out, the strength of my grip (I think she made this last one up), my breathing, then perches on my bed for a few minutes, clucking at me in a caring way, telling me the gossip. I know who's going out with whom, where Dr Paul's buying a new house, how long it takes to get to Newquay airport. And while I was locked away in my cave – Maggie's words, which make me wonder what she thinks I've been doing – the weather was atrocious. Who'd have guessed? Rain bombs on Boscastle, Tintagel, and St Ives, several months of rain in just a few hours, with houses and streets and cars washed away, people made homeless, businesses destroyed. Some old people even died.

Maggie looks askance at me when she says this, clearly thinking that as I'm old she's perhaps been tactless. But she goes on, nevertheless. Scarborough, too, and Mumbles, and Dublin. The Thames Barrier's been raised every day for the last two weeks, and the Underground's out of action. The Royal Family's been out and about in waders, seeing the damage and rallying the nation.

I've heard enough and close my eyes. Maggie leaves me to rest.

∽

Flora's visit was yesterday. Maggie bustles into the room with a gift from the twins (raspberry jam made by Dugald and chocolate shortbread baked by Fergus, arranged artfully on gold tissue paper in a shoe box) and asks how I feel about having a special visitor.

'Special?' I croak.

'If you're up to it. You can refuse, you know, although we all think it would do you good.'

I raise my eyebrows.

'Doctor Paul included. You need taking out of yourself.' She lifts me with one arm and straightens the pillow with her free hand. 'No good brooding on your ordeal, terrible though it was.'

I wonder what she knows of my 'ordeal.' I have been, officially, a missing person; my face and name have been in all the newspapers, on all the TV news bulletins. My disappearance has been 'out of character.' How kind. How tactful not to mention my earlier disappearance, when I ran away to Anne's cottage.

'We need to start getting you back into society, seeing family and friends. Anyway, it's your husband. What do you think?'

Interesting question. Flora must have told them we were separated. Not for the first time I wonder why Hugo hasn't asked me for a divorce.

I hold my breath for a few seconds, then let it go, a controlled out-breath, giving myself time to gather my thoughts.

'When?' I manage.

'This afternoon. OK?' She stands at the end of my bed and regards me seriously. 'You don't have to. Only if you're up to it.'

I close my eyes and nod. I'm up to Hugo.

⁂

Hugo creeps carefully into the room, as if stepping on broken glass barefoot. He's holding a bunch of flowers. We eye each other warily.

'How's the baby?' I whisper.

He starts, then collects himself in that way I remember so well: the smile, the head dipped slightly to one side, the twinkle, all the signs he used to give when covering his tracks. 'Nearly seven now,' he says. 'Charlie.' The mask falls. 'Actually, we're no longer together, me and Juliette. I see him on Sundays.' He pauses, fiddling with the cellophane and tissue paper of the white roses and scented lilies – imported flowers not in season in January. 'I've missed you, Roly. You don't know how much.' He glances back at me. 'I'm glad you're all right.'

'…not all right…' I croak.

'Alive. You know what I mean. Look –' He settles himself on the bed and places his hand – huge, red, hairy – on my withered forearm, white and flaccid, the skin hanging off in folds. 'Let's get you better and get you home.'

He stares expressionless into my eyes, and I can't tell what he's thinking.

'The police found your car at Tiverton,' he says.

I nod.

He gently squeezes my hand.

ↄ

Hugo and Flora are visiting me together this evening. They've managed to get rooms in a decent hotel only a few minutes' walk away. It has an outdoor swimming pool.

'Chilly?' I ask.

'Not bad,' says Flora. 'A few good lengths warm you up.'

I can't imagine anything worse. My internal thermostat is still faulty, and I get chilled just lying in my bed in an overheated ward.

I listen to them chatting. I don't join in. I'm so very tired. But I derive quiet pleasure from listening to their conversation. It would be even better if the twins were to visit, but I can't ask for miracles. This is enough, for now.

They're discussing the storms, and the links to global warming. Storms like these are clear evidence of climate change. We all know this; it's accepted as fact these days.

You can only do what you can do, says Hugo, and Flora agrees. For instance, he says, I reduced my carbon footprint by building sustainably. Flora glances across my bed at him, her expression anxiously willing him not to say more, but he carries blithely on. He planted an orchard and dug a pond and goes almost everywhere by train. He's not flown anywhere for two years, at least. Then he remembers he's talking to me and harrumphs and looks at his watch and says that maybe it's time for a cup of tea.

Those who have already perished, I want to ask, what about them? But there's only so much Flora and Hugo can take. Their compassion banks are nearly empty. They're sorry for the state of the world, for habitats and species driven to extinction, for people battling with extreme climate events, but they're sorriest for me. You can only do what you can do.

They tell me that the world's not come to an end, not yet; I misread the signs. They tell me we're all quite safe; there is no danger. I see pity in their eyes. The pity is for me, not for those who have already perished. They think I lost my grip on reality.

They're right, of course. The world didn't end last week. From what I can see from my bed it doesn't look as if it'll end next week either. Spring is on its way, the days are warm and mild, and it's only mid-January.

So I panicked, apparently. There's no apocalypse, they tell me. Earth isn't trying to shake us off like a virus. She's not trying to starve or burn or drown us. She wants to work with us, says Hugo, and Flora nods earnestly and squeezes my hand.

'You mustn't let your imagination run away with you,' say Hugo and Flora in different ways at different times. They repeat this over and over, as if that's our only problem. 'Of course we understand,' says Flora. 'But our prime concern is for you. We have to get you better.' She kisses me, then quietly leaves the room. She needs to phone her children.

Hugo moves on, conversationally. He clearly thinks he's sorted this out, this little problem of my overactive imagination. It's not that he doesn't appreciate nature, after all. He's looking forward to gardening alongside me again, he says, helping me grow our own food. He's proposing polytunnels to protect our crops from the erratic weather. And because of the lack of bees and hoverflies we can try hand-pollinating like they do in China. It's all worked out. He doesn't want me to worry about a thing.

We won't travel very much, says Hugo; the unpredictable weather makes air travel unreliable, and, anyway, we all need to reduce our carbon emissions, don't we, hmm? – and the trains are overcrowded because of the unreliable planes. He much prefers to spend time at home these days, he says, pottering around and keeping an eye on things. He does a good job of talking up the joys of a quiet life at home and talking down the benefits of travel. He likes the idea of Scotland for holidays, and in due course we may move up there to a place he knows that I will absolutely love. It's remote but beautiful. Wonderful views. Good fishing as well.

He can't have thought very hard about being isolated in our seventies. It sounds a terrible idea. What about food? Medical care? Seeing our family? And Hugo's so gregarious, I can't imagine he'd last a week with just me for company.

'And the youngsters,' he adds. 'They're going to save us all, they're so inspiring. All those strikes and things. Although they really shouldn't be gluing themselves to roads or anywhere.'

'Maybe,' I say. 'It's complicated.' A conversation for another time. I take a breath. 'Hugo, I need to know something.'

He waits, smoothing the blanket between us with his right hand. His left hand holds mine.

I struggle to get the words out. My chest is tight with anxiety. 'Have you – have you – did you ever forgive Jonnie?'

Hugo holds my gaze. His eyes are soft, kind. 'Oh, Roly. A long time ago.'

'He wasn't wrong,' I whisper, almost belligerently.

'No, he wasn't wrong. He was ahead of his time.' This shocks me, and I can't think what to say. When did Hugo come to this conclusion? And why did he never tell me?... Unless – and now I feel a frisson of self-doubt, a quiet echo of my anguish in the cave – unless he did try to tell me, in his own way, back when we weren't listening.

Hugo squeezes my hand gently. 'And you, Roly? Have you forgiven him?'

'Whatever for?' I ask in astonishment.

'For leaving you.'

'Oh!'

Hugo waits.

I think about forgiveness, about letting go, about moving on.

I think about Jonnie, perfect and not perfect, Jonnie who can no longer be argued with.

I think about Earth, huge and beautiful, unstoppable in her rebalancing, in her demands for clemency, Earth who cannot be reasoned with.

After a moment, he reaches into his inner pocket and draws out an envelope.

'I want you to look at this, Roly.'

It's a photograph of us on our wedding day, coming down the church path. It was always my favourite wedding photo, until, well… In it I am twenty-three years old, beautiful, blonde, laughing up into the face of my handsome and adored bridegroom, who is grinning down at me. Rose petals swirl around us, gusted by the gentle breeze that made the day perfect for June, not too hot, a quintessentially English summer day. I am holding a sheaf of white roses and lilies; my veil has been swept out over my shoulder by the breeze. I am so very happy. We were the perfect couple, everyone said so, and so we believed.

'I've always kept it. You know.' He pauses and scrunches up his face, looking away from me, glancing out of the window, at the door, at the cards from neighbours and Ollie, at the luxury lavender bath set from Boots sent by Anne. 'It's, I mean, it's important.' He glances back at me and clears his throat. He almost looks as if he's about to cry.

I make a huge effort to speak. 'Patronising bastard,' I whisper.

'Oh, God, I know…' He screws up his eyes, closes them, opens them again. 'I know, Roly. God, I'm so sorry. I don't know…' He rummages in his trouser pocket, brings out a crumpled handkerchief, and wipes his eyes. 'I took you for granted, I am the biggest… I'm a bloody fool. You were right, Roly.'

He looks down at me, helpless on my bed. I wonder which bit of our life he thinks I was right about.

'I did think I could have my cake and eat it,' he says. 'Too big for my own boots. What an idiot. A prize idiot. I didn't know how lucky I was. My God, Roly, I'm sorry.'

To my surprise, I find tears trickling down my cheeks. I've believed I'm no longer surprised by anything, and yet these tears surprise me, and I try to hold them back, conscious of the physical pain in my chest and my desperate sense of yearning and loss. I've never stopped loving him, yet we can never go back to how we were. I'm not the same. I've been pared back, peeled to the bone.

I swallow back my tears, enough to whisper: 'I pushed you away.'

'Oh, Roly.'

'I'm sorry, for being so angry, for…' I can't find the words or the breath to describe everything I regret and suddenly my chest is leaden, my throat tight, and I see, as if from a great distance, a poor old woman in a hospital bed, and an old man holding her hand, and the pity of it and the beauty of it and the love in it makes me so very sad, and so very happy.

Hugo gently kisses my forehead.

'We've got everything to play for,' he says. 'Breathe, Roly,' he whispers. 'Breathe.'

Acknowledgements

This book has been a long time coming, from its first faint imaginings over ten years ago, to this story today. So, thank you, all my family, for your support and encouragement over the years: my husband and children, Ian, Alexandra, Christopher, and Nathaniel; my sisters Sarah, Rebecca and Jodie; and my wider family and friends, who encouraged me to keep writing (even when there seemed to be nothing to show!).

Thank you too, fellow writers, especially members of the Bristol Climate Writers, my friends the Harbourside Heroes, and those I have met through the Society of Authors and at various events, including Novel Nights, BristolCon, and the Flash Fiction Festival. Writing is a lonely pursuit, and it's always a treat to get together with other writers and to be inspired by your dedication, craft, talent, and brilliant writing. I have also been inspired by ClimateCultures, a network of creatives and scientists determined to bring climate and ecology to the fore in fiction, art, and music. Thank you too, friends at Green Christian, for your inspirational commitment to ecological justice.

My thanks go to Cheryl Robson, publisher and editor and her team at Aurora Metro who picked this book as a winner of the Virginia Prize for Fiction; and to Cheryl, again, and to editor Jill Russo, for your astute comments on this book and your eagle-like editorial eyes. It's tremendously exciting to see this book in print when once it was only a glimmer of an idea.

The Virginia Prize for Fiction is named in honour of the literary icon Virginia Woolf who lived near to the publisher's offices in Richmond-upon-Thames from 1914–1924. Her first novel *The Voyage Out* was published in 1915. Virginia and husband Leonard set up the Hogarth Press and ran it from their house in Paradise Road in Richmond, publishing authors such as T.S. Eliot, E.M. Forster and Katherine Mansfield.

Established in 2009, the biennial Virginia Prize competition is open to women and non-binary writers, of any nationality, writing in English, aged 18 and over.

The competition accepts completed, unpublished novels for adults or YA readers of at least 45,000 words in length. You can find out more about the competition at:

www.aurorametro.com/virginia-prize-for-fiction/

In 2017, publisher Cheryl Robson and our sister charity Aurora Metro Arts & Media launched a crowdfunding campaign to commemorate Virginia Woolf with a full-sized statue of the author. In 2022, the sculpture in bronze by Laury Dizengremel was finally unveiled in Richmond and has become a popular attraction.

Read more about it at:

www.aurorametro.org.uk/virginia-woolf-statue

Read more from Virginia Prize Winners

Pomegranate Sky by Louise Soraya Black
9781906582104 £8.99

Kipling and Trix by Mary Hamer
9781906582340 £9.99

The Leipzig Affair by Fiona Rintoul
9781906582975 £8.99

The Dragonfly by Kate Dunn
9781911501039 £9.99

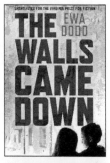

The Walls Came Down by Eva Dodd
9781911501152 £9.99

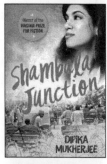

Shambala Junction by Dipika Mukherjee
9781910798393 £9.99

Volta by Nikki Dudley
9781912430550 £9.99

Bone Rites by Natalie Bayley
9781912430871 £11.99

To find out about our other titles visit
www.aurorametro.com